THOREAU
PEOPLE, PRINCIPLES, AND POLITICS

By Milton Meltzer

A Pictorial History of the Negro in America (with Langston Hughes)
Mark Twain Himself
Milestones to American Liberty
A Thoreau Profile (with Walter Harding)

THOREAU

PEOPLE, PRINCIPLES, AND POLITICS

Edited and with an Introduction by
MILTON MELTZER

American Century Series

HILL AND **WANG** · NEW YORK

A division of Farrar, Straus and Giroux

To my brothers,
Allan and Marshall

CONTENTS

INTRODUCTION

Thoreau was born in time to hear reminiscences of the American Revolution from local survivors of those battles, and he died as the Civil War was creating another generation of veterans. In the years between, great changes took place in national life. The patriarchal quiet of the countryside began to recede under a tumultuous wave of industrialization. While Thoreau was at Concord Academy and Harvard, tie-wig Federalists in government gave way to rude, brawling Jacksonians. As Fremont opened up the West, Thoreau explored Walden's shores. Thoreau looked up from the placid pond to see newly arrived Irish immigrants building the Fitchburg railroad a hundred rods past his cabin. Gold was discovered in California, and by the time *A Week on the Concord and Merrimack Rivers* was issued, the mad rush across greater rivers had started. A year later the Fugitive Slave Law was passed, and as proofs of *Walden* came from the press, the bloody troubles in Kansas were in the headlines.

In Thoreau's lifetime, too, there were wars—against the Indians and against the Mexicans. But though he was old enough, he fought in neither of these dubious battles. He was committed to another war, his private war against the herd-spirit, against materialism and conformity, against smugness and hypocrisy, against injustice and slavery.

This book makes available for the first time a selection of Thoreau's writings on man and society. The essays on philosophical and political themes are the foundation of the book. It begins with Thoreau's discussion of the utopian schemes of the early nineteenth century, moves on to the issue of free speech, the duty of civil disobedience, the struggle against slavery, and the defence of John Brown, and concludes with the posthumous "Life Without Principle." From *Walden*, which is really the poem of Thoreau's philosophy, I have selected the second chapter, "Where I Lived and What I Lived For." Introductory notes are provided for each essay. With the essays I have included over one hundred passages from Thoreau's *Journal* and a few excerpts from his letters, which also show Thoreau as protestant and reformer.

The arrangement of the selections is chronological, a method which permits the reader to watch the writer's growth. "Our thoughts are the epochs of our life," Thoreau said. "The more you have thought and written on a given theme, the more you can still write. Thought breeds thought. It grows under your hands."

An important part of Thoreau's writing has not been included in this book. His early reputation was built upon his observations of nature. Indeed, for a considerable time after his death his social philosophy was ignored. Only later did the connection between his exploration of wildness in nature and his exploration of man in society become apparent. A true picture of Thoreau is to be seen only by looking at him in every aspect, but this book will, it is hoped, illuminate at least one side of the man.

Thoreau spoke only for himself; the truths he uttered still speak to man's condition. "These same questions that disturb and puzzle and confound us," he said, "have in their turn occurred to all wise men; not one has been omitted; and each has answered them, according to his ability, by his words and his life."

Many a man has dated a new era in his life from the reading of Thoreau's answers; his words have gone round the world.

The Reverend Martin Luther King, Jr., President of the Southern Christian Leadership Conference, has said that it was during his reading of Thoreau's "Civil Disobedience" in his college days that he became convinced that "non-co-operation with evil is as much a moral obligation as is co-operation with good. No other person has been more eloquent and passionate in making this understood than Henry David Thoreau. As a result of his writings and personal witness we are the heirs of a legacy of creative protest. The teachings of Thoreau are alive today, indeed, they are more alive today than ever before. A sit-in at lunch counters, a freedom ride into Mississippi, a peaceful protest in Albany, Georgia, a bus boycott in Montgomery, Alabama—all are outgrowths of Thoreau's insistence that evil must be resisted and no moral man can patiently adjust to injustice."

Mohandas K. Gandhi recorded that when he read *Walden* in 1906 he adopted some of its ideas. He said, "I recommended the study of Thoreau to all my friends who were helping me in the cause of Indian independence. Why, I actually took the name of my movement from Thoreau's essay, 'On the Duty of Civil Disobedience. . . .' There is no doubt that Thoreau's ideas greatly influenced my movement in India."

Nor is there any doubt that the campaigners against the nuclear deterrent in this country and abroad have taken not only principle but courage from the man who knew that sometimes one has to stand alone.

Contrary to popular impression, Thoreau never asked anyone to live the way he did. He sought no imitators; he hoped disciples would follow of their own accord. "Let everyone mind his own business," he said, "and endeavor to be what he was made." Many of us, of course, spend a lifetime without ever finding out what we are. Have any of us, Thoreau asks bluntly, yet lived a whole human life?

At the heart of these selections is Thoreau's belief in action according to principle. This it is which "changes things and relations," he said; "it is essentially revolutionary." Thoreau was a reformer, but his first concern was not society; it was man himself. ("If I am not I, who will be?") He was an individualist concerned with principles and problems who went to the core of man's nature and the possibility of his self-discovery. "However mean your life is, meet it and live it; do not shun it and call it hard names. Love your life, poor as it is. Why should we be in such deep haste to succeed and in such desperate enterprises? If a man does not keep pace with his companions, perhaps it is because he hears a different drummer. Let him step to the music which he hears, however measured or far away."

Thoreau's life was slow-paced, and quiet. The real events of his history were all internal. Born in Concord in 1817, he was taken from town to town in his first five or six years as his father roved about in search of a livelihood. In 1823 the family settled finally in Concord where his father found a modest living in the making of pencils and his mother helped by running a boarding house. Thoreau was schooled at Concord Academy and at Harvard. At that time, to young men of his education, only the professions or business were possible, but none of these appealed to him. He tried teaching for a few years, but though his school prospered he gave it up. Encouraged by Emerson, who had moved to Concord, he began to write, keeping a journal. His first poem and essay appeared in *The Dial* in 1840, and soon he was contributing to other magazines. But in that day it was almost impossible for anyone to make a living at writing. Thoreau proved it for himself during an eight-month stay in New York in 1843. Back in Concord, he helped his father make pencils and pieced out a living with odd jobs as mason, gardener, carpenter, house painter, and day laborer.

The great adventure of his life came in 1845 when he built his cabin at Walden Pond on land provided by Emerson. He hoped that living a simple life would leave him time for writing. He stayed at the pond for two years, two months, and two days, writing his first book, *A Week on the Concord and Merrimack Rivers*, and a large part of his second, *Walden*. He was no hermit at Walden, for he often visited family and friends who were not two miles off, and many came to talk with him in his cabin.

In 1847, leaving Walden to become a "sojourner in civilized life again," he went to live for a year in Emerson's house while the master was away in Europe. It was the second time he had exchanged board and room there for a handyman's work. Now, too, he took up professional surveying as another trade. It got him out into his beloved fields and woods and still left him time to sit in his room and return to himself.

He traveled much in Concord, and a little outside the town. His lecturing took him north to New Hampshire and south to Philadelphia. But during his busiest season he appeared in only seven cities. He spoke most often (nineteen times) at the Concord

Lyceum, and that was for no fee at all. His private excursions began with the 1838 trip to Maine and the voyage on the Concord and Merrimack which he made with his brother John the next year. Excursions to Canada, Cape Cod, and the White Mountains provided the raw material for articles (published posthumously in book form). In 1861, as his long struggle with tuberculosis became more severe, he made a last trip, this time to Minnesota in the vain hope of regaining his health. A year later, on May 6, 1862, at the age of forty-four, he died in the family home on Main Street.

What matters to us in this brief life were the thoughts which came to Thoreau and, above all, the way he wrote them down. For he was first of all a writer. Few of his ideas were original. His power lies in the freshness, beauty, passion of his expressions. Most of his thinking was done on the walks he took into the fields and woods around Concord, making it his everyday business "to extract the honey from the flowers of the world." Sometimes he went out with a friend, much more often alone. And nearly every day, from 1837 to within a few months of his death, he worked at his journal, testing his ideas, his feelings, his impressions of nature and man and society, writing and rewriting this two million word record of his experiences and growth.

In his own lifetime, almost no one seemed to be listening to Thoreau. The first printing in 1849 of his *A Week on the Concord and Merrimack Rivers* was one thousand copies. Fewer than three hundred of these were sold in four years, and Thoreau had to pay the publisher 290 dollars for the remaining copies. The failure of *A Week* postponed publication of *Walden* for five years, and when it appeared in 1854 two thousand copies were sold—in five years. These two books and a scattering of articles and poems were all that he published, and for a generation after his death, that seemed to be the end.

But it was not. Thoreau's reputation matured and expanded slowly until now it reaches into every land. *Walden* has gone into over 150 editions, and has been translated into many languages. He wrote while the heat was in him, and his words still inflame our minds.

Readers may want to compare their own response to Thoreau's

political and philosophical ideas with the evaluations of others. Sherman Paul's *Thoreau: A Collection of Critical Essays* (Englewood Cliffs, 1962) is a selection of pieces by some of the most perceptive critics of the twentieth century. Walter Harding's *Thoreau: A Century of Criticism* (Dallas, 1954) is an anthology of twenty-four widely known critical articles. Three major critical studies are Joseph Wood Krutch's *Henry David Thoreau* (New York, 1948), Sherman Paul's *The Shores of America* (Urbana, 1958), and Leo Stoller's *After Walden: Thoreau's Changing Views on Economic Man* (Stanford, 1957).

For currently available biographies of Thoreau the reader is referred to Henry Seidel Canby's *Thoreau* (Boston, 1939) and to Milton Meltzer's and Walter Harding's *A Thoreau Profile* (New York, 1962).

For the full texts of Thoreau's work, the reader can turn to *The Complete Journals of Henry D. Thoreau* (New York, 1963), in two volumes; *The Correspondence of Henry David Thoreau* (New York, 1958), edited by Carl Bode and Walter Harding; and *The Collected Poems* (Chicago, 1943), edited by Carl Bode.

There are several editions, some in paperback, of *Walden, A Week on the Concord and Merrimack Rivers, Cape Cod, The Maine Woods,* and *Excursions.*

I wish to express my deep appreciation to Jane Meltzer and Anne Coldewey for typing the manuscript. I owe another debt to Walter Harding for his leadership in Thoreau scholarship and his friendly advice.

THOREAU
PEOPLE, PRINCIPLES, AND POLITICS

JOURNAL AND LETTERS
1837–1847

We can afford to lend a willing ear occasionally to those earnest reformers of the age. Let us treat them hospitably. Shall we be charitable only to the poor? What though they are fanatics? Their errors are likely to be generous errors, and these may be they who will put to rest the American Church and the American government, and awaken better ones in their stead.

Let us not meanly seek to maintain our delicate lives in chambers or in legislative halls by a timid watchfulness of the rude mobs that threaten to pull down our baby-houses. Let us not think to raise a revenue which shall maintain our domestic quiet by an impost on the liberty of speech. Let us not think to live by the principle of self-defense. Have we survived our accidents hitherto, think you, by virtue of our good swords—that three-foot lath that dangles by your side, or those brazen-mouthed pieces under the burying hill which the trainers keep to hurrah with in the April and July mornings? Do our protectors burrow under the burying-ground hill, on the edge of the beanfield which you all know, gorging themselves once a year with powder and smoke, and kept bright and in condition by a chafing of oiled rags and rotten stone? Have we resigned the protection of our hearts and civil liberties to that feathered race of wading birds and marching men who drill but once a month?—and I mean no reproach to our Concord train-bands, who certainly make a handsome appearance—and dance well. Do we enjoy the sweets of domestic life undisturbed, because the naughty boys are all shut up in that whitewashed "stone-yard," as it is called, and see the Concord meadows only through a grating.

No, let us live amid the free play of the elements. Let the dogs bark, let the cocks crow, and the sun shine, and the winds blow!

✧   ✧   ✧

Scholars have for the most part a diseased way of looking at the world. They mean by it a few cities and unfortunate assemblies of men and women, who might all be concealed in the grass of the prairies. They describe this world as old or new, healthy or diseased, according to the state of their libraries—a little dust more or less on their shelves. When I go abroad from under this shingle or slate roof, I find several things which they have not considered. Their conclusions seem imperfect.

JOURNAL / DECEMBER 27, 1837

Revolutions are never sudden. Not one man, nor many men, in a few years or generations, suffice to regulate events and dispose mankind for the revolutionary movement. The hero is but the crowning stone of the pyramid—the keystone of the arch. Who was Romulus or Remus, Hengist or Horsa, that we should attribute to them Rome or England? They are famous or infamous because the progress of events has chosen to make them its steppingstones. But we would know where the avalanche commenced, or the hollow in the rock whence springs the Amazon. The most important is apt to be some silent and unobtrusive fact in history. In 449 three Saxon cyules arrived on the British coast, "Three scipen gode comen mid than flode, three hundred cnihten." The pirate of the British coast was no more the founder of a state than the scourge of the German shore.

JOURNAL / NOVEMBER 22, 1839

We do all stand in the front ranks of the battle every moment of our lives; where there is a brave man, there is the thickest of the fight, there the post of honor. Not he who procures a substitute to go to Florida is exempt from service; he gathers his laurels in another field. Waterloo is not the only battleground: as many and fatal guns are pointed at my breast now as are contained in the English arsenals.

JOURNAL / DECEMBER 1839

Men have made war from a deeper instinct than peace. War is but the compelling of peace.

When the world is declared under martial law, every Esau retakes his birthright, and what there is in him does not fail to appear. He wipes off all old scores and commences a new account. The world is interested to know how any soul will demean itself in so novel a position. But when war, too, like commerce and husbandry, gets to be a routine, and men go about it as indented apprentices, the hero degenerates into a marine, and the standing army into a standing jest.

JOURNAL / DECEMBER 1839

The bravest deed, which for the most part is left quite out of history, which alone wants the staleness of a deed done and the uncertainty of a deed doing, is the life of a great man. To perform exploits is to be temporarily bold, as becomes a courage that ebbs and flows, the soul quite vanquished by its own deed subsiding into indifference and cowardice; but the exploit of a brave life consists in its momentary completeness.

JOURNAL / FEBRUARY 11, 1840

The ring leader of the mob will soonest be admitted into the councils of state.

JOURNAL / FEBRUARY 26, 1840

The most important events make no stir on their first taking place, nor indeed in their effects directly. They seem hedged

3

about by secrecy. It is concussion, or the rushing together of air to fill a vacuum, which makes a noise. The great events to which all things consent, and for which they have prepared the way, produce no explosion, for they are gradual, and create no vacuum which requires to be suddenly filled; as a birth takes place in silence, and is whispered about the neighborhood, but an assassination, which is at war with the constitution of things, creates a tumult immediately.

Corn grows in the night.

JOURNAL / JANUARY 24, 1841

Wealth, no less than knowledge, is power. Among the Bedouins the richest man is the sheik; among savages he who has most iron and wampum is chief; and in England and America he is the merchant prince.

JOURNAL / FEBRUARY 28, 1841

As for these [utopian] communities, I think I had rather keep bachelor's hall in hell than go to board in heaven. Do you think your virtue will be boarded with you? It will never live on the interest of your money, depend upon it. The boarder has no home. In heaven I hope to bake my own bread and clean my own linen. The tomb is the only boardinghouse in which a hundred are served at once. In the catacomb we may dwell together and prop one another without loss.

JOURNAL / APRIL 7, 1841

The times have no heart. The true reform can be undertaken any morning before unbarring our doors. It calls no convention. I can do two-thirds the reform of the world myself. When two neighbors begin to eat corn bread, who before ate wheat, then the gods smile from ear to ear, for it is very pleasant to them. When an individual takes a sincere step, then all the gods attend, and his single deed is sweet.

JOURNAL / APRIL 26, 1841

The charm of the Indian to me is that he stands free and unconstrained in Nature, is her inhabitant and not her guest, and wears her easily and gracefully. But the civilized man has the habits of the house. His house is a prison, in which he finds himself oppressed and confined, not sheltered and protected. He walks as if he sustained the roof; he carries his arms as if the walls would fall in and crush him, and his feet remember the cellar beneath. His muscles are never relaxed. It is rare that he overcomes the house, and learns to sit at home in it, and roof and floor and walls support themselves, as the sky and trees and earth.

JOURNAL / FEBRUARY 19, 1842

I am amused to see from my window here how busily man has divided and staked off his domain. God must smile at his puny fences running hither and thither everywhere over the land.

JOURNAL / MARCH 19, 1842

When I walk in the fields of Concord and meditate on the destiny of this prosperous slip of the Saxon family, the unexhausted energies of this new country, I forget that this which is now Concord was once Musketaquid, and that the American race has had its destiny also. Everywhere in the fields, in the corn and grain land, the earth is strewn with the relics of a race which has vanished as completely as if trodden in with the earth. I find it good to remember the eternity behind me as well as the eternity before. Wherever I go, I tread in the tracks of the Indian. I pick up the bolt which he has but just dropped at my feet. And if I consider destiny, I am on his trail. I scatter his hearthstones with my feet, and pick out of the embers of his fire the simple but enduring implements of the wigwam and the chase. In planting my corn in the same furrow which yielded its increase to his support so long, I displace some memorial of him.

I have been walking this afternoon over a pleasant field planted with winter rye, near the house, where this strange people once had their dwelling place. Another species of mortal men, but little less wild to me than the musquash they hunted. Strange spirits, daemons, whose eyes could never meet mine; with another nature and another fate than mine. The crows flew over the edge of the woods, and, wheeling over my head, seemed to rebuke, as dark-winged spirits more akin to the Indian than I. Perhaps only the present disguise of the Indian. If the new has a meaning, so has the old.

*   *   *

The pines and the crows are not changed, but instead that Philip and Paugus stand on the plain, here are Webster and Crockett. Instead of the council house is the legislature. What a new aspect have new eyes given to the land! Where is this country but in the hearts of its inhabitants? Why, there is only so much of Indian America left as there is of the American Indian in the character of this generation.

JOURNAL / MARCH 26, 1842

It is hard to be a good citizen of the world in any great sense; but if we do render no interest or increase to mankind out of that talent God gave us, we can at least preserve the principle unimpaired. One would like to be making large dividends to society out [of] that deposited capital in us, but he does well for the most part if he proves a secure investment only, without adding to the stock.

LETTER TO HELEN THOREAU / JULY 21, 1843

I believe that I have not told you anything about Lucretia Mott. It was a good while ago that I heard her at the Quaker Church in Hester St. She is a preacher, and it was advertised that she would be present on that day. I liked all the proceedings very well—their plainly greater harmony and sincerity than elsewhere. They do nothing in a hurry. Every one that walks up the aisle in his square coat and expansive hat—has a history, and comes from a house to a house. The women come in one after another in their Quaker bonnets and handkerchiefs, looking all like sisters and so many chickadees. At length, after a long silence, waiting for the spirit, Mrs. Mott rose, took off her bonnet, and began to utter very deliberately what the spirit suggested. Her self-possession was something to say, if all else failed—but it did not. Her subject was the abuse of the Bible—and thence she straightway digressed to slavery and the degradation of woman. It was a good speech—transcendentalism in its mildest form. She sat down at length, and after a long and decorous silence in which some seemed to be really digesting her words, the elders shook hands and the meeting dispersed. On the whole I liked their ways, and the plainness of their meetinghouse. It looked as if it was indeed made for service.

PARADISE (TO BE) REGAINED
1843

In May 1843 Thoreau left Concord to try to earn his way in New York's literary market. His base of operations was Judge William Emerson's home on Staten Island, where he tutored the children—a post arranged by the judge's brother, Ralph Waldo. The year ended with only three pieces in print, and Thoreau returned to Concord. One of these essays was the extended review, "Paradise (to Be) Regained." Emerson had asked Thoreau to review for The Dial *a book by a German immigrant, J. A. Etzler,* The Paradise Within the Reach of All Men, Without Labour, by Powers of Nature and Machinery. An Address to All Intelligent Men. (*Part First. Second English Edition, London, 1842.*) Thoreau submitted his piece not to* The Dial *but to the* Democratic Review, *a lively literary magazine which expressed the views of the radical wing of Andrew Jackson's party. The editors objected at first to Thoreau's advocacy of individual rather than group reform, but finally printed his opinions in the November 1843 issue.*

Prescriptions for a paradise on earth were compounded almost daily in that era of reform. Robert Owen had founded New Harmony in Indiana in 1825; Thoreau's friends had organized Brook Farm in 1841; and during his 1843 expedition to New York Thoreau had run into Albert Brisbane, on his way to New Jersey to establish the North American Phalanx. The latter was one of some forty communal settlements which Brisbane had founded to implement Fourier's ideas of social reconstruction. Horace Greeley, Thoreau's friend and literary agent, used the columns in his New York Tribune *to champion Fourierism.*

In his review Thoreau did justice to the mechanical marvels imagined by Etzler. He did not make the mistake of dismissing as airy science fiction technological possibilities which were eventually to be realized. Etzler's chief fault, he said, was that his utopia aimed "to secure the greatest degree of gross comfort and pleasure merely." A moral reform must take place first, Thoreau believed, which would use the incalculable power of love to change the world. "But," he noted, "though the wisest men in all ages have labored to publish this force, and every human heart is, sooner or later, more or less, made to feel it, yet how little is actually applied to social ends!" (M.M.)

We learn that Mr. Etzler is a native of Germany, and originally published his book in Pennsylvania ten or twelve years ago; and now a second English edition, from the original American one, is demanded by his readers across the water—owing, we suppose, to the recent spread of Fourier's doctrines. It is one of the signs of the times. We confess that we have risen from reading this book with enlarged ideas, and grander conceptions of our duties in this world. It did expand us a little. It is worth attending to, if only that it entertains large questions. Consider what Mr. Etzler proposes:

Fellow men! I promise to show the means of creating a paradise within ten years, where everything desirable for human life may be had by every man in superabundance, without labor, and without pay; where the whole face of nature shall be changed into the most beautiful forms, and man may live in the most magnificent palaces, in all imaginable refinements of luxury, and in the most delightful gardens; where he may accomplish, without labor, in one year, more than hitherto could be done in thousands of years; may level mountains, sink valleys, create lakes, drain lakes and swamps, and intersect the land everywhere with beautiful canals, and roads for transporting heavy loads of many thousand tons, and for traveling one thousand miles in twenty-four hours; may cover the ocean with floating islands movable in any desired direction with immense power and celerity, in perfect security, and with all comforts and luxuries, bearing gardens and palaces, with thousands of families, and provided with rivulets of sweet water; may explore the interior of the globe, and travel from pole to pole in a fortnight; provide himself with means, unheard of yet, for increasing his knowledge of the world, and so his intelligence; lead a life of continual happiness, of enjoyments yet unknown; free

9

himself from almost all the evils that afflict mankind, except death, and even put death far beyond the common period of human life, and finally render it less affecting. Mankind may thus live in and enjoy a new world, far superior to the present, and raise themselves far higher in the scale of being.

It would seem from this, and various indications beside, that there is a transcendentalism in mechanics as well as in ethics. While the whole field of the one reformer lies beyond the boundaries of space, the other is pushing his schemes for the elevation of the race to its utmost limits. While one scours the heavens, the other sweeps the earth. One says he will reform himself, and then nature and circumstances will be right. Let us not obstruct ourselves, for that is the greatest friction. It is of little importance though a cloud obstruct the view of the astronomer, compared with his own blindness. The other will reform nature and circumstances, and then man will be right. Talk no more vaguely, says he, of reforming the world—I will reform the globe itself. What matters it whether I remove this humor out of my flesh, or this pestilent humor from the fleshy part of the globe? Nay, is not the latter the more generous course? At present the globe goes with a shattered constitution in its orbit. Has it not asthma, and ague, and fever, and dropsy, and flatulence, and pleurisy, and is it not afflicted with vermin? Has it not its healthful laws counteracted, and its vital energy which will yet redeem it? No doubt the simple powers of nature, properly directed by man, would make it healthy and a paradise; as the laws of man's own constitution but wait to be obeyed, to restore him to health and happiness. Our panaceas cure but few ails, our general hospitals are private and exclusive. We must set up another Hygeia than is now worshiped. Do not the quacks even direct small doses for children, larger for adults, and larger still for oxen and horses? Let us remember that we are to prescribe for the globe itself.

This fair homestead has fallen to us, and how little have we done to improve it, how little have we cleared and hedged and ditched! We are too inclined to go hence to a "better land," without lifting a finger, as our farmers are moving to Ohio soil; but would it not be more heroic and faithful to till and redeem this New England soil of the world? The still youthful energies of the globe have only to be directed in their proper channel. Every gazette brings accounts of the untutored freaks of the wind—shipwrecks and hurricanes which the mariner and planter accept as special or general providences; but they touch our consciences, they remind us of our sins. Another deluge would disgrace mankind. We confess we never had much respect for that antediluvian race. A thoroughbred business man cannot enter heartily upon the business of life without first looking into his accounts. How many things are now at loose ends! Who knows which way the wind will blow tomorrow? Let us not succumb to nature. We will marshall the clouds and restrain tempests; we will bottle up pestilent exhalations; we will probe for earthquakes, grub them up, and give vent to the dangerous gas; we will disembowel the volcano, and extract its poison, take its seed out. We will wash water, and warm fire, and cool ice, and underprop the earth. We will teach birds to fly, and fishes to swim, and ruminants to chew the cud. It is time we had looked into these things.

And it becomes the moralist, too, to inquire what man might do to improve and beautify the system; what to make the stars shine more brightly, the sun more cheery and joyous, the moon more placid and content. Could he not heighten the tints of flowers and the melody of birds? Does he perform his duty to the inferior races? Should he not be a god to them? What is the part of the magnanimity to the whale and the beaver? Should we not fear to exchange places with them for a day, lest by their behavior they should shame us? Might we not treat with magnanimity the shark and the tiger, not descend to meet them on their own level, with spears of shark's teeth and bucklers of tiger's skin? We slander the hyena; man is the fiercest and cruelest animal. Ah! he is of little faith; even the erring comets and meteors would thank him, and return his kindness in their kind.

How meanly and grossly do we deal with nature. Could we not have a less gross labor? What else do these fine inventions suggest—magnetism, the daguerreotype, electricity? Can we not do more than cut and trim the forest?—can we not assist in its interior economy, in the circulation of the sap? Now we work superficially and violently. We do not suspect how much might

11

be done to improve our relation to animated nature even; what kindness and refined courtesy there might be.

There are certain pursuits which, if not wholly poetic and true, do at least suggest a nobler and finer relation to nature than we know. The keeping of bees, for instance, is a very slight interference. It is like directing the sunbeams. All nations, from the remotest antiquity, have thus fingered nature. There are Hymettus and Hybla, and how many bee-renowned spots beside! There is nothing gross in the idea of these little herds—their hum like the faintest low of kine in the meads. A pleasant reviewer has lately reminded us that in some places they are led out to pasture where the flowers are most abundant. "Columella tells us," says he, "that the inhabitants of Arabia sent their hives into Attica to benefit by the later-blowing flowers." Annually are the hives, in immense pyramids, carried up the Nile in boats, and suffered to float slowly down the stream by night, resting by day, as the flowers put forth along the banks; and they determine the richness of any locality, and so the profitableness of delay, by the sinking of the boat in the water. We are told, by the same reviewer, of a man in Germany, whose bees yielded more honey than those of his neighbors, with no apparent advantage; but at length he informed them that he had turned his hives one degree more to the east, and so his bees, having two hours the start in the morning, got the first sip of honey. True, there is treachery and selfishness behind all this, but these things suggest to the poetic mind what might be done.

Many examples there are of a grosser interference, yet not without their apology. We saw last summer, on the side of a mountain, a dog employed to churn for a farmer's family, traveling upon a horizontal wheel; and though he had sore eyes, an alarming cough, and withal a demure aspect, yet their bread did get buttered for all that. Undoubtedly, in the most brilliant successes, the first rank is always sacrificed. Much useless traveling of horses, *in extenso*, has of late years been improved for man's behoof, only two forces being taken advantage of—the gravity of the horse, which is the centripetal, and his centrifugal inclination to go ahead. Only these two elements in the calculation. And is not the creature's whole economy better economized thus? Are not all

finite beings better pleased with motions relative than absolute?
And what is the great globe itself but such a wheel—a larger
treadmill—so that our horse's freest steps over prairies are often-
times balked and rendered of no avail by the earth's motion on
its axis? But here he is the central agent and motive-power; and,
for variety of scenery, being provided with a window in front,
do not the ever-varying activity and fluctuating energy of the
creature himself work the effect of the most varied scenery on a
country road? It must be confessed that horses at present work
too exclusively for men, rarely men for horses; and the brute
degenerates in man's society.

It will be seen that we contemplate a time when man's will
shall be law to the physical world, and he shall no longer be
deterred by such abstractions as time and space, height and depth,
weight and hardness, but shall indeed be the lord of creation.
"Well," says the faithless reader, " 'life is short, but art is long';
where is the power that will effect all these changes?" This it is
the very object of Mr. Etzler's volume to show. At present, he
would merely remind us that there are innumerable and immeas-
urable powers already existing in nature, unimproved on a large
scale, or for generous and universal ends, amply sufficient for
these purposes. He would only indicate their existence, as a surveyor makes known the existence of a water-power on any
stream; but for their application he refers us to a sequel to this
book, called the *Mechanical System.* A few of the most obvious
and familiar of these powers are the Wind, the Tide, the Waves,
the Sunshine. Let us consider their value.

First, there is the power of the Wind, constantly exerted over
the globe. It appears from observation of a sailing vessel, and
from scientific tables, that the average power of the wind is equal
to that of one horse for every one hundred square feet. We do
not attach much value to this statement of the comparative power
of the wind and horse, for no common ground is mentioned on
which they can be compared. Undoubtedly, each is incomparably
excellent in its way, and every general comparison made for such
practical purposes as are contemplated, which gives a preference
to the one, must be made with some unfairness to the other. The
scientific tables are, for the most part, true only in a tabular

13

sense. We suspect that a loaded wagon, with a light sail, ten feet square, would not have been blown so far by the end of the year, under equal circumstances, as a common racer or dray horse would have drawn it. And how many crazy structures on our globe's surface, of the same dimensions, would wail for dry rot if the traces were hitched to them, even their windward side? Plainly this is not the principle of comparison. But even the steady and constant force of the horse may be rated as equal to his weight at least. Yet we should prefer to let the zephyrs and gales bear, with all their weight, upon our fences, than that Dobbin, with feet braced, should lean ominously against them for a season.

Nevertheless, here is an almost incalculable power at our disposal, yet how trifling the use we make of it! It only serves to turn a few mills, blow a few vessels across the ocean, and a few trivial ends besides. What a poor compliment do we pay to our indefatigable and energetic servant!

Men having discovered the power of falling water, which, after all, is comparatively slight, how eagerly do they seek out and improve these *privileges!* Let a difference of but a few feet in level be discovered on some stream near a populous town, some slight occasion for gravity to act, and the whole economy of the neighborhood is changed at once. Men do indeed speculate about and with this power as if it were the only privilege. But meanwhile this aerial stream is falling from far greater heights with more constant flow, never shrunk by drought, offering mill sites wherever the wind blows—a Niagara in the air, with no Canada side; only the application is hard.

There are the powers, too, of the Tide and Waves, constantly ebbing and flowing, lapsing and relapsing, but they serve man in but few ways. They turn a few tide-mills, and perform a few other insignificant and accidental services only. We all perceive the effect of the tide; how imperceptibly it creeps up into our harbors and rivers, and raises the heaviest navies as easily as the lightest chip. Everything that floats must yield to it. But man, slow to take nature's constant hint of assistance, makes slight and irregular use of this power, in careening ships and getting them afloat when aground.

This power may be applied in various ways. A large body, of the heaviest materials that will float, may first be raised by it, and being attached to the end of a balance reaching from the land, or from a stationary support fastened to the bottom, when the tide falls, the whole weight will be brought to bear upon the end of the balance. Also, when the tide rises, it may be made to exert a nearly equal force in the opposite direction. It can be employed wherever a *point d'appui* can be obtained.

Verily, the land would wear a busy aspect at the spring and neap tide, and these island ships, these *terrae infirmae*, which realize the fables of antiquity, affect our imagination. We have often thought that the fittest locality for a human dwelling was on the edge of the land—that there the constant lesson and impression of the sea might sink deep into the life and character of the landsman, and perhaps impart a marine tint to his imagination. It is a noble word, that *mariner*—one who is conversant with the sea. There should be more of what it signifies in each of us. It is a worthy country to belong to—we look to see him not disgrace it. Perhaps we should be equally mariners and terreners, and even our Green Mountains need some of that sea-green to be mixed with them.

The computation of the power of the Waves is less satisfactory. While only the average power of the wind and the average height of the tide were taken before, now the extreme height of the waves is used, for they are made to rise ten feet above the level of the sea, to which, adding ten more for depression, we have twenty feet, or the extreme height of a wave. Indeed, the power of the waves, which is produced by the wind blowing obliquely and at disadvantage upon the water, is made to be, not only three thousand times greater than that of the tide, but one hundred times greater than that of the wind itself, meeting its object at right angles. Moreover, this power is measured by the area of the vessel, and not by its length mainly, and it seems to be forgotten that the motion of the waves is chiefly undulatory, and exerts a power only within the limits of a vibration, else the very continents, with their extensive coasts, would soon be set adrift.

Finally, there is the power to be derived from Sunshine, by the principle on which Archimedes contrived his burning mirrors—a multiplication of mirrors reflecting the rays of the sun upon the same spot till the requisite degree of heat is obtained. The principal application of this power will be to the boiling of water and production of steam. So much for these few and more obvious powers, already used to a trifling extent. But there are innumerable others in nature not described nor discovered. These, however, will do for the present. This would be to make the sun and the moon equally our satellites. For, as the moon is the cause of the tides, and the sun the cause of the wind, which, in turn, is the cause of the waves, all the work of this planet would be performed by these far influences.

We may store up water in some eminent pond, and take out of this store, at any time, as much water through the outlet as we want to employ, by which means the original power may react for many days after it has ceased. . . . Such reservoirs of moderate elevation or size need not be made artificially, but will be found made by nature very frequently, requiring but little aid for their completion. They require no regularity of form. Any valley, with lower grounds in its vicinity, would answer the purpose. Small crevices may be filled up. Such places may be eligible for the beginning of enterprises of this kind.

The greater the height, of course, the less water required. But suppose a level and dry country; then hill and valley, and "eminent pond," are to be constructed by main force; or, if the springs are unusually low, then dirt and stones may be used, and the disadvantage arising from friction will be counterbalanced by their greater gravity. Nor shall a single rood of dry land be sunk in such artificial ponds as may be wanted, but their surfaces "may be covered with rafts decked with fertile earth, and all kinds of vegetables which may grow there as well as anywhere else."

And, finally, by the use of thick envelopes retaining the heat, and other contrivances, "the power of steam caused by sunshine may react at will, and thus be rendered perpetual, no matter how often or how long the sunshine may be interrupted."

Here is power enough, one would think, to accomplish somewhat. These are the Powers below. O ye millwrights, ye engineers, ye operatives and speculators of every class, never again

16

PARADISE (TO BE) REGAINED

complain of a want of power: it is the grossest form of infidelity. The question is, not how we shall execute, but what. Let us not use in a niggardly manner what is thus generously offered.

Consider what revolutions are to be effected in agriculture. First, in the new country a machine is to move along, taking out trees and stones to any required depth, and piling them up in convenient heaps; then the same machine, "with a little alteration," is to plane the ground perfectly, till there shall be no hills nor valleys, making the requisite canals, ditches, and roads as it goes along. The same machine, "with some other little alteration," is then to sift the ground thoroughly, supply fertile soil from other places if wanted, and plant it; and finally the same machine, "with a little addition," is to reap and gather in the crop, thresh and grind it, or press it to oil, or prepare it any way for final use. For the description of these machines we are referred to *Etzler's Mechanical System*, pages 11 to 27. We should be pleased to see that *Mechanical System*. We have great faith in it. But we cannot stop for applications now.

Who knows but by accumulating the power until the end of the present century, using meanwhile only the smallest allowance, reserving all that blows, all that shines, all that ebbs and flows, all that dashes, we may have got such a reserved accumulated power as to run the earth off its track into a new orbit, some summer, and so change the tedious vicissitude of the seasons? Or, perchance, coming generations will not abide the dissolution of the globe, but, availing themselves of future inventions in aerial locomotion, and the navigation of space, the entire race may migrate from earth, to settle some vacant and more western planet, it may be still healthy, perchance unearthy, not composed of dirt and stones, whose primary strata only are strewn, and where no weeds are sown. It took but little art, a simple application of natural laws, a canoe, a paddle, and a sail of matting, to people the isles of the Pacific, and a little more will people the shining isles of space. Do we not see in the firmament the lights carried along the shore by night, as Columbus did? Let us not despair nor mutiny.

The dwellings also ought to be very different from what is known, if the full benefit of our means be enjoyed. They are to be of a struc-

17

ture for which we have no name yet. They are to be neither palaces, nor temples, nor cities, but a combination of all, superior to whatever is known.

Earth may be baked into bricks, or even vitrified stone by heat—we may bake large masses of any size and form, into stone and vitrified substance of the greatest durability, lasting even thousands of years, out of clayey earth, or of stones ground to dust, by the application of burning mirrors. This is to be done in the open air without other preparation than gathering the substance, grinding and mixing it with water and cement, molding or casting it, and bringing the focus of the burning mirrors of proper size upon the same.

The character of the architecture is to be quite different from what it ever has been hitherto; large solid masses are to be baked or cast in one piece, ready-shaped in any form that may be desired. The building may, therefore, consist of columns two hundred feet high and upwards, of proportionate thickness, and of one entire piece of vitrified substance; huge pieces are to be molded so as to join and hook on to each other firmly, by proper joints and folds, and not to yield in any way without breaking.

Foundries, of any description, are to be heated by burning mirrors, and will require no labor, except the making of the first molds and the superintendence for gathering the metal and taking the finished articles away.

Alas! in the present state of science, we must take the finished articles away; but think not that man will always be the victim of circumstances.

The countryman who visited the city, and found the streets cluttered with bricks and lumber, reported that it was not yet finished; and one who considers the endless repairs and reforming of our houses might well wonder when they will be done. But why may not the dwellings of men on this earth be built, once for all, of some durable material, some Roman or Etruscan masonry, which will stand, so that time shall only adorn and beautify them? Why may we not finish the outward world for posterity, and leave them leisure to attend to the inner? Surely all the gross necessities and economies might be cared for in a few years. All might be built and baked and stored up, during this, the term-time of the world, against the vacant eternity, and the globe go provisioned and furnished, like our public vessels, for its voyage through space, as through some Pacific Ocean, while we would "tie up the rudder and sleep before the wind," as those who sail from Lima to Manila.

But, to go back a few years in imagination, think not that life in these crystal palaces is to bear any analogy to life in our present humble cottages. Far from it. Clothed, once for all, in some "flexible stuff," more durable than George Fox's suit of leather, composed of "fibers of vegetables," "glutinated" together by some "cohesive substances," and made into sheets, like paper, of any size or form, man will put far from him corroding care and the whole host of ills.

The twenty-five halls in the inside of the square are to be each two hundred feet square and high; the forty corridors, each one hundred feet long and twenty wide; the eighty galleries, each from 1,000 to 1,250 feet long; about 7,000 private rooms, the whole surrounded and intersected by the grandest and most splendid colonnades imaginable; floors, ceilings, columns, with their various beautiful and fanciful intervals, all shining, and reflecting to infinity all objects and persons, with splendid luster of all beautiful colors and fanciful shapes and pictures.

All galleries, outside and within the halls, are to be provided with many thousand commodious and most elegant vehicles, in which persons may move up and down like birds, in perfect security, and without exertion. . . . Any member may procure himself all the common articles of his daily wants by a short turn of some crank, without leaving his apartment.

One or two persons are sufficient to direct the kitchen business. They have nothing else to do but to superintend the cookery, and to watch the time of the victuals being done, and then to remove them, with the table and vessels, into the dining hall, or to the respective private apartments, by a slight motion of the hand at some crank. . . . *Any very extraordinary desire of any person may be satisfied by going to the place where the thing is to be had; and anything that requires a particular preparation in cooking or baking may be done by the person who desires it.*

This is one of those instances in which the individual genius is found to consent, as indeed it always does, at last, with the universal. This last sentence has a certain sad and sober truth, which reminds us of the scripture of all nations. All expression of truth does at length take this deep ethical form. Here is hint of a place the most eligible of any in space, and of a servitor, in

19

comparison with whom all other helps dwindle into insignificance. We hope to hear more of him anon, for even a Crystal Palace would be deficient without his invaluable services.

And as for the environs of the establishment:

There will be afforded the most enrapturing views to be fancied, out of the private apartments, from the galleries, from the roof, from its turrets and cupolas—gardens, as far as the eye can see, full of fruits and flowers, arranged in the most beautiful order, with walks, colonnades, aqueducts, canals, ponds, plains, amphitheatres, terraces, fountains, sculptural works, pavilions, gondolas, places for public amusement, etc., to delight the eye and fancy, the taste and smell. . . . The walks and roads are to be paved with hard vitrified large plates, so as to be always clean from all dirt in any weather or season. . . .

The walks may be covered with porticoes adorned with magnificent columns, statues, and sculptural works; all of vitrified substance, and lasting forever. At night the roof and the inside and outside of the whole square are illuminated by gaslight, which, in the mazes of many-colored crystal-like colonnades and vaultings, is reflected with brilliancy that gives to the whole a luster of precious stones, as far as the eye can see. Such are the future abodes of men. . . . Such is the life reserved to true intelligence, but withheld from ignorance, prejudice, and stupid adherence to custom.

Thus is Paradise to be Regained, and that old and stern decree at length reversed. Man shall no more earn his living by the sweat of his brow. All labor shall be reduced to "a short turn of some crank," and "taking the finished articles away." But there is a crank—oh, how hard to be turned! Could there not be a crank upon a crank—an infinitely small crank?—we would fain inquire. No, alas! not. But there is a certain divine energy in every man, but sparingly employed as yet, which may be called the crank within, the crank after all—the prime mover in all machinery— quite indispensable to all work. Would that we might get our hands on its handle! In fact, no work can be shirked. It may be postponed indefinitely, but not infinitely. Nor can any really important work be made easier by cooperation or machinery. Not one particle of labor now threatening any man can be routed without being performed. It cannot be hunted out of the vicinity like jackals and hyenas. It will not run. You may begin by sawing the little sticks, or you may saw the great sticks first, but sooner or later you must saw them both.

We will not be imposed upon by this vast application of forces. We believe that most things will have to be accomplished still by the application called Industry. We are rather pleased, after all, to consider the small private, but both constant and accumulated, force which stands behind every spade in the field. This it is that makes the valleys shine and the deserts really bloom. Sometimes, we confess, we are so degenerate as to reflect with pleasure on the days when men were yoked like cattle, and drew a crooked stick for a plow. After all, the great interests and methods were the same.

It is a rather serious objection to Mr. Etzler's schemes that they require time, men, and money, three very superfluous and inconvenient things for an honest and well-disposed man to deal with. "The whole world," he tells us, "might therefore be really changed into a paradise, within less than ten years, commencing from the first year of an association for the purpose of constructing and applying the machinery." We are sensible of a startling incongruity when the time and money are mentioned in this connection. The ten years which are proposed would be a tedious while to wait if every man were at his post and did his duty, but quite too short a period if we are to take time for it. But this fault is by no means peculiar to Mr. Etzler's schemes. There is far too much hurry and bustle, and too little patience and privacy, in all our methods, as if something were to be accomplished in centuries. The true reformer does not want time, nor money, nor cooperation, nor advice. What is time but the stuff delay is made of? And depend upon it, our virtue will not live on the interest of our money. He expects no income, but outgoes; so soon as we begin to count the cost, the cost begins. And as for advice, the information floating in the atmosphere of society is as evanescent and unserviceable to him as gossamer for clubs of Hercules. There is absolutely no common sense; it is common nonsense. If we are to risk a cent or a drop of our blood, who then shall advise us? For ourselves, we are too young for experience. Who is old enough? We are older by faith than by experience. In the unbending of the arm to do the deed there is experience worth all the maxims in the world.

21

It will now be plainly seen that the execution of the proposals is not proper for individuals. Whether it be proper for government at this time, before the subject has become popular, is a question to be decided; all that is to be done is to step forth, after mature reflection, to confess loudly one's conviction, and to constitute societies. Man is powerful but in union with many. Nothing great, for the improvement of his own condition or that of his fellow men, can ever be effected by individual enterprise.

Alas! this is the crying sin of the age, this want of faith in the prevalence of a man. Nothing can be effected but by one man. He who wants help wants everything. True, this is the condition of our weakness, but it can never be the means of our recovery. We must first succeed alone, that we may enjoy our success together. We trust that the social movements which we witness indicate an aspiration not to be thus cheaply satisfied. In this matter of reforming the world, we have little faith in corporations; not thus was it first formed.

But our author is wise enough to say that the raw materials for the accomplishment of his purposes are "iron, copper, wood, earth chiefly, and a union of men whose eyes and understanding are not shut up by preconceptions." Ay, this last may be what we want mainly—a company of "odd fellows" indeed.

"Small shares of twenty dollars will be sufficient"—in all, from "200,000 to 300,000"—"to create the first establishment for a whole community of from 3,000 to 4,000 individuals;" at the end of five years we shall have a principal of two hundred millions of dollars, and so paradise will be wholly regained at the end of the tenth year. But, alas! the ten years have already elapsed, and there are no signs of Eden yet, for want of the requisite funds to begin the enterprise in a hopeful manner. Yet it seems a safe investment. Perchance they could be hired at a low rate, the property being mortgaged for security, and, if necessary, it could be given up in any stage of the enterprise, without loss, with the fixtures.

But we see two main difficulties in the way: first, the successful application of the powers by machinery (we have not yet seen the *Mechanical System*), and, secondly, which is infinitely harder, the application of man to the work by faith. This it is, we fear, which will prolong the ten years to ten thousand at least. It will take a power more than "eighty thousand times greater than all the men on earth could effect with their nerves" to persuade men to use that which is already offered them. Even a greater than this physical power must be brought to bear upon that moral power. Faith, indeed, is all the reform that is needed; it is itself a reform. Doubtless, we are as slow to conceive of Paradise as of Heaven, of a perfect natural as of a perfect spiritual world. We see how past ages have loitered and erred. "Is perhaps our generation free from irrationality and error? Have we perhaps now the summit of human wisdom, and need no more to look out for mental or physical improvement?" Undoubtedly, we are never so visionary as to be prepared for what the next hour may bring forth.

Μέλλει τὸ θεῖον δ᾽ἐστι τοιοῦτον φύσει.

The Divine is about to be, and such is its nature. In our wisest moments we are secreting a matter, which, like the lime of the shellfish, encrusts us quite over, and well for us if, like it, we cast our shells from time to time, though they be pearl and of the fairest tint. Let us consider under what disadvantages Science has hitherto labored before we pronounce thus confidently on her progress.

Mr. Etzler is not one of the enlightened practical men, the pioneers of the actual, who move with the slow, deliberate tread of science, conserving the world; who execute the dreams of the last century, though they have no dreams of their own; yet he deals in the very raw but still solid material of all inventions. He has more of the practical than usually belongs to so bold a schemer, so resolute a dreamer. Yet his success is in theory, and not in practice, and he feeds our faith rather than contents our understanding. His book wants order, serenity, dignity, every-thing—but it does not fail to impart what only man can impart to man of much importance, his own faith. It is true his dreams are not thrilling nor bright enough, and he leaves off to dream where he who dreams just before the dawn begins. His castles in the air fall to the ground because they are not built lofty enough; they should be secured to heaven's roof. After all, the theories and speculations of men concern us more than their puny accomplishment. It is with a certain coldness and languor that we loiter about the actual and so-called practical. How little do the most wonderful inventions of modern times detain us. They insult nature. Every machine, or particular application, seems a slight outrage against universal laws. How many fine inventions are there which do not clutter the ground? We think that those only succeed which minister to our sensible and animal wants, which bake or brew, wash or warm or the like. But are those of no account which are patented by fancy and imagination, and succeed so admirably in our dreams that they give the tone still to our waking thoughts? Already nature is serving all those uses which science slowly derives on a much higher and grander scale to him that will be served by her. When the sunshine falls on the path of the poet, he enjoys all those pure benefits and pleasures which the arts slowly and partially realize from age to age. The winds which fan his cheek waft him the sum of that profit and happiness which their lagging inventions supply.

The chief fault of this book is that it aims to secure the greatest degree of gross comfort and pleasure merely. It paints a Mahometan's heaven, and stops short with singular abruptness when we think it is drawing near to the precincts of the Christian's,—and we trust we have not made here a distinction without a difference. Undoubtedly if we were to reform this outward life truly and thoroughly, we should find no duty of the inner omitted. It would be employment for our whole nature; and what we should do thereafter would be as vain a question as to ask the bird what it will do when its nest is built and its brood reared. But a moral reform must take place first, and then the necessity of the other will be superseded, and we shall sail and plow by its force alone. There is a speedier way than the *Mechanical System* can show to fill up marshes, to drown the roar of the waves, to tame hyenas, secure agreeable environs, diversify the land, and refresh it with "rivulets of sweet water," and that is by the power of rectitude and true behavior. It is only for a little while, only occasionally, methinks, that we want a garden. Surely a good man need not be at the labor to level a hill for the sake of a prospect, or raise fruits and flowers, and construct floating islands, for the sake of a paradise. He enjoys better prospects than lie behind any hill.

Where an angel travels, it will be paradise all the way; but where Satan travels, it will be burning marl and cinders. What says Veeshnoo Sarma? "He whose mind is at ease is possessed of all riches. Is it not the same to one whose foot is enclosed in a shoe, as if the whole surface of the earth were covered with leather?"

He who is conversant with the supernal powers will not worship these inferior deities of the wind, waves, tide, and sunshine. But we would not disparage the importance of such calculations as we have described. They are truths in physics, because they are true in ethics. The moral powers no one would presume to calculate. Suppose we could compare the moral with the physical, and say how many horsepower the force of love, for instance, blowing on every square foot of a man's soul, would equal. No doubt we are well aware of this force; figures would not increase our respect for it; the sunshine is equal to but one ray of its heat. The light of the sun is but the shadow of love. "The souls of men loving and fearing God," says Raleigh, "receive influence from that divine light itself, whereof the sun's clarity, and that of the stars, is by Plato called but a shadow. *Lumen est umbra Dei, Deus est Lumen Luminis.* Light is the shadow of God's brightness, who is the light of light," and, we may add, the heat of heat. Love is the wind, the tide, the waves, the sunshine. Its power is incalculable; it is many horsepower. It never ceases, it never slacks; it can move the globe without a resting place; it can warm without fire; it can feed without meat; it can clothe without garments; it can shelter without roof; it can make a paradise within which will dispense with a paradise without. But though the wisest men in all ages have labored to publish this force, and every human heart is, sooner or later, more or less, made to feel it, yet how little is actually applied to social ends! True, it is the motive power of all successful social machinery; but as in physics we have made the elements do only a little drudgery for us, steam to take the place of a few horses; wind, of a few oars, water, of a few cranks and handmills—as the mechanical forces have not yet been generously and largely applied to make the physical world answer to the ideal, so the power of love has been but meanly and sparingly applied as yet. It has patented only such

25

machines as the almshouse, the hospital, and the Bible Society, while its infinite wind is still blowing, and blowing down these very structures, too, from time to time. Still less are we accumulating its power, and preparing to act with greater energy at a future time. Shall we not contribute our shares to this enterprise, then?

HERALD OF FREEDOM
1844

One of the very few men Thoreau could praise wholeheartedly was Nathaniel Peabody Rogers, a New Hampshire lawyer turned abolitionist editor. His weekly newspaper, Herald of Freedom, *was read in the Thoreau household and admired especially by Henry, who flew the same "no organization" flag. Rogers's intense individualism clashed with William Lloyd Garrison's conviction that organized slavery required an organized abolitionist movement to overthrow it. Thoreau took sides in the conflict in his spirited but oblique article supporting Rogers as a man and a stylist; it appeared in* The Dial *of April 1844. Rogers went under, however, losing his editorship and his influence in the antislavery movement, which moved into the broader channel of a political strategy ready to use expediency to win popular support. (M.M.)*

We had occasionally, for several years, met with a number of this spirited journal, edited, as abolitionists need not to be informed, by Nathaniel P. Rogers, once a counselor-at-law in Plymouth, still farther up the Merrimack, but now, in his riper years, come down the hills thus far, to be the Herald of Freedom to these parts. We had been refreshed not a little by the cheap cordial of his editorials, flowing like his own mountain torrents, now clear and sparkling, now foaming and gritty, and always spiced with the essence of the fir and the Norway pine; but never

27

dark nor muddy, nor threatening with smothered murmurs, like the rivers of the plain. The effect of one of his effusions reminds us of what the hydropathists say about the electricity in fresh spring water, compared with that which has stood overnight, to suit weak nerves. We do not know of another notable and public instance of such pure, youthful, and hearty indignation at all wrong. The Church itself must love it, if it have any heart, though he is said to have dealt rudely with its sanctity. His clean attachment to the right, however, sanctions the severest rebuke we have read.

Mr. Rogers seems to us to have occupied an honorable and manly position in these days, and in this country, making the press a living and breathing organ to reach the hearts of men, and not merely "fine paper and good type," with its civil pilot sitting aft, and magnanimously waiting for the news to arrive—the vehicle of the earliest news, but the *latest intelligence*—recording the indubitable and last results, the marriages and deaths, alone. This editor was wide awake, and standing on the beak of his ship; not as a scientific explorer under government, but a Yankee sealer rather, who makes those unexplored continents his harbors in which to refit for more adventurous cruises. He was a fund of news and freshness in himself—had the gift of speech, and the knack of writing; and if anything important took place in the Granite State, we might be sure that we should hear of it in good season. No other paper that we know kept pace so well with one forward wave of the restless public thought and sentiment of New England, and asserted so faithfully and ingenuously the largest liberty in all things. There was beside more unpledged poetry in his prose than in the verses of many an accepted rhymer; and we were occasionally advertised by a mellow hunter's note from his trumpet, that, unlike most reformers, his feet were still where they should be, on the turf, and that he looked out for a serener natural life into the turbid arena of politics. Nor was slavery always a somber theme with him, but invested with the colors of his wit and fancy, and an evil to be abolished by other means than sorrow and bitterness of complaint. He will fight this fight with what cheer may be.

But to speak of his composition. It is a genuine Yankee style,

without fiction—real guessing and calculating to some purpose—
and reminds us occasionally, as does all free, brave, and original
writing, of its great master in these days, Thomas Carlyle. It has
a life above grammar, and a meaning which need not be parsed to
be understood. But like those same mountain torrents, there is
rather too much slope to his channel, and the rainbow sprays and
evaporations go double-quick time to heaven, while the body of
his water falls headlong to the plain. We could have more pause
and deliberation, occasionally, if only to bring his tide to a head—
more frequent expansions of the stream—still, bottomless, mountain tarns, perchance inland seas, and at length the deep ocean
itself.

Some extracts will show in what sense he was a poet as well
as a reformer. He thus raises the antislavery "war whoop" in
New Hampshire, when an important convention is to be held,
sending the summons:

> To none but the wholehearted, fully committed, cross-the-Rubicon
> spirits. . . . From rich 'old Cheshire,' from Rockingham, with her
> horizon setting down away to the salt sea . . . from where the sun
> sets behind Kearsarge, even to where he rises gloriously over *Moses
> Norris's* own town of *Pittsfield*—and from Amoskeag to Ragged
> Mountains—Coos—Upper Coos, home of the everlasting hills—send
> out your bold advocates of human rights, wherever they lay, scattered
> by lonely lake, or Indian stream, or "Grant," or "Location," from the
> trout-haunted brooks of the Amoriscoggin, and where the adventur-
> ous streamlet takes up its mountain march for the St. Lawrence.
> Scattered and insulated men wherever the light of philanthropy and
> liberty has beamed in upon your solitary spirits, come down to us
> like your streams and clouds and our own Grafton, all about among
> your dear hills, and your mountain-flanked valleys—whether you
> *home* along the swift Ammonoosuck, the cold Pemigewassett, or the
> ox-bowed Connecticut. . . .
> We are slow, brethren, dishonorably slow, in a cause like ours. Our
> feet should be as "hinds' feet." "Liberty lies bleeding." The leaden-
> colored wing of slavery obscures the land with its baleful shadow. Let
> us come together, and inquire at the hand of the Lord what is to be
> done.

And again, on occasion of a New England Convention in the
Second-Advent Tabernacle, in Boston, he desires to try one more
blast, as it were, "on Fabyan's White Mountain horn":

Ho, then, people of the Bay State—men, women, and children; children, women, and men, scattered friends of the *friendless*, wheresoever ye inhabit—if habitations ye have, as such friends have not *always*—along the sea-beat border of Old Essex and the Puritan Landing, and up beyond sight of the sea cloud, among the inland hills, where the sun rises and sets upon the dry land, in that vale of the Connecticut, too fair for human content and too fertile for virtuous industry—where deepens the haughtiest of earth's streams, on its seaward way, proud with the pride of old Massachusetts. Are there any friends of the friendless Negro haunting such a valley as this? In God's name, I fear there are none, or few; for the very scene looks apathy and oblivion to the genius of humanity. I blow you the summons, though. Come, if any of you are there.

And gallant little Rhode Island; *transcendent* abolitionists of the tiny Commonwealth. I need not call you. You are *called* the year round, and, instead of sleeping in your tents, stand harnessed, and with trumpets in your hands—every one!

Connecticut! Yonder, the home of the Burleighs, the Monroes, and the Hudsons, and the native land of old George Benson! are you ready? "All ready!"

Maine here, off east, looking from my mountain post like an everglade. Where is your Sam. Fessenden, who stood storm-proof 'gainst New Organization in '38. Has he too much name as a jurist and orator, to be found at a New England Convention in '43? God forbid! Come one and all of you from "Down East" to Boston, on the thirtieth, and let the sails of your coasters whiten all the sea-road. Alas! there are scarce enough of you to man a fishing boat. Come up mighty in your fewness.

Such timely, pure, and unpremeditated expressions of a public sentiment, such publicity of genuine indignation and humanity, as abound everywhere in this journal, are the most generous gifts which a man can make.

WENDELL PHILLIPS
BEFORE THE CONCORD LYCEUM
1845

Believing in "the largest liberty in all things," Thoreau came again and again to the defense of men whose right to be heard was threatened. A few months after standing up for Rogers against Garrison's attack, he joined Emerson in defying the Concord churchmen who refused their buildings for a meeting to mark the anniversary of Negro emancipation in the British West Indies. Thoreau rang the bell in the courthouse to rally the townsfolk to hear Emerson's address. That was August 1, 1844. By wintertime a free speech controversy of some years' duration had come to a head in the Concord Lyceum. The conservative town squires who argued for exclusion of controversial issues were defeated by the liberals, who elected Thoreau and Emerson to the governing board. The new men moved promptly to invite Wendell Phillips to lecture on slavery. Thoreau reported the speech for The Liberator, *in a letter printed March 28, 1845. (M.M.)*

Mr. Editor: We have now, for the third winter, had our spirits refreshed, and our faith in the destiny of the Commonwealth strengthened, by the presence and the eloquence of Wendell Phillips; and we wish to tender to him our thanks and our sympathy. The admission of this gentleman into the Lyceum has been strenuously opposed by a respectable portion of our fellow citizens, who themselves, we trust—whose descendants, at least, we know—will be as faithful conservers of the true order, when-

31

ever that shall be the order of the day—and in each instance
the people have voted that they *would hear him*, by coming
themselves and bringing their friends to the lecture room, and
being very silent that they *might* hear. We saw some men and
women, who had long ago *come out, going in* once more through
the free and hospitable portals of the Lyceum; and many of our
neighbors confessed that they had had a "sound season" this once.

It was the speaker's aim to show what the State, and above all
the Church, had to do, and now, alas! have done, with Texas and
slavery, and how much, on the other hand, the individual should
have to do with Church and State. These were fair themes, and
not mistimed, and his words were addressed to "fit audience, *and
not* few."

We must give Mr. Phillips the credit of being a clean, erect,
and what was once called a consistent man. He at least is not
responsible for slavery, nor for American Independence; for the
hypocrisy and superstition of the Church, nor the timidity and
selfishness of the State; nor for the indifference and willing
ignorance of any. He stands so distinctly, so firmly, and so effectively alone, and one honest man is so much more than a host,
that we cannot but feel that he does himself injustice when he
reminds us of "the American Society, which he represents." It
is rare that we have the pleasure of listening to so clear and
orthodox a speaker, who obviously has so few cracks or flaws
in his moral nature—who, having words at his command in a
remarkable degree, has much more than words, if these should
fail, in his unquestionable earnestness and integrity—and, aside
from their admiration at his rhetoric, secures the genuine respect
of his audience. He unconsciously tells his biography as he
proceeds, and we see him early and earnestly deliberating on
these subjects, and wisely and bravely, without counsel or consent of any, occupying a ground at first from which the varying
tides of public opinion cannot drive him.

No one could mistake the genuine modesty and truth with
which he affirmed, when speaking of the framers of the Constitution, "I am wiser than they," who with him has improved these
sixty years' experience of its working; or the uncompromising
consistency and frankness of the prayer which concluded—not

like the Thanksgiving proclamations, with, "God save the Commonwealth of Massachusetts," but—God dash it into a thousand
pieces, till there shall not remain a fragment on which a man can
stand, and dare not tell his name, referring to the case of Frederick ——.* To our disgrace we know not what to call him, unless
Scotland will lend us the spoils of one of her Douglasses, out of
history or fiction, for a season, till we be hospitable and brave
enough to hear his proper name—a fugitive slave in one more
sense than we; who has proved himself the possessor of a fair
intellect, and has won a colorless reputation in these parts,
and who, we trust, will be as superior to degradation from the
sympathies of Freedom as from the antipathies of Slavery. When,
said Mr. Phillips, he communicated to a New Bedford audience,
the other day, his purpose of writing his life, and telling his name,
and the name of his master, and the place he ran from, the
murmur ran round the room, and was anxiously whispered by
the sons of the Pilgrims: "He had better not!" And it was echoed
under the shadow of Concord monument: "He had better not!"

We would fain express our appreciation of the freedom and
steady wisdom, so rare in the reformer, with which he declared
that he was not born to abolish slavery, but to do right. We have
heard a few, a very few, good political speakers, who afforded
us the pleasure of great intellectual power and acuteness, of
soldierlike steadiness, and of a graceful and natural oratory; but
in this man the audience might detect a sort of moral principle
and integrity, which was more stable than their firmness, more
discriminating than his own intellect, and more graceful than his
rhetoric, which was not working for temporary or trivial ends.
It is so rare and encouraging to listen to an orator who is content
with another alliance than with the popular party, or even with
the sympathizing school of the martyrs, who can afford sometimes to be his own auditor if the mob stay away, and hears
himself without reproof, that we feel ourselves in danger of
slandering all mankind by affirming that here is one who is at the
same time an eloquent speaker and a righteous man.

Perhaps, on the whole, the most interesting fact elicited by
these addresses, is the readiness of the people at large, of what-

* Frederick Douglass, fugitive slave.

ever sect or party, to entertain, with good will and hospitality, the most revolutionary and heretical opinions, when frankly and adequately, and in some sort cheerfully, expressed. Such clear and candid declaration of opinion served like an electuary to whet and clarify the intellect of all parties, and furnished each one with an additional argument for that right he asserted.

We consider Mr. Phillips one of the most conspicuous and efficient champions of a true Church and State now in the field, and would say to him, and such as are like him, "God speed you." If you know of any champion in the ranks of his opponents who has the valor and courtesy even of paynim chivalry, if not the Christian graces and refinement of this knight, you will do us a service by directing him to these fields forthwith, where the lists are now open, and he shall be hospitably entertained. For as yet the Redcross Knight has shown us only the gallant device upon his shield, and his admirable command of his steed, prancing and curveting in the empty lists; but we wait to see who, in the actual breaking of lances, will come tumbling upon the plain.

CIVIL DISOBEDIENCE
1849

It was on a July evening in 1846, a year after he had gone to live in a hut by Walden Pond, that Thoreau was put in jail for refusing to pay his poll tax. He had stopped paying the tax four years earlier, unwilling to support a state that sanctioned slavery, but for some reason nothing had been done about it until the night when Sam Staples, Concord's jailer, picked Henry up as he strolled into town to collect a repaired shoe from the cobbler. If it had been a test case of the poll-tax law he wanted, Thoreau was not to have his chance, for before the night in jail was over, his Aunt Maria had paid the tax, and by morning Henry was free to put on the mended shoe and go off huckleberrying.

Brief as his prison hours were, they led to his best known and most influential essay. Only a few months before he went to jail the United States had begun a war with Mexico. Thoreau held it was promoted by relatively a few slaveholders, using the government as their tool for extending slavery into new territory. A man of conscience could not be associated with this American government without disgrace, Thoreau said in "Civil Disobedience," nor could he for an instant recognize that political organization as his government which was the slave's government also.

"Civil Disobedience" reached only a handful of listeners in its first form, a lecture entitled "The Rights and Duties of the Individual in Relation to Government," delivered twice at the Concord Lyceum, early in 1848. The next year Elizabeth Peabody's Aesthetic Papers made its first and only appearance, and included, along with pieces by Emerson and Hawthorne, Thoreau's lecture, retitled "Resistance to Civil Government." If anyone read the essay, they made no men-

35

tion of it. It was ignored until four years after Thoreau's death when, as "Civil Disobedience," it was included in his A Yankee in Canada, With Anti-Slavery and Reform Papers. In 1890 Thoreau's British biographer, Henry S. Salt, gave it a place in a Thoreau collection, and by 1903 it appeared by itself in a cheap paperback in England. It took twenty-five more years before Thoreau's own countrymen printed it separately, although in an expensive limited edition of three hundred copies. Now, of course, the essay has been included in many anthologies of great writing and enjoys frequent reprinting by libertarian editors.

"Civil Disobedience" has had a universal appeal. What it says goes beyond the Mexican War and the slavery struggle with which it was immediately concerned. Thoreau spoke to the issue of the moral law in conflict with government law. He argued that "it is not desirable to cultivate a respect for the law, so much as for the right." The law is not to be respected merely because it is the law, but only because it is right and just. If unjust laws exist, civil disobedience is an effective way to oppose and change them. "Under a government which imprisons any man unjustly, the true place for a just man is also a prison." In the Nürnberg trials that followed the fall of Nazism, the precedent was set for punishing individuals who failed to practice civil disobedience when they carried out orders civilized man regarded as crimes against humanity.

The doctrine of civil disobedience was not originated by Thoreau. But his expression of it eventually moved people around the world to practice it against local and national tyrannies. Gandhi in South Africa and India, the resistance movement of Nazi-occupied Europe, the freedom riders and sit-downers from New York to Mississippi, the anti-nuclear war pickets in Eniwetok, Groton, and Scotland have responded to the words uttered in Concord over a hundred years ago. (M.M.)

I heartily accept the motto, "That government is best which governs least"; and I should like to see it acted up to more rapidly and systematically. Carried out, it finally amounts to this, which also I believe: "That government is best which governs not at all"; and when men are prepared for it, that will be the kind of government which they will have. Government is at best but an expedient; but most governments are usually, and all governments

36

governed by self-interest

are sometimes, inexpedient. The objections which have been brought against a standing army—and they are many and weighty, and deserve to prevail—may also at last be brought against a standing government. The standing army is only an arm of the standing government. The government itself, which is only the mode which the people have chosen to execute their will, is equally liable to be abused and perverted before the people can act through it. Witness the present Mexican war, the work of comparatively a few individuals using the standing government as their tool; for, in the outset, the people would not have consented to this measure.

This American government—what is it but a tradition, though a recent one, endeavoring to transmit itself unimpaired to posterity, but each instant losing some of its integrity? It has not the vitality and force of a single living man; for a single man can bend it to his will. It is a sort of wooden gun to the people themselves. But it is not the less necessary for this; for the people must have some complicated machinery or other, and hear its din, to satisfy that idea of government which they have. Governments show thus how successfully men can be imposed on, even impose on themselves, for their own advantage. It is excellent, we must all allow. Yet this government never of itself furthered any enterprise, but by the alacrity with which it got out of its way. It does not keep the country free. It does not settle the West. It does not educate. The character inherent in the American people has done all that has been accomplished; and it would have done somewhat more if the government had not sometimes got in its way. For government is an expedient by which men would fain succeed in letting one another alone; and, as has been said, when it is most expedient, the governed are most let alone by it. Trade and commerce, if they were not made of india rubber, would never manage to bounce over the obstacles which legislators are continually putting in their way; and, if one were to judge these men wholly by the effects of their actions and not partly by their intentions, they would deserve to be classed and punished with those mischievous persons who put obstructions on the railroads.

But to speak practically and as a citizen, unlike those who call

37

themselves no-government men, I ask for, not at once no government, but at once a better government. Let every man make known what kind of government would command his respect, and that will be one step toward obtaining it.

After all, the practical reason why, when the power is once in the hands of the people, a majority are permitted, and for a long period continue, to rule is not because they are most likely to be in the right, nor because this seems fairest to the minority, but because they are physically the strongest. But a government in which the majority rule in all cases cannot be based on justice, even as far as men understand it. Can there not be a government in which majorities do not virtually decide right and wrong, but conscience?—in which majorities decide only those questions to which the rule of expediency is applicable? Must the citizen ever for a moment, or in the least degree, resign his conscience to the legislator? Why has every man a conscience, then? I think that we should be men first, and subjects afterward. It is not desirable to cultivate a respect for the law, so much as for the right. The only obligation which I have a right to assume is to do at any time what I think right. It is truly enough said that a corporation has no conscience; but a corporation of conscientious men is a corporation with a conscience. Law never made men a whit more just; and, by means of their respect for it, even the well disposed are daily made the agents of injustice. A common and natural result of an undue respect for law is that you may see a file of soldiers—colonel, captain, corporal, privates, powder monkeys, and all—marching in admirable order over hill and dale to the wars, against their wills, ay, against their common sense and consciences, which makes it very steep marching indeed, and produces a palpitation of the heart. They have no doubt that it is a damnable business in which they are concerned; they are all peaceably inclined. Now, what are they? Men at all? or small movable forts and magazines, at the service of some unscrupulous man in power? Visit the navy yard, and behold a marine, such a man as an American government can make, or such as it can make a man with its black arts—a mere shadow and reminiscence of humanity, a man laid out alive and standing, and already, as one may say, buried under arms with funeral accompaniments, though it may be:

> Not a drum was heard, not a funeral note,
> As his corse to the rampart we hurried;
> Not a soldier discharged his farewell shot
> O'er the grave where our hero we buried.

The mass of men serve the state thus, not as men mainly, but as machines, with their bodies. They are the standing army, and the militia, jailers, constables, posse comitatus, etc. In most cases there is no free exercise whatever of the judgment or of the moral sense; but they put themselves on a level with wood and earth and stones; and wooden men can perhaps be manufactured that will serve the purpose as well. Such command no more respect than men of straw or a lump of dirt. They have the same sort of worth only as horses and dogs. Yet such as these even are commonly esteemed good citizens. Others—as most legislators, politicians, lawyers, ministers, and officeholders—serve the state chiefly with their heads; and, as they rarely make any moral distinctions, they are as likely to serve the devil, without intending it, as God. A very few—as heroes, patriots, martyrs, reformers in the great sense, and men—serve the state with their consciences also, and so necessarily resist it for the most part; and they are commonly treated as enemies by it. A wise man will only be useful as a man, and will not submit to be "clay," and "stop a hole to keep the wind away," but leave that office to his dust at least:

> I am too high-born to be propertied,
> To be a secondary at control,
> Or useful serving man and instrument
> To any sovereign state throughout the world.

He who gives himself entirely to his fellow men appears to them useless and selfish; but he who gives himself partially to them is pronounced a benefactor and philanthropist.

How does it become a man to behave toward this American government today? I answer that he cannot without disgrace be associated with it. I cannot for an instant recognize that political organization as my government which is the slave's government also.

All men recognize the right of revolution; that is, the right to refuse allegiance to, and to resist, the government when its tyranny or its inefficiency are great and unendurable. But almost all say that such is not the case now. But such was the case, they think, in the Revolution of '75. If one were to tell me that this was a bad government because it taxed certain foreign commodities brought to its ports, it is most probable that I should not make an ado about it, for I can do without them. All machines have their friction; and possibly this does enough good to counterbalance the evil. At any rate, it is a great evil to make a stir about it. But when the friction comes to have its machine, and oppression and robbery are organized, I say, let us not have such a machine any longer. In other words, when a sixth of the population of a nation which has undertaken to be the refuge of liberty are slaves, and a whole country is unjustly overrun and conquered by a foreign army and subjected to military law, I think that it is not too soon for honest men to rebel and revolutionize. What makes this duty the more urgent is the fact that the country so overrun is not our own, but ours is the invading army.

Paley, a common authority with many on moral questions, in his chapter on the "Duty of Submission to Civil Government," resolves all civil obligation into expediency; and he proceeds to say that "so long as the interest of the whole society requires it, that is, so long as the established government cannot be resisted or changed without public inconveniency, it is the will of God . . . that the established government be obeyed—and no longer. This principle being admitted, the justice of every particular case of resistance is reduced to a computation of the quantity of the danger and grievance on the one side, and of the probability and expense of redressing it on the other." Of this, he says, every man shall judge for himself. But Paley appears never to have contemplated those cases to which the rule of expediency does not apply, in which a people, as well as an individual, must do justice, cost what it may. If I have unjustly wrested a plank from a drowning man, I must restore it to him though I drown myself.

This, according to Paley, would be inconvenient. But he that would save his life, in such a case, shall lose it.] This people must cease to hold slaves, and to make war on Mexico, though it cost them their existence as a people.]

In their practice, nations agree with Paley; but does any one think that Massachusetts does exactly what is right at the present crisis?

> A drab of state, a cloth-o'-silver slut,
> To have her train borne up, and her soul trail in the dirt.

Practically speaking, the opponents to a reform in Massachusetts are not a hundred thousand politicians at the South, but a hundred thousand merchants and farmers here, who are more interested in commerce and agriculture than they are in humanity, and are not prepared to do justice to the slave and to Mexico, cost what it may. I quarrel not with far-off foes, but with those who, near at home, cooperate with, and do the bidding of, those far away, and without whom the latter would be harmless. We are accustomed to say that the mass of men are unprepared; but improvement is slow because the few are not materially wiser or better than the many. It is not so important that many should be as good as you, as that there be some absolute goodness somewhere; for that will leaven the whole lump. There are thousands who are in opinion opposed to slavery and to the war, who yet in effect do nothing to put an end to them; who, esteeming themselves children of Washington and Franklin, sit down with their hands in their pockets and say that they know not what to do, and do nothing; who even postpone the question of freedom to the question of free trade, and quietly read the prices-current along with the latest advices from Mexico, after dinner, and, it may be, fall asleep over them both. What is the price-current of an honest man and patriot today? They hesitate, and they regret, and sometimes they petition; but they do nothing in earnest and with effect. They will wait, well disposed, for others to remedy the evil, that they may no longer have it to regret. At most, they give only a cheap vote and a feeble countenance and Godspeed to the right as it goes by them. There are nine hundred and ninety-nine patrons of virtue to one virtuous man. But it is easier

41

to deal with the real possessor of a thing than with the temporary guardian of it.

All voting is a sort of gaming, like checkers or backgammon, with a slight moral tinge to it, a playing with right and wrong, with moral questions; and betting naturally accompanies it. The character of the voters is not staked. I cast my vote, perchance, as I think right; but I am not vitally concerned that that right should prevail. I am willing to leave it to the majority. Its obligation, therefore, never exceeds that of expediency. Even voting for the right is doing nothing for it. It is only expressing to men feebly your desire that it should prevail. A wise man will not leave the right to the mercy of chance, nor wish it to prevail through the power of the majority. There is but little virtue in the action of masses of men. When the majority shall at length vote for the abolition of slavery, it will be because they are indifferent to slavery, or because there is but little slavery left to be abolished by their vote. They will then be the only slaves. Only his vote can hasten the abolition of slavery who asserts his own freedom by his vote.

I hear of a convention to be held at Baltimore, or elsewhere, for the selection of a candidate for the Presidency, made up chiefly of editors and men who are politicians by profession; but I think, what is it to any independent, intelligent, and respectable man what decision they may come to? Shall we not have the advantage of his wisdom and honesty, nevertheless? Can we not count upon some independent votes? Are there not many individuals in the country who do not attend conventions? But no: I find that the respectable man, so called, has immediately drifted from his position, and despairs of his country, when his country has more reason to despair of him. He forthwith adopts one of the candidates thus selected as the only available one, thus proving that he is himself available for any purposes of the demagogue. His vote is of no more worth than that of any unprincipled foreigner or hireling native who may have been bought. O for a man who is a man, and, as my neighbor says, has a bone in his back which you cannot pass your hand through! Our statistics are at fault: the population has been returned too large. How many men are there to a square thousand miles in

this country? Hardly one. Does not America offer any induce-
ment for men to settle here? The American has dwindled into an
Odd Fellow—one who may be known by the development of
his organ of gregariousness, and a manifest lack of intellect and
cheerful self-reliance; whose first and chief concern, on coming
into the world, is to see that the almshouses are in good repair;
and, before yet he has lawfully donned the virile garb, to collect
a fund for the support of the widows and orphans that may be;
who, in short, ventures to live only by the aid of the Mutual
Insurance company, which has promised to bury him decently.

It is not a man's duty, as a matter of course, to devote himself
to the eradication of any, even the most enormous, wrong; he
may still properly have other concerns to engage him; but it is
his duty, at least, to wash his hands of it, and, if he gives it no
thought longer, not to give it practically his support. If I devote
myself to other pursuits and contemplations, I must first see, at
least, that I do not pursue them sitting upon another man's
shoulders. I must get off him first, that he may pursue his contemplations, too. See what gross inconsistency is tolerated. I have
heard some of my townsmen say, "I should like to have them
order me out to help put down an insurrection of the slaves, or
to march to Mexico—see if I would go." And yet these very
men have each, directly by their allegiance, and so indirectly, at
least, by their money, furnished a substitute. The soldier is applauded who refuses to serve in an unjust war by those who do
not refuse to sustain the unjust government which makes the war;
is applauded by those whose own act and authority he disregards
and sets at naught; as if the state were penitent to that degree
that it hired one to scourge it while it sinned, but not to that
degree that it left off sinning for a moment. Thus, under the
name of Order and Civil Government, we are all made at last
to pay homage to and support our own meanness. After the first
blush of sin comes its indifference; and from immoral it becomes,
as it were, unmoral, and not quite necessary to that life which
we have made.

The broadest and most prevalent error requires the most dis-
interested virtue to sustain it. The slight reproach to which the
virtue of patriotism is commonly liable, the noble are most likely

43

to incur. Those who, while they disapprove of the character and measures of a government, yield to it their allegiance and support are undoubtedly its most conscientious supporters, and so frequently the most serious obstacles to reform. Some are petitioning the State to dissolve the Union, to disregard the requisitions of the President. Why do they not dissolve it themselves—the union between themselves and the State—and refuse to pay their quota into its treasury? Do not they stand in the same relation to the State that the State does to the Union? And have not the same reasons prevented the State from resisting the Union which have prevented them from resisting the State?

How can a man be satisfied to entertain an opinion merely, and enjoy it? Is there any enjoyment in it if his opinion is that he is aggrieved? If you are cheated out of a single dollar by your neighbor, you do not rest satisfied with knowing that you are cheated, or with saying that you are cheated, or even with petitioning him to pay you your due; but you take effectual steps at once to obtain the full amount, and see that you are never cheated again. Action from principle, the perception and the performance of right, changes things and relations; it is essentially revolutionary, and does not consist wholly with anything which was. It not only divides States and churches, it divides families; ay, it divides the individual, separating the diabolical in him from the divine.

Unjust laws exist: shall we be content to obey them, or shall we endeavor to amend them, and obey them until we have succeeded, or shall we transgress them at once? Men generally, under such a government as this, think that they ought to wait until they have persuaded the majority to alter them. They think that, if they should resist, the remedy would be worse than the evil. But it is the fault of the government itself that the remedy is worse than the evil. It makes it worse. Why is it not more apt to anticipate and provide for reform? Why does it not cherish its wise minority? Why does it cry and resist before it is hurt? Why does it not encourage its citizens to be on the alert to point out its faults, and do better than it would have them? Why does it always crucify Christ, and excommunicate Copernicus and Luther, and pronounce Washington and Franklin rebels?

One would think that a deliberate and practical denial of its authority was the only offense never contemplated by government; else, why has it not assigned its definite, its suitable and proportionate, penalty? If a man who has no property refuses but once to earn nine shillings for the State, he is put in prison for a period unlimited by any law that I know, and determined only by the discretion of those who placed him there; but if he should steal ninety times nine shillings from the State, he is soon permitted to go at large again. 7

If the injustice is part of the necessary friction of the machine of government, let it go, let it go: perchance it will wear smooth —certainly the machine will wear out. If the injustice has a spring, or a pulley, or a rope, or a crank, exclusively for itself, then perhaps you may consider whether the remedy will not be worse than the evil; but if it is of such a nature that it requires you to be the agent of injustice to another, then, I say, break the law. Let your life be a counterfriction to stop the machine. What I have to do is to see, at any rate, that I do not lend myself to the wrong which I condemn.

As for adopting the ways which the State has provided for remedying the evil, I know not of such ways. They take too much time, and a man's life will be gone. I have other affairs to attend to. I came into this world, not chiefly to make this a good place to live in, but to live in it, be it good or bad. A man has not everything to do, but something; and because he cannot do everything, it is not necessary that he should do something wrong. It is not my business to be petitioning the Governor or the Legislature any more than it is theirs to petition me; and if they should not hear my petition, what should I do then? But in this case the State has provided no way: its very Constitution is the evil. This may seem to be harsh and stubborn and unconciliatory; but it is to treat with the utmost kindness and consideration the only spirit that can appreciate or deserves it. So is all change for the better, like birth and death, which convulse the body.

I do not hesitate to say that those who call themselves Abolitionists should at once effectually withdraw their support, both in person and property, from the government of Massachusetts, and not wait till they constitute a majority of one before they

45

suffer the right to prevail through them. I think that it is enough if they have God on their side, without waiting for that other one. Moreover, any man more right than his neighbors constitutes a majority of one already.

— I meet this American government, or its representative, the State government, directly, and face to face, once a year—no more—in the person of its tax gatherer. This is the only mode in which a man situated as I am necessarily meets it; and it then says distinctly, Recognize me; and the simplest, the most effectual, and, in the present posture of affairs, the indispensablest mode of treating with it on this head, of expressing your little satisfaction with and love for it, is to deny it then. My civil neighbor, the tax gatherer, is the very man I have to deal with— for it is, after all, with men and not with parchment that I quarrel—and he has voluntarily chosen to be an agent of the government. How shall he ever know well what he is and does as an officer of the government, or as a man, until he is obliged to consider whether he shall treat me, his neighbor, for whom he has respect, as a neighbor and well-disposed man, or as a maniac and disturber of the peace, and see if he can get over this obstruction to his neighborliness without a ruder and more impetuous thought or speech corresponding with his action. I know this well, that if one thousand, if one hundred, if ten men whom I could name— if ten *honest* men only—ay, if *one* HONEST man, in this State of Massachusetts, *ceasing to hold slaves,* were actually to withdraw from this copartnership, and be locked up in the county jail therefor, it would be the abolition of slavery in America. For it matters not how small the beginning may seem to be: what is once well done is done forever. But we love better to talk about it: that we say is our mission. Reform keeps many scores of newspapers in its service, but not one man. If my esteemed neighbor, the State's ambassador, who will devote his days to the settlement of the question of human rights in the council chamber, instead of being threatened with the prisons of Carolina, were to sit down the prisoner of Massachusetts, that State which is so anxious to foist the sin of slavery upon her sister—though at present she can discover only an act of inhospitality to be the ground of a quarrel with her—the Legislature would not wholly waive the subject the following winter.

Under a government which imprisons any unjustly, the true place for a just man is also a prison. The proper place today, the only place which Massachusetts has provided for her freer and less desponding spirits, is in her prisons, to be put out and locked out of the State by her own act, as they have already put themselves out by their principles. It is there that the fugitive slave and the Mexican prisoner on parole and the Indian come to plead the wrongs of his race should find them; on that separate, but more free and honorable, ground where the State places those who are not *with* her but *against* her—the only house in a slave State in which a free man can abide with honor. If any think that their influence would be lost there and their voices no longer afflict the ear of the State, that they would not be as an enemy within its wall, they do not know by how much truth is stronger than error, nor how much more eloquently and effectively he can combat injustice who has experienced a little in his own person. Cast your whole vote, not a strip of paper merely, but your whole influence. A minority is powerless while it conforms to the majority; it is not even a minority then; but it is irresistible when it clogs by its whole weight. If the alternative is to keep all just men in prison, or give up war and slavery, the State will not hesitate which to choose. If a thousand men were not to pay their tax bills this year, that would not be a violent and bloody measure, as it would be to shed innocent blood. This is, in fact, the definition of a peaceable revolution, if any such is possible. If the tax gatherer, or any other public officer, asks me, as one has done, "But what shall I do?" my answer is, "If you really wish to do anything, resign your office." When the subject has refused allegiance, and the officer has resigned his office, then the revolution is accomplished. But even suppose blood should flow. Is there not a sort of blood shed when the conscience is wounded? Through this wound a man's real manhood and immortality flow out, and he bleeds to an everlasting death. I see this blood flowing now.

I have contemplated the imprisonment of the offender, rather

47

than the seizure of his goods—though both will serve the same purpose—because they who assert the purest right, and consequently are most dangerous to a corrupt State, commonly have not spent much time in accumulating property. To such the State renders comparatively small service, and a slight tax is wont to appear exorbitant, particularly if they are obliged to earn it by special labor with their hands. If there were one who lived wholly without the use of money, the State itself would hesitate to demand it of him. But the rich man—not to make any invidious comparison—is always sold to the institution which makes him rich. Absolutely speaking, the more money, the less virtue; for money comes between a man and his objects, and obtains them for him; and it was certainly no great virtue to obtain it. It puts to rest many questions which he would otherwise be taxed to answer; while the only new question which it puts is the hard but superfluous one, how to spend it. Thus his moral ground is taken from under his feet. The opportunities of living are diminished in proportion as what are called the "means" are increased. The best thing a man can do for his culture when he is rich is to endeavor to carry out those schemes which he entertained when he was poor. Christ answered the Herodians according to their condition. "Show me the tribute money," said he—and one took a penny out of his pocket; if you use money which has the image of Caesar on it, and which he has made current and valuable, that is, *if you are men of the State,* and gladly enjoy the advantages of Caesar's government, then pay him back some of his own when he demands it. "Render therefore to Caesar that which is Caesar's, and to God those things which are God's"—leaving them no wiser than before as to which was which; for they did not wish to know.

When I converse with the freest of my neighbors, I perceive that, whatever they may say about the magnitude and seriousness of the question and their regard for the public tranquillity, the long and the short of the matter is that they cannot spare the protection of the existing government, and they dread the consequences to their property and families of disobedience to it. For my own part, I should not like to think that I ever rely on the protection of the State. But, if I deny the authority of the State

48

when it presents its tax bill, it will soon take and waste all my property, and so harass me and my children without end. This is hard. This makes it impossible for a man to live honestly, and at the same time comfortably, in outward respects. It will not be worth the while to accumulate property; that would be sure to go again. You must hire or squat somewhere, and raise but a small crop, and eat that soon. You must live within yourself, and depend upon yourself always tucked up and ready for a start, and not have many affairs. A man may grow rich in Turkey even, if he will be in all respects a good subject of the Turkish government. Confucius said: "If a state is governed by the principles of reason, poverty and misery are subjects of shame; if a state is not governed by the principles of reason, riches and honors are the subjects of shame." No: until I want the protection of Massachusetts to be extended to me in some distant Southern port, where my liberty is endangered, or until I am bent solely on building up an estate at home by peaceful enterprise, I can afford to refuse allegiance to Massachusetts, and her right to my property and life. It costs me less in every sense to incur the penalty of disobedience to the State than it would to obey. I should feel as if I were worth less in that case.

Some years ago the State met me in behalf of the Church, and commanded me to pay a certain sum toward the support of a clergyman whose preaching my father attended, but never I myself. "Pay," it said, "or be locked up in the jail." I declined to pay. But, unfortunately, another man saw fit to pay it. I did not see why the schoolmaster should be taxed to support the priest, and not the priest the schoolmaster; for I was not the State's schoolmaster, but I supported myself by voluntary subscription. I did not see why the lyceum should not present its tax bill, and have the State to back its demand, as well as the Church. However, at the request of the selectmen, I condescended to make some such statement as this in writing: "Know all men by these presents, that I, Henry Thoreau, do not wish to be regarded as a member of any incorporated society which I have not joined." This I gave to the town clerk; and he has it. The State, having thus learned that I did not wish to be regarded as a member of that church, has never made a like demand on me since; though it said that it must adhere to its original presumption that time. If I had known how to name them, I should then have signed off in detail from all the societies which I never signed on to; but I did not know where to find a complete list.

I have paid no poll tax for six years. I was put into a jail once on this account, for one night; and, as I stood considering the walls of solid stone, two or three feet thick, the door of wood and iron, a foot thick, and the iron grating which strained the light, I could not help being struck with the foolishness of that institution which treated me as if I were mere flesh and blood and bones, to be locked up. I wondered that it should have concluded at length that this was the best use it could put me to, and had never thought to avail itself of my services in some way. I saw that, if there was a wall of stone between me and my townsmen, there was a still more difficult one to climb or break through before they could get to be as free as I was. I did not for a moment feel confined, and the walls seemed a great waste of stone and mortar. I felt as if I alone of all my townsmen had paid my tax. They plainly did not know how to treat me, but behaved like persons who are underbred. In every threat and in every compliment there was a blunder; for they thought that my chief desire was to stand the other side of that stone wall. I could not but smile to see how industriously they locked the door on my meditations, which followed them out again without let or hindrance, and they were really all that was dangerous. As they could not reach me, they had resolved to punish my body; just as boys, if they cannot come at some person against whom they have a spite, will abuse his dog. I saw that the State was half-witted, that it was timid as a lone woman with her silver spoons, and that it did not know its friends from its foes, and I lost all my remaining respect for it, and pitied it.

Thus the State never intentionally confronts a man's sense, intellectual or moral, but only his body, his senses. It is not armed with superior wit or honesty, but with superior physical strength. I was not born to be forced. I will breathe after my own fashion. Let us see who is the strongest. What force has a multitude? They only can force me who obey a higher law than I. They force me to become like themselves. I do not hear of men being forced to live this way or that by masses of men. What sort of life were that to live? When I meet a government which says to me, "Your money or your life," why should I be in haste to give it my money? It may be in a great strait, and not know what to do: I cannot help that. It must help itself; do as I do. It is not worth the while to snivel about it. I am not responsible for the successful working of the machinery of society. I am not the son of the engineer. I perceive that, when an acorn and a chestnut fall side by side, the one does not remain inert to make way for the other, but both obey their own laws, and spring and grow and flourish as best they can, till one, perchance, overshadows and destroys the other. If a plant cannot live according to its nature, it dies; and so a man.

The night in prison was novel and interesting enough. The prisoners in their shirt sleeves were enjoying a chat and the evening air in the doorway when I entered. But the jailer said, "Come, boys, it is time to lock up"; and so they dispersed, and I heard the sound of their steps returning into the hollow apartments. My roommate was introduced to me by the jailer as "a first-rate fellow and a clever man." When the door was locked, he showed me where to hang my hat, and how he managed matters there. The rooms were whitewashed once a month; and this one, at least, was the whitest, most simply furnished, and probably the neatest apartment in the town. He naturally wanted to know where I came from, and what brought me there; and when I had told him, I asked him in my turn how he came there, presuming him to be an honest man, of course; and, as the world goes, I believe he was. "Why," said he, "they accuse me of burning a barn; but I never did it." As near as I could discover, he had probably gone to bed in a barn when drunk, and smoked his pipe there; and so a barn was burned. He had the reputation of being a clever man, had been there some three months waiting for his trial to come on, and would have to wait as much longer; but he was quite domesticated and contented, since he got his board for nothing, and thought that he was well treated.

He occupied one window, and I the other; and I saw that if one stayed there long, his principal business would be to look out the window. I had soon read all the tracts that were left there, and examined where former prisoners had broken out, and where a grate had been sawed off, and heard the history of the various occupants of that room; for I found that even here there was a history and a gossip which never circulated beyond the walls of the jail. Probably this is the only house in the town where verses are composed, which are afterward printed in a circular form, but not published. I was shown quite a long list of verses which were composed by some young men who had been detected in an attempt to escape, who avenged themselves by singing them.

I pumped my fellow prisoner as dry as I could, for fear I should never see him again; but at length he showed me which was my bed, and left me to blow out the lamp.

It was like traveling into a far country, such as I had never expected to behold, to lie there for one night. It seemed to me that I never had heard the town clock strike before, nor the evening sounds of the village; for we slept with the windows open, which were inside the grating. It was to see my native village in the light of the Middle Ages, and our Concord was turned into a Rhine stream, and visions of knights and castles passed before me. They were the voices of old burghers that I heard in the streets. I was an involuntary spectator and auditor of whatever was done and said in the kitchen of the adjacent village inn—a wholly new and rare experience to me. It was a closer view of my native town. I was fairly inside of it. I never had seen its institutions before. This is one of its peculiar institutions; for it is a shire town. I began to comprehend what its inhabitants were about.

In the morning our breakfasts were put through the hole in the door, in small oblong-square tin pans, made to fit, and holding a pint of chocolate, with brown bread, and an iron spoon. When they called for the vessels again, I was green enough to return what bread I had left; but my comrade seized it, and said that I should lay that up for lunch or dinner. Soon after he was let to work at haying in a neighboring field, whither he went every day, and would not be back till noon; so he bade me good day, saying that he doubted if he should see me again.

When I came out of prison—for some one interfered, and

paid that tax—I did not perceive that great changes had taken place on the common, such as he observed who went in a youth and emerged a tottering and gray-headed man; and yet a change had to my eyes come over the scene—the town, and State, and country—greater than any that mere time could effect. I saw yet more distinctly the State in which I lived. I saw to what extent the people among whom I lived could be trusted as good neighbors and friends; that their friendship was for summer weather only; that they did not greatly propose to do right; that they were a distinct race from me by their prejudices and superstitions, as the Chinamen and Malays are; that in their sacrifices to humanity they ran no risks, not even to their property; that after all they were not so noble but they treated the thief as he had treated them, and hoped, by a certain outward observance and a few prayers, and by walking in a particular straight though useless path from time to time, to save their souls. This may be to judge my neighbors harshly; for I believe that many of them are not aware that they have such an institution as the jail in their village.

It was formerly the custom in our village, when a poor debtor came out of jail, for his acquaintances to salute him, looking through their fingers, which were crossed to represent the grating of a jail window, "How do you do?" My neighbors did not thus salute me, but first looked at me, and then at one another, as if I had returned from a long journey. I was put into jail as I was going to the shoemaker's to get a shoe which was mended. When I was let out the next morning, I proceeded to finish my errand, and, having put on my mended shoe, joined a huckleberry party, who were impatient to put themselves under my conduct; and in half an hour—for the horse was soon tackled—was in the midst of a huckleberry field, on one of our highest hills, two miles off, and then the State was nowhere to be seen.

This is the whole history of "My Prisons."

I have never declined paying the highway tax, because I am as desirous of being a good neighbor as I am of being a bad subject; and as for supporting schools, I am doing my part to educate my fellow countrymen now. It is for no particular item in the tax bill that I refuse to pay it. I simply wish to refuse allegiance to the State, to withdraw and stand aloof from it effectually. I do not care to trace the course of my dollar, if I could, till it buys a man or a musket to shoot one with—the dollar is innocent—but I am concerned to trace the effects of my allegiance. In fact, I quietly declare war with the State, after my fashion, though I will still make what use and get what advantage of her I can, as is usual in such cases.

If others pay the tax which is demanded of me, from a sympathy with the State, they do but what they have already done in their own case, or rather they abet injustice to a greater extent than the State requires. If they pay the tax from a mistaken interest in the individual taxed, to save his property or prevent his going to jail, it is because they have not considered wisely how far they let their private feelings interfere with the public good.

This, then, is my position at present. But one cannot be too much on his guard in such a case, lest his action be biased by obstinacy or an undue regard for the opinions of men. Let him see that he does only what belongs to himself and to the hour.

I think sometimes, Why, this people mean well, they are only ignorant; they would do better if they knew how: why give your neighbors this pain to treat you as they are not inclined to? But I think again, This is no reason why I should do as they do, or permit others to suffer much greater pain of a different kind. Again, I sometimes say to myself, When many millions of men, without heat, without ill will, without personal feeling of any kind, demand of you a few shillings only, without the possibility, such is their constitution, of retracting or altering their present demand, and without the possibility, on your side, of appeal to any other millions, why expose yourself to this overwhelming brute force? You do not resist cold and hunger, the winds and the waves, thus obstinately; you quietly submit to a thousand similar necessities. You do not put your head into the fire. But just in proportion as I regard this as not wholly a brute force, but partly a human force, and consider that I have relations to those millions as to so many millions of men, and not of mere brute or inanimate things, I see that appeal is possible, first and instantaneously, from them to the Maker of them, and, secondly, from them to themselves. But if I put my head deliberately into the fire, there is no appeal to fire or to the Maker of fire, and I have only myself to blame. If I could convince myself that I have any right to be satisfied with men as they are, and to treat them accordingly, and not according, in some respects, to my requisitions and expectations of what they and I ought to be, then, like a good Mussulman and fatalist, I should endeavor to be satisfied with things as they are, and say it is the will of God. And, above all, there is this difference between resisting this and a purely brute or natural force, that I can resist this with some effect; but I cannot expect, like Orpheus, to change the nature of the rocks and trees and beasts.

I do not wish to quarrel with any man or nation. I do not wish to split hairs, to make fine distinctions, or set myself up as better than my neighbors. I seek rather, I may say, even an excuse for conforming to the laws of the land. I am but too ready to conform to them. Indeed, I have reason to suspect myself on this head; and each year, as the tax gatherer comes round, I find myself disposed to review the acts and position of the general and State governments, and the spirit of the people, to discover a pretext for conformity.

> We must affect our country as our parents,
> And if at any time we alienate
> Our love or industry from doing it honor,
> We must respect effects and teach the soul
> Matter of conscience and religion,
> And not desire of rule or benefit.

I believe that the State will soon be able to take all my work of this sort out of my hands, and then I shall be no better a patriot than my fellow countrymen. Seen from a lower point of view, the Constitution, with all its faults, is very good; the law and the courts are very respectable; even this State and this American government are, in many respects, very admirable, and rare things, to be thankful for, such as a great many have described them; but seen from a point of view a little higher, they are what I have described them; seen from a higher still, and the highest, who shall say what they are, or that they are worth looking at or thinking of at all?

However, the government does not concern me much, and I

Lowest level our govt. is good. But from the highest level it is not necessarily our good at all.

shall bestow the fewest possible thoughts on it. It is not many moments that I live under a government, even in this world. If a man is thought-free, fancy-free, imagination-free, that which *is not* never for a long time appearing *to be* to him, unwise rulers or reformers cannot fatally interrupt him.

I know that most men think differently from myself; but those whose lives are by profession devoted to the study of these or kindred subjects content me as little as any. Statesmen and legislators, standing so completely within the institution, never distinctly and nakedly behold it. They speak of moving society, but have no resting place without it. They may be men of a certain experience and discrimination, and have no doubt invented ingenious and even useful systems, for which we sincerely thank them; but all their wit and usefulness lie within certain not very wide limits. They are wont to forget that the world is not governed by policy and expediency. Webster never goes behind government, and so cannot speak with authority about it. His words are wisdom to those legislators who contemplate no essential reform in the existing government; but for thinkers, and those who legislate for all time, he never once glances at the subject. I know of those whose serene and wise speculations on this theme would soon reveal the limits of his mind's range and hospitality. Yet, compared with the cheap professions of most reformers, and the still cheaper wisdom and eloquence of politicians in general, his are almost the only sensible and valuable words, and we thank Heaven for him. Comparatively, he is always strong, original, and, above all, practical. Still, his quality is not wisdom, but prudence. The lawyer's truth is not Truth, but consistency or a consistent expediency. Truth is always in harmony with herself, and is not concerned chiefly to reveal the justice that may consist with wrongdoing. He well deserves to be called, as he has been called, the Defender of the Constitution. There are really no blows to be given by him but defensive ones. He is not a leader, but a follower. His leaders are the men of '87. "I have never made an effort," he says, "and never propose to make an effort; I have never countenanced an effort, and never mean to countenance an effort, to disturb the arrangement as originally made, by which the various States came into the Union." Still thinking of the sanction which the Constitution gives to slavery, he says, "Because it was a part of the original compact—let it stand." Notwithstanding his special acuteness and ability, he is unable to take a fact out of its merely political relations, and behold it as it lies absolutely to be disposed of by the intellect— what, for instance, it behooves a man to do here in America today with regard to slavery—but ventures, or is driven, to make some such desperate answer as the following, while professing to speak absolutely, and as a private man—from which, what new and singular code of social duties might be inferred? "The manner," says he, "in which the governments of those States where slavery exists are to regulate it is for their own consideration, under their responsibility to their constituents, to the general laws of propriety, humanity, and justice, and to God. Associations formed elsewhere, springing from a feeling of humanity, or any other cause, have nothing whatever to do with it. They have never received any encouragement from me, and they never will."

They who know of no purer sources of truth, who have traced up its stream no higher, stand, and wisely stand, by the Bible and the Constitution, and drink at it there with reverence and humility; but they who behold where it comes trickling into this lake or that pool, gird up their loins once more, and continue their pilgrimage toward its fountainhead.

No man with a genius for legislation has appeared in America. They are rare in the history of the world. There are orators, politicians, and eloquent men by the thousand; but the speaker has not yet opened his mouth to speak who is capable of settling the much-vexed questions of the day. We love eloquence for its own sake, and not for any truth which it may utter or any heroism it may inspire. Our legislators have not yet learned the comparative value of free trade and of freedom, of union, and of rectitude, to a nation. They have no genius or talent for comparatively humble questions of taxation and finance, commerce and manufactures and agriculture. If we were left solely to the wordy wit of legislators in Congress for our guidance, uncorrected by the seasonable experience and the effectual complaints of the people, America would not long retain her rank among the nations. For eighteen hundred years, though perchance I have no right to say it, the New Testament has been written; yet where is the legislator who has wisdom and practical talent enough to avail himself of the light which it sheds on the science of legislation?

The authority of government, even such as I am willing to submit to—for I will cheerfully obey those who know and can do better than I, and in many things even those who neither know nor can do so well—is still an impure one: to be strictly just, it must have the sanction and consent of the governed. It can have no pure right over my person and property but what I concede to it. The progress from an absolute to a limited monarchy, from a limited monarchy to a democracy, is a progress toward a true respect for the individual. Even the Chinese philosopher was wise enough to regard the individual as the basis of the empire. Is a democracy, such as we know it, the last improvement possible in government? Is it not possible to take a step further towards recognizing and organizing the rights of man? There will never be a really free and enlightened State until the State comes to recognize the individual as a higher and independent power, from which all its own power and authority are derived, and treats him accordingly. I please myself with imagining a State at last which can afford to be just to all men, and to treat the individual with respect as a neighbor; which even would not think it inconsistent with its own repose if a few were to live aloof from it, not meddling with it, nor embraced by it, who fulfilled all the duties of neighbors and fellow men. A State which bore this kind of fruit, and suffered it to drop off as fast as it ripened, would prepare the way for a still more perfect and glorious State, which also I have imagined, but not yet anywhere seen.

JOURNAL
1850-1854

JOURNAL / 1850

I do not prefer one religion or philosophy to another. I have no sympathy with the bigotry and ignorance which make transient and partial and puerile distinctions between one man's faith or form of faith and another's—as Christian or heathen. I pray to be delivered from narrowness, partiality, exaggeration, bigotry. To the philosopher all sects, all nations, are alike. I like Brahma, Hari, Buddha, the Great Spirit, as well as God.

⚡   ⚡   ⚡

Wherever a man goes, men will pursue and paw him with their dirty institutions.

⚡   ⚡   ⚡

As to conforming outwardly and living your own life inwardly, I have not a very high opinion of that course. Do not let your right hand know what your left hand does in that line of business. I have no doubt it will prove a failure.

⚡   ⚡   ⚡

Man and his affairs—Church and State and school, trade and commerce and agriculture—Politics—for that is the word for them all here today—I am pleased to see how little space it oc-

59

cupies in the landscape. It is but a narrow field. That still narrower highway yonder leads to it. I sometimes direct the traveler.

✓   ✓   ✓

A squaw came to our door today with two papooses, and said, "Me want a pie." Theirs is not common begging. You are merely the rich Indian who shares his goods with the poor. They merely offer you an opportunity to be generous and hospitable.

Equally simple was the observation which an Indian made at Mr. Hoar's door the other day, who went there to sell his baskets. "No, we don't want any," said the one who went to the door. "What! do you mean to starve us?" asked the Indian in astonishment, as he was going out (*sic*) the gate. The Indian seems to have said: I too will do like the white man; I will go into business. He sees his white neighbors well off around him, and he thinks that if he only enters on the profession of basketmaking, riches will flow in unto him as a matter of course; just as the lawyer weaves arguments, and by some magical means wealth and standing follow. He thinks that when he has made the baskets, he has done his part; now it is yours to buy them. He has not discovered that it is necessary for him to make it worth your while to buy them, or make some which it will be worth your while to buy. With great simplicity he says to himself: I too will be a man of business; I will go into trade. It isn't enough simply to make baskets. You have got to sell them.

✓   ✓   ✓

Here and there still you will find a man with Indian blood in his veins, an eccentric farmer descended from an Indian chief; or you will see a solitary pure-blooded Indian, looking as wild as ever among the pines, one of the last of the Massachusetts tribes, stepping into a railroad car with his gun.

Still here and there an Indian squaw with her dog, her only companion, lives in some lone house, insulted by schoolchildren, making baskets and picking berries her employment. You will meet her on the highway, with few children or none, with melancholy face, history, destiny; stepping after her race; who has stayed to tuck them up in their long sleep. For whom berries condescend to grow. I have not seen one on the Musketaquid for many a year, and some who came up in their canoes and camped on its banks a dozen years ago had to ask me where it came from. A lone Indian woman without children, accompanied by her dog, wearing the shroud of her race, performing the last offices for her departed race. Not yet absorbed into the elements again; a daughter of the soil; one of the nobility of the land. The white man an imported weed—burdock and mullein, which displace the groundnut.

JOURNAL / NOVEMBER 17, 1850

It is a strange age of the world this, when empires, kingdoms, and republics come abegging to our doors and utter their complaints at our elbows. I cannot take up a newspaper but I find that some wretched government or other, hard pushed and on its last legs, is interceding with me, the reader, to vote for it— more importunate than an Italian beggar. Why does it not keep its castle in silence, as I do? The poor President, what with preserving his popularity and doing his duty, does not know what to do. If you do not read the newspapers, you may be impeached for treason. The newspapers are the ruling power. What Congress does is an afterclap. Any other government is reduced to a few marines at Fort Independence. If a man neglects to read the *Daily Times*, government will go on its knees to him; this is the only treason in these days. The newspapers devote some of their columns specially to government and politics without charge, and this is all that saves it, but I never read those columns.

JOURNAL / 1851

When formerly I was looking about to see what I could do for a living, some sad experience in conforming to the wishes of friends being fresh in my mind to tax my ingenuity, I thought often and seriously of picking huckleberries; that surely I could do, and its small profits might suffice, so little capital it required, so little distraction from my wonted thoughts, I foolishly thought. While my acquaintances went unhesitatingly into trade or the professions, I thought of this occupation as most like theirs; ranging the hills all summer to pick the berries which came in my way, which I might carelessly dispose of; so to keep the flocks of King Admetus. My greatest skill has been to want but little. I also dreamed that I might gather the wild herbs, or carry evergreens to such villagers as loved to be reminded of the woods, and so find my living got. But I have since learned that trade curses everything it handles; and though you trade in messages from heaven, the whole curse of trade attaches to the business.

JOURNAL / FEBRUARY 16, 1851

Do we call this the land of the free? What is it to be free from King George IV and continue the slaves of prejudice? What is it [to] be born free and equal, and not to live? What is the value of any political freedom, but as a means to moral freedom? Is it a freedom to be slaves or a freedom to be free, of which we boast? We are a nation of politicians, concerned about the outsides of freedom, the means and outmost defenses of freedom. It is our children's children who may perchance be essentially free. We tax ourselves unjustly. There is a part of us which is not represented. It is taxation without representation. We quarter troops upon ourselves. In respect to virtue or true manhood, we are essentially provincial, not metropolitan—mere Jonathans. We are provincial, because we do not find at home our standards; because we do not worship truth but the reflection of truth; because we are absorbed in and narrowed by trade and commerce and agriculture, which are but means and not the end. We are essentially provincial, I say, and so is the English Parliament. Mere country bumpkins they betray themselves when any more important questions arise for them to settle. Their natures are subdued to what they work in!

JOURNAL / MAY 1, 1851

Nations! What are nations? Tartars! and Huns! and Chinamen! Like insects they swarm. The historian strives in vain to make them memorable. It is for want of a man that there are so many men. It is individuals that populate the world.

JOURNAL / AUGUST 21, 1851

To a great extent the feudal system still prevails there [in Canada], and I saw that I should be a bad citizen, that any man who thought for himself and was only reasonably independent would naturally be a rebel. You could not read or hear of their laws without seeing that it was a legislating for a few and not for all. That certainly is the best government where the inhabitants are least often reminded of the government. (Where a man cannot be a poet even without danger of being made poet-laureate! Where he cannot be healthily neglected, and grow up a man, and not an Englishman merely!) Where it is the most natural thing in the world for a government that does not understand you, to let you alone. Oh, what a government were there, my countrymen! It is a government, that English one—and most other European ones—that cannot afford to be forgotten, as you would naturally forget them, that cannot let you go alone, having learned to walk. It appears to me that a true Englishman can only speculate within bounds; he has to pay his respects to so many things that before he knows it he has paid all he is worth. The principal respect in which our government is more tolerable is in the fact that there is so much less of government with us. In the States it is only once in a dog's age that a man need remember his government, but here he is reminded of it every day. Government parades itself before you. It is in no sense the servant but the master.

JOURNAL / SEPTEMBER 19, 1851

And now (perchance at half past four) I hear the sound of some far-off factory bell arousing the operatives to their early labors. It sounds very sweet here. It is very likely some valley which I have never visited; yet now I hear this, which is its only matin bell, sweet and inspiring as if it summoned holy men and maids to worship and not factory girls and men to resume their trivial toil, as if it were the summons of some religious or even poetic community. My first impression is that it is the matin bell of some holy community who in a distant valley dwell, a band of spiritual knights—thus sounding far and wide, sweet and sonorous, in harmony with their own morning thoughts. What else could I suppose fitting this earth and hour? Some man of high resolve, devoted soul, has touched the rope; and by its peals how many men and maids are waked from peaceful slumbers to fragrant morning thoughts! Why should I fear to tell that it is Knight's factory bell at Assabet? A few melodious peals and all is still again.

JOURNAL / SEPTEMBER 21, 1851

The retirement in which Green has lived for nearly eighty years in Carlisle is a retirement very different from and much greater than that in which the pioneer dwells at the West; for the latter dwells within sound of the surf of those billows of migration which are breaking on the shores around him, or near him, of the West, but those billows have long since swept over the spot which Green inhabits, and left him in the calm sea. There is somewhat exceedingly pathetic to think of in such a life as he must have lived—with no more to redeem it—such a life as an average Carlisle man may be supposed to live drawn out to eighty years. And he has died, perchance, and there is nothing but the mark of his cider mill left. Here was the cider mill, and there the orchard, and there the hog pasture; and so men lived, and ate, and drank, and passed away—like vermin. Their long life was mere duration. As respectable is the life of the woodchucks, which perpetuate their race in the orchard still. That is the life of these selectmen (!) spun out. They will be forgotten in a few years, even by such as themselves, like vermin. They will be known only like Kibbe, who is said to have been a large man who weighed two hundred and fifty, who had five or six heavy daughters who rode to Concord meetinghouse on horseback, taking turns—they were so heavy that only one could ride at once. What, then, would redeem such a life? We only know that they ate, and drank, and built barns, and died and were buried, and still, perchance, their tombstones cumber the ground. But if I could know that there was ever entertained over their cellar-hole some divine thought, which came as a messenger of the gods, that he who resided here acted once in his life from a noble impulse, rising superior to his groveling and penurious life, if only a single verse of poetry or of poetic prose had ever been written or spoken or conceived here beyond a doubt, I should not think it in vain that man had lived here. It would to some extent be true then that God had lived here. That all his life he lived only as a farmer—as the most valuable stock only on a farm—and in no moments as a man!

JOURNAL / SEPTEMBER 25, 1851

Since I perambulated the bounds of the town, I find that I have in some degree confined myself—my vision and my walks. On whatever side I look off, I am reminded of the mean and narrow-minded men whom I have lately met there. What can be uglier than a country occupied by groveling, coarse, and low-lived men? No scenery will redeem it. What can be more beautiful than any scenery inhabited by heroes? Any landscape would be glorious to me if I were assured that its sky was arched over a single hero. Hornets, hyenas, and baboons are not so great a curse to a country as men of a similar character.

JOURNAL / SEPTEMBER 27, 1851

We of Massachusetts boast a good deal of what we do for the education of our people, of our district-school system; and yet our district schools are as it were but infant-schools, and we have no system for the education of the great mass who are grown up. I have yet to learn that one cent is spent by this town, this political community called Concord, directly to educate the great mass of its inhabitants who have long since left the district school; for the Lyceum, important as it is comparatively, though absolutely trifling, is supported by individuals. There are certain refining and civilizing influences, as works of art, journals and books, and scientific instruments, which this community is amply rich enough to purchase, which would educate this village, elevate its tone of thought, and, if it alone improved these opportunities, easily make it the center of civilization in the known world, put us on a level as to opportunities at once with London and Arcadia, and secure us a culture at once superior to both: Yet we spend sixteen thousand dollars on a town house, a hall for our political meetings mainly, and nothing to educate ourselves who are grown up. Pray is there nothing in the market, no advantages, no intellectual food worth buying? Have Paris and London and New York and Boston nothing to dispose of which this village might try and appropriate to its own use? Might not this great villager adorn his villa with a few pictures and statues, enrich himself with a choice library as available, without being cumbrous, as any in the world, with scientific instruments for such as have a taste to use them? Yet we are contented to be countrified, to be provincial. I am astonished to find that in this nineteenth century, in this land of free schools, we spend absolutely nothing as a town on our own education, cultivation, civilization. Each town, like each individual, has its own character—some more, some less, cultivated. I know many towns so mean-spirited and benighted that it would be a disgrace to belong to them. I believe that some of our New England villages within thirty miles of Boston are as boorish and barbarous communities as there are on the face of the earth. And how much superior are the best of them? If London has any refinement, any information to sell, why should we not buy it? Would not the town of Carlisle do well to spend sixteen thousand dollars on its own education at once, if it could only find a schoolmaster for itself? It has one man, as I hear, who takes the *North American Review*. That will never civilize them, I fear. Why should not the town itself take the London and Edinburgh Reviews, and put itself in communication with whatever sources of light and intelligence there are in the world? Yet Carlisle is very little behind Concord in these respects. I do not know but it spends its proportional part on education. How happens it that the only libraries which the towns possess are the district-school libraries—books for children only, or for readers who must needs be written down to? Why should they not have a library, if not so extensive, yet of the same stamp and more select than the British Museum? It is not that the town cannot well afford to buy these things, but it is unaspiring and ignorant of its own wants. It sells milk, but it only builds larger barns with the money which it gets for its milk. Undoubtedly every New England village is as able to surround itself with as many civilizing influences of this kind [as] the members of the English nobility; and here there need be no peasantry. If the *London Times* is the best newspaper in the world, why does not the village of Concord take it, that its inhabitants may read it, and not the second best? If the South Sea explorers have at length got their story ready, and Congress has neglected to make it accessible to the people, why does not Concord purchase one for its grown-up children?

JOURNAL / OCTOBER 1, 1851

Just put a fugitive slave, who has taken the name of Henry Williams, into the cars for Canada. He escaped from Stafford County, Virginia, to Boston last October; has been in Shadrach's place at the Cornhill Coffee House; had been corresponding through an agent with his master, who is his father, about buying himself, his master asking $600, but he having been able to raise only $500. Heard that there were writs out for two Williamses, fugitives, and was informed by his fellow servants and employer that Augerhole Burns and others of the police had called for him when he was out. Accordingly fled to Concord last night on foot, bringing a letter to our family from Mr. Lovejoy of Cambridge and another which Garrison had formerly given him on another occasion. He lodged with us, and waited in the house till funds were collected with which to forward him. Intended to dispatch him at noon through to Burlington, but when I went to buy his ticket, saw one at the depot who looked and behaved so much like a Boston policeman that I did not venture that time. An intelligent and very well-behaved man, a mulatto.

JOURNAL / NOVEMBER 10, 1851

In relation to politics, to society, aye, to the whole outward world, I am tempted to ask, Why do *they* lay such stress on a particular experience which you have had?—that, after twenty-five years, you should meet Cyrus Warren again on the sidewalk! Haven't I budged an inch, then? This daily routine should go on, then, like those—it must be conceded—vital functions of digestion, circulation of the blood, etc., which in health we know nothing about. A wise man is as unconscious of the movements in the body politic as he is of the process of digestion and the circulation of the blood in the natural body. These processes are *infra*-human. I sometimes awake to a half-consciousness of these things going on about me—as politics, society, business, etc., etc.—as a man may become conscious of some of the processes of digestion, in a morbid state, and so have the dyspepsia, as it is called. It appears to me that those things which most engage the attention of men, as politics, for instance, are vital functions of human society, it is true, but should [be] unconsciously performed, like the vital functions of the natural body. It is as if a thinker submitted himself to be rasped by the great gizzard of creation. Politics is, as it were, the gizzard of society, full of grit and gravel, and the two political parties are its two opposite halves, which grind on each other. Not only individuals but states have thus a confirmed dyspepsia, which expresses itself, you can imagine by what sort of eloquence. Our life is not altogether a forgetting, but also, alas, to a great extent a remembering, of that which perchance we should never have been conscious of—the consciousness of what should not be permitted to disturb a man's waking hours. As for society, why should we not meet, not always as dyspeptics, but sometimes as eupeptics?

JOURNAL / JANUARY 26, 1852

As I stand under the hill beyond J. Hosmer's and look over the plains westward toward Acton and see the farmhouses nearly half a mile apart, few and solitary, in these great fields between these stretching woods, out of the world, where the children have to go far to school; the still, stagnant, heart-eating, life-everlasting, and gone-to-seed country, so far from the post office where the weekly paper comes, wherein the new-married wife cannot live for loneliness, and the young man has to depend upon his

horse for society; see young J. Hosmer's house, whither he returns with his wife in despair after living in the city—I standing
in Tarbell's road, which he alone cannot break out—the world
in winter for most walkers reduced to a sled track winding far
through the drifts, all springs sealed up and no digressions; where
the old man thinks he may possibly afford to rust it out, not
having long to live, but the young man pines to get nearer the
post office and the Lyceum, is restless and resolves to go to California, because the depot is a mile off (he hears the rattle of the
cars at a distance and thinks the world is going by and leaving
him); where rabbits and partridges multiply, and muskrats are
more numerous than ever, and none of the farmer's sons are willing to be farmers, and the apple trees are decayed, and the cellar-
holes are more numerous than the houses, and the rails are covered
with lichens, and the old maids wish to sell out and move into the
village, and have waited twenty years in vain for this purpose
and never finished but one room in the house, never plastered
nor painted, inside or out, lands which the Indian was long since
dispossessed [of], and how the farms are run out, and what were
forests are grainfields, what were grainfields, pastures; dwellings
which only those Arnolds of the wilderness, those *coureurs de
bois*, the baker and the butcher visit, to which at least the latter
penetrates for the annual calf—and as he returns the cow lows
after; whither the villager never penetrates, but in huckleberry
time, perchance, and if he does not, who does?—where some
men's breaths smell of rum, having smuggled in a jugful to al-
leviate their misery and solitude; where the owls give a regular
serenade—I say, standing there and seeing these things, I cannot
realize that this is that hopeful young America which is famous
throughout the world for its activity and enterprise, and this is
the most thickly settled and Yankee part of it. What must be the
condition of the *old* world! The sphagnum must by this time
have concealed it from the eye.

JOURNAL / FEBRUARY 26, 1852

We are told today that civilization is making rapid progress;
the tendency is ever upward; substantial justice is done even by

human courts; you may trust the good intentions of mankind. We read tomorrow in the newspapers that the French nation is on the eve of going to war with England to give employment to her army. What is the influence of men of principle, or how numerous are they? How many moral teachers has society? This Russian war is popular. Of course so many as she has will resist her. How many resist her? How many have I heard speak with warning voice? utter wise warnings? The preacher's standard of morality is no higher than that of his audience. He studies to conciliate his hearers and never to offend them. Does the threatened war between France and England evince any more enlightenment than a war between two savage tribes, as the Iroquois and the Hurons? Is it founded in better reason?

JOURNAL / APRIL 21, 1852

We have heard enough nonsense about the pyramids. If Congress should vote to rear such structures on the prairies today, I should not think it worth the while, nor be interested in the enterprise. It was the foolish undertaking of some tyrant. "But," says my neighbor, "when they were built, all men believed in them and were inspired to build them." Nonsense! nonsense! I believe that they were built essentially in the same spirit in which the public works of Egypt, of England, and America are built today—the Mahmoudi Canal, the Tubular Bridge, Thames Tunnel, and the Washington Monument. The inspiring motive in the actual builders of these works is garlic, or beef, or potatoes. For meat and drink and the necessaries of life men can be hired to do many things. "Ah," says my neighbor, "but the stones are fitted with such nice joints!" But the joints were nicer yet before they were disjointed in the quarry. Men are wont to speak as if it were a noble work to build a pyramid—to set, forsooth, a hundred thousand Irishmen at work at fifty cents a day to piling stone. As if the good joints could ennoble it, if a noble motive was wanting! To ramble round the world to see that pile of stones which ambitious Mr. Cheops, an Egyptian booby, like some Lord Timothy Dexter, caused a hundred thousand poor devils to pile up for low wages, which contained for all treasure the thigh bone of a cow. The tower of Babel has been a good deal laughed at. It was just as sensible an undertaking as the pyramids, which, because they were completed and have stood to this day, are admired. I don't believe they made a better joint than Mr. Crab, the joiner, can.

JOURNAL /APRIL 24, 1852

I know two species of men. The vast majority are men of society. They live on the surface; they are interested in the transient and fleeting; they are like driftwood on the flood. They ask forever and only the news, the froth and scum of the eternal sea. They use policy; they make up for want of matter with manner. They have many letters to write. Wealth and the approbation of men is to them success. The enterprises of society are something final and sufficing for them. The world advises them, and they listen to its advice. They live wholly an evanescent life, creatures of circumstance. It is of prime importance to them who is the President of the day. They have no knowledge of truth, but by an exceedingly dim and transient instinct, which stereotypes the Church and some other institutions. They swell, they are ever right in my face and eyes like gnats; they are like motes, so near the eyes that, looking beyond, they appear like blurs; they have their being between my eyes and the end of my nose. The terra firma of my existence lies far beyond, behind them and their improvements. If they write, the best of them deal in "elegant literature." Society, man, has no prize to offer me that can tempt me; not one. That which interests a town or city or any large number of men is always something trivial, as politics. It is impossible for me to be interested in what interests men generally. Their pursuits and interests seem to me frivolous. When I am most myself and see the clearest, men are least to be seen; they are like *muscae volitantes,* and that they are seen at all is the proof of imperfect vision. These affairs of men are so narrow as to afford no vista, no distance; it is a shallow foreground only, no large extended views to be taken. Men put to me frivolous questions: When did I come? Where am I going? That was a more pertinent question—what I lectured for?— which one auditor put once to another. What an ordeal it were to make men pass through, to consider how many ever put to you a vital question! Their knowledge of something better gets no further than what is called religion and spiritual knockings.

JOURNAL / MAY 4, 1852

This excitement about Kossuth is not interesting to me, it is so superficial. It is only another kind of dancing or of politics. Men are making speeches to him all over the country, but each expresses only the thought, or the want of thought, of the multitude. No man stands on truth. They are merely banded together as usual, one leaning on another and all together on nothing; as the Hindus made the world rest on an elephant, and the elephant on a tortoise, and had nothing to put under the tortoise. You can pass your hand under the largest mob, a nation in revolution even, and, however solid a bulk they may make, like a hail cloud in the atmosphere, you may not meet so much as a cobweb of support. They may not rest, even by a point, on eternal foundations. But an individual standing on truth you cannot pass your hand under, for his foundations reach to the center of the universe. So superficial these men and their doings, it is life on a leaf of a chip which has nothing but air or water beneath. I love to see a man with a taproot, though it make him difficult to transplant. It is unimportant what these men do. Let them try forever, they can effect nothing. Of what significance the things you can forget?

JOURNAL / JUNE 15, 1852

The motive of the laborer should be not to get his living, to get a good job, but to perform well a certain work. A town must pay its engineers so well that they shall not feel that they are working for low ends, as for a livelihood merely, but for scientific ends. Do not hire a man who does your work for money, but him who does it for love, and pay him well

72

JOURNAL / JUNE 26, 1852

But it should not be by their architecture but by their abstract thoughts that a nation should seek to commemorate itself. How much more admirable the Bhagavad-Gita than all the ruins of the East! Methinks there are few specimens of architecture so perfect as a verse of poetry. Architectural remains are beautiful not intrinsically and absolutely, but from association. They are the luxury of princes. A simple and independent mind does not toil at the bidding of any prince, nor is its material silver and gold, or marble. The American's taste for architecture, whether Grecian or Gothic, is like his taste for olives and wine, though the last may be made of logwood. Consider the beauty of New York architecture—and there is no very material difference between this and Baalbec—a vulgar adornment of what is vulgar. To what end pray is so much stone hammered? An insane ambition to perpetuate the memory of themselves by the amount of hammered stone they leave. Such is the glory of nations. What if equal pains were taken to smooth and polish their manners? Is not the builder of more consequence than the material? One sensible act will be more memorable than a monument as high as the moon. I love better to see stones in place. The grandeur of Thebes was a vulgar grandeur. She was not simple, and why should I be imposed on by the hundred gates of her prison? More sensible is a rod of stone wall that bounds an honest man's field than a hundred-gated Thebes that has mistaken the true end of life, that places hammered marble before honesty. The religion and civilization which are barbaric and heathenish build splendid temples, but Christianity does not. It needs no college-bred architect. All the stone a nation hammers goes toward its tomb only. It buries itself alive. The too exquisitely cultured I avoid as I do the theatre. Their life lacks reality. They offer me wine instead of water. They are surrounded by things that can be bought.

JOURNAL / JUNE 29, 1852

In my experience nothing is so opposed to poetry—not crime—as business. It is a negation of life.

73

Just after sunrise this morning I noticed Hayden walking beside his team, which was slowly drawing a heavy hewn stone swung under the axle, surrounded by an atmosphere of industry, his day's work begun. Honest, peaceful industry, conserving the world, which all men respect, which society has consecrated. A reproach to all sluggards and idlers. Pausing abreast the shoulders of his oxen and half turning round, with a flourish of his merciful whip, while they gained their length on him. And I thought, such is the labor which the American Congress exists to protect— honest, manly toil. His brow has commenced to sweat. Honest as the day is long. One of the sacred band doing the needful but irksome drudgery. Toil that makes his bread taste sweet, and keeps society sweet. The day went by, and at evening I passed a rich man's yard, who keeps many servants and foolishly spends much money while he adds nothing to the common stock, and there I saw Hayden's stone lying beside a whimsical structure intended to adorn this Lord Timothy Dexter's mansion, and the dignity forthwith departed from Hayden's labor, in my eyes. I am frequently invited to survey farms in a rude manner, a very (sic) and insignificant labor, though I manage to get more out of it than my employers; but I am never invited by the community to do anything quite worth the while to do. How much of the industry of the boor, traced to the end, is found thus to be subserving some rich man's foolish enterprise! There is a coarse, boisterous, money-making fellow in the north part of the town who is going to build a bank wall under the hill along the edge of his meadow. The powers have put this into his head to keep him out of mischief, and he wishes me to spend three weeks digging there with him. The result will be that he will perchance get a little more money to hoard, or leave for his heirs to spend foolishly when he is dead. Now, if I do this, the community will commend me as an industrious and hard-working man; but, as I choose to devote myself to labors which yield more real profit, though but little money, they regard me as a loafer. But, as I do not need this police of meaningless labor to regulate me, and do not see anything absolutely praiseworthy in his undertaking, however amusing it may be to him, I prefer to finish my education at a different school.

JOURNAL / JULY 29, 1852

It is commonly said that history is a history of war, but it is at the same time a history of development. Savage nations—any of our Indian tribes, for instance—would have enough stirring incidents in their annals, wars and murders enough, surely, to make interesting anecdotes without end, such a chronicle of startling and monstrous events as fill the daily papers and suit the appetite of barrooms; but the annals of such a tribe do not furnish the materials for history.

JOURNAL / AUGUST 29, 1852

We boast that we belong to the nineteenth century, and are making the most rapid strides of any nation. But consider how little this village does for its own culture. We have a comparatively decent system of common schools, schools for infants only, as it were, but, excepting the half-starved Lyceum in the winter, no school for ourselves. It is time that we had uncommon schools, that we did not leave off our education when we begin to be men. Comparatively few of my townsmen evince any interest in their own culture, however much they may boast of the school tax they pay. It is time that villages were universities, and their elder inhabitants the fellows, with leisure—if they are indeed so well off—to pursue liberal studies as long as they live. In this country the village should in many respects take the place of the nobleman who has gone by the board. It should be the patron of the fine arts. It is rich enough; it only wants the refinement. It can spend money enough on such things as farmers value, but it is thought utopian to propose spending money enough for things which more intelligent men know to be of far more worth. If we live in the nineteenth century, why should we not enjoy the advantages which the nineteenth century has to offer? Why should our life be in any respect provincial? As the nobleman of cultivated taste surrounds himself with whatever conduces to his culture—books, paintings, statuary, etc.—so let the village do. This town—how much has it ever spent directly on its own culture? To act collectively is according to the spirit of our institutions, and I am confident that, as our circumstances are more flourishing, our means are greater. New England can hire all the wise men in the world to come and teach her, and board them round the while, and not be provincial at all. That is the uncommon school we want. The one hundred and twenty-five dollars which is subscribed in this town every winter for a Lyceum is better spent than any other equal sum. Instead of noblemen, let us have noble towns or villages of men. This town has just spent sixteen thousand dollars for a town house. Suppose it had been proposed to spend an equal sum for something which will tend far more to refine and cultivate its inhabitants, a library, for instance. We have sadly neglected our education. We leave it to Harper and Brothers and Redding and Co.

JOURNAL / OCTOBER 15, 1852

How Father Le Jeune pestered the poor Indians with his God at every turn (they must have thought it his one idea), only getting their attention when they required some external aid to save them from starving! Then, indeed, they were good Christians.

JOURNAL / OCTOBER 25, 1852

The constitution of the Indian mind appears to be the very opposite to that of the white man. He is acquainted with a different side of nature. He measures his life by winters, not summers. His year is not measured by the sun, but consists of a certain number of moons, and his moons are measured not by days, but by nights. He has taken hold of the dark side of nature; the white man, the bright side.

JOURNAL / DECEMBER 28, 1852

It is worth the while to apply what wisdom one has to the conduct of his life, surely. I find myself oftenest wise in little things and foolish in great ones. That I may accomplish some particular petty affair well, I live my whole life coarsely. A broad margin of leisure is as beautiful in a man's life as in a book. Haste makes waste, no less in life than in housekeeping. Keep the time, observe the hours of the universe, not of the cars. What are threescore years and ten hurriedly and coarsely lived to moments of divine leisure in which your life is coincident with the life of the universe? We live too fast and coarsely, just as we eat too fast, and do not know the true savor of our food. We consult our will and understanding and the expectation of men, not our genius. I can impose upon myself tasks which will crush me for life and prevent all expansion, and this I am but too inclined to do.

One moment of life costs many hours, hours not of business but of preparation and invitation. Yet the man who does not betake himself at once and desperately to sawing is called a loafer, though he may be knocking at the doors of heaven all the while, which shall surely be opened to him. That aim in life is highest which requires the highest and finest discipline. How much, what infinite, leisure it requires, as of a lifetime, to appreciate a single phenomenon! You must camp down beside it as for life, having reached your land of promise, and give yourself wholly to it. It must stand for the whole world to you, symbolical of all things. The least partialness is your own defect of sight and cheapens the experience fatally. Unless the humming of a gnat is as the music of the spheres, and they are naught to me. It is not communications to serve for a history—which are science—but the great story itself, that cheers and satisfies us.

JOURNAL / JANUARY 6, 1853

About ten minutes before 10:00 A.M. I heard a very loud sound, and felt a violent jar, which made the house rock and the loose articles on my table rattle, which I knew must be either a powder mill blown up or an earthquake. Not knowing but another and more violent might take place, I immediately ran downstairs, but I saw from the door a vast expanding column of whitish smoke rising in the west directly over the powder mills four miles distant. It was unfolding its volumes above, which made it widest there. In three or four minutes it had all risen and spread itself into a lengthening, somewhat copper-colored cloud parallel with the horizon from north to south, and about ten minutes after the explosion it passed over my head, being several miles long from north to south and distinctly dark and smoky toward the north, not nearly so high as the few cirrhi in the sky. I jumped into a man's wagon and rode toward the mills. In a few minutes more, I saw behind me, far in the east, a faint salmon-colored cloud carrying the news of the explosion to the sea, and perchance over [the] head of the absent proprietor.

Arrived probably before half past ten. There were perhaps thirty or forty wagons there. The kernel mill had blown up first, and killed three men who were in it, said to be turning a roller with a chisel. In three seconds after, one of the mixing houses exploded. The kernel house was swept away, and fragments, mostly but a foot or two in length, were strewn over the hills and meadows, as if sown, for thirty rods, and the slight snow then on the ground was for the most part melted around. The mixing house, about ten rods west, was not so completely dispersed, for most of the machinery remained, a total wreck. The press house, about twelve rods east, had two thirds [of] its boards off, and a mixing house next westward from that which blew up had lost some boards on the east side. The boards fell out (*i.e.* of those buildings which did not blow up), the air within apparently rushing out to fill up the vacuum occasioned by the explosions; and so, the powder being bared to the fiery particles in the air, another building explodes. The powder on the floor of the bared press house was six inches deep in some places, and the crowd were thoughtlessly going into it. A few windows were broken thirty or forty rods off. Timber six inches square and eighteen feet long was thrown over a hill eighty feet high at least —a dozen rods; thirty rods was about the limit of fragments. The drying house, in which was a fire, was perhaps twenty-five rods distant and escaped. Every timber and piece of wood which was blown up was as black as if it had been dyed, except where it had broken on falling; other breakages were completely concealed by the color. I mistook what had been iron hoops in the woods for leather straps. Some of the clothes of the men were in the tops of the trees, where undoubtedly their bodies had been and left them. The bodies were naked and black, some limbs and bowels here and there, and a head at a distance from its trunk. The feet were bare; the hair singed to a crisp. I smelt the powder half a mile before I got there. Put the different buildings thirty rods apart, and then but one will blow up at a time.

JOURNAL / MARCH 10, 1853

It is essential that a man confine himself to pursuits—a scholar, for instance, to studies—which lie next to and conduce to his life, which do not go against the grain, either of his will or his imagination. The scholar finds in his experience some studies to be most fertile and radiant with light, others dry, barren, and dark. If he is wise, he will not persevere in the last, as a plant in a cellar will strive toward the light. He will confine the observations of his mind as closely as possible to the experience or life of his senses. His thought must live with and be inspired with the life of the body. The deathbed scenes and observations even of the best and wisest afford but a sorry picture of our humanity. Some men endeavor to live a constrained life, to subject their whole lives to their wills, as he who said he would give a sign if he were conscious after his head was cut off—but he gave no sign. Dwell as near as possible to the channel in which your life flows. A man may associate with such companions, he may pursue such employments, as will darken the day for him. Men choose darkness rather than light.

JOURNAL / APRIL 3, 1853

I have no time to read newspapers. If you chance to live and move and have your being in that thin stratum in which the events which make the news transpire—thinner than the paper on which it is printed—then these things will fill the world for you; but if you soar above or dive below that plane, you cannot remember nor be reminded of them.

JOURNAL / MAY 8, 1853

I have devoted most of my day to Mr. Alcott. He is broad and genial, but indefinite; some would say feeble; forever feeling about vainly in his speech and touching nothing. But this is a very negative account of him, for he thus suggests far more than the sharp and definite practical mind. The feelers of his thought diverge—such is the breadth of their grasp—not converge; and in his society almost alone I can express at my leisure, with more or less success, my vaguest but most cherished fancy or thought. There are never any obstacles in the way of our meeting. He has no creed. He is not pledged to any institution. The sanest man I ever knew; the fewest crotchets, after all, has he.

JOURNAL / JUNE 17, 1853

Here have been three ultrareformers, lecturers on Slavery, Temperance, the Church, etc., in and about our house and Mrs. Brooks's the last three or four days—A. D. Foss, once a Baptist minister in Hopkinton, N.H.; Loring Moody, a sort of traveling pattern-working chaplain; and H. C. Wright, who shocks all the old women with his infidel writings. Though Foss was a stranger to the others, you would have thought them old and familiar cronies. (They happened here together by accident.) They addressed each other constantly by their Christian names, and rubbed you continually with the greasy cheeks of their kindness. They would not keep their distance, but cuddle up and lie spoon fashion with you, no matter how hot the weather nor how narrow the bed—chiefly ——. I was awfully pestered with his benignity; feared I should get greased all over with it past restoration; tried to keep some starch in my clothes. He wrote a book called *A Kiss for a Blow,* and he behaved as if there were no alternative between these, or as if I had given him a blow. I would have preferred the blow, but he was bent on giving me the kiss, when there was neither quarrel nor agreement between us. I wanted that he should straighten his back, smooth out those ogling wrinkles of benignity about his eyes, and, with a healthy reserve, pronounce something in a downright manner. It was difficult to keep clear in his slimy benignity, with which he sought to cover you before he swallowed you and took you fairly into his bowels. It would have been far worse than the fate of Jonah. I do not wish to get any nearer to a man's bowels than usual. They lick you as a cow her calf. They would fain wrap you about with their bowels. —— addressed me as "Henry" within one minute from the time I first laid eyes on him, and when I spoke, he said with drawling, sultry sympathy, "Henry, I know all you would say; I understand you perfectly; you need not explain anything to me"; and to another, "I am going to dive into Henry's inmost depths." I said, "I trust you will not strike your head against the bottom." He could tell in a dark room, with his eyes blinded and in perfect stillness, if there was one there whom he loved. One of the most attractive things about the flowers is their beautiful reserve. The truly beautiful and noble puts its lover, as it were, at an infinite distance, while it attracts him more strongly than ever. I do not like the men who come so near with their bowels. It is the most disagreeable kind of snare to be caught in. Men's bowels are far more slimy than their brains. They must be ascetics indeed who approach you by this side. What a relief to have heard the ring of one healthy reserved tone! With such a forgiving disposition, as if he were all the while forgiving you for existing. Considering our condition or habit of soul—maybe corpulent and asthmatic— maybe dying of atrophy, with all our bones sticking out—is it kindness to embrace a man? They lay their sweaty hand on your shoulder, or your knee, to magnetize you.

JOURNAL / JUNE 18, 1853

Saw tonight Lewis the blind man's horse, which works on the sawing machine at the depot, now let out to graze along the road, but at each step he lifts his hind legs convulsively high from the ground, as if the whole earth were a treadmill continually slipping away from under him while he climbed its convex surface. It was painful to witness, but it was symbolical of the moral condition of his master and of all artisans in contradistinction from artists, all who are engaged in any routine; for to them also the whole earth is a treadmill, and the routine results instantly in a similar painful deformity. The horse may bear the mark of his servitude on the muscles of his legs, the man on his brow.

JOURNAL / JUNE 26, 1853

Such is oftenest the young man's introduction to the forest and wild. He goes thither at first as a hunter and fisher, until at last the naturalist or poet distinguishes that which attracted him and leaves the gun and fishing rod behind. The mass of men are still and always young in this respect. I have been surprised to observe that the only obvious employment which ever to my knowledge detained at Walden Pond for a whole half-day, unless it was in the way of business, any of my "fellow citizens," whether fathers or children of the town, with just one exception, was fishing. They might go there a thousand times, perchance, before the sediment of fishing would sink to the bottom and leave their purpose pure—before they began to angle for the pond itself. Thus, even in civilized society, the embryo man (speaking intellectually) passes through the hunter stage of development. They did not think they were lucky or well paid for their time unless they got a long string of fish, though they had the opportunity of seeing the pond all the while. They measured their success by the length of a string of fish. The Governor faintly remembers the pond, for he went afishing there when he was a boy, but now he is too old and dignified to go afishing, and so he knows it no longer. If the Legislature regards it, it is chiefly to regulate the number of hooks to be used in fishing there; but they know nothing about the hook of hooks.

JOURNAL / AUGUST 10, 1853

Alcott spent the day with me yesterday. He spent the day before with Emerson. He observed that he had got his wine and now he had come after his venison. . . . He has offered his services to the Abolition Society, to go about the country and speak for freedom as their agent, but they declined him. This is very much to their discredit; they should have been forward

82

to secure him. Such a connection with him would confer unexpected dignity on their enterprise. But they cannot tolerate a
man who stands by a head above them. They are as bad—Garrison and Phillips, etc.—as the overseers and faculty of Harvard
College. They require a man who will train well *under* them.
Consequently they have not in their employ any but small men—
trainers.

JOURNAL / OCTOBER 12, 1853

Today I have had the experience of borrowing money for a
poor Irishman who wishes to get his family to this country. One
will never know his neighbors till he has carried a subscription
paper among them. Ah! it reveals many and sad facts to stand in
this relation to them. To hear the selfish and cowardly excuses
some make—that *if* they help any, they must help the Irishman
who lives with them—and him they are sure never to help!
Others, with whom public opinion weighs, will think of it, trusting
you never will raise the sum and so they will not be called on
again; who give stingily after all. What a satire in the fact that
you are much more inclined to call on a certain slighted and so-
called crazy woman in moderate circumstances rather than on
the president of the bank! But some are generous and save the
town from the distinction which threatened it, and *some* even
who do not lend, plainly would if they could.

JOURNAL / OCTOBER 22, 1853

Yesterday, toward night, gave Sophia and mother a sail as far
as the battleground. One-eyed John Goodwin, the fisherman, was
loading into a handcart and conveying home the piles of driftwood which of late he had collected with his boat. It was a
beautiful evening, and a clear amber sunset lit up all the eastern
shores; and that man's employment, so simple and direct—though
he is regarded by most as a vicious character—whose whole
motive was so easy to fathom—thus to obtain his winter's wood
—charmed me unspeakable. So much do we love actions that are
simple. They are all poetic. We, too, would fain be so employed.
So unlike the pursuits of most men, so artificial or complicated.

Consider how the broker collects his winter's wood, what sport he makes of it, what is his boat and handcart! Postponing instant life, he makes haste to Boston in the cars, and there deals in stocks, not quite relishing his employment—and so earns the money with which he buys his fuel. And when, by chance, I meet him about this indirect and complicated business, I am not struck with the beauty of his employment. It does not harmonize with the sunset. How much more the former consults his genius, some genius at any rate! Now I should love to get my fuel so—I have got some so—but though I may be glad to have it, I do not love to get it in any other way less simple and direct. For if I buy one necessary of life, I cheat myself to some extent, I deprive myself of the pleasure, the inexpressible joy, which is the un-failing reward of satisfying any want of our nature simply and truly.

No *trade* is simple, but artificial and complex. It postpones life and substitutes death. It goes against the grain. If the first genera-tion does not die of it, the third or fourth does. In face of all statistics, I will never believe that it is the descendants of trades-men who keep the state alive, but of simple yeomen or laborers. This, indeed, statistics say of the city reinforced by the country. The oldest, wisest politician grows not more human so, but is merely a gray wharf rat at last. He makes a habit of disregarding the moral right and wrong for the legal or political, commits a slow suicide, and thinks to recover by retiring onto a farm at last. This simplicity it is, and the vigor it imparts, that enables the simple vagabond, though he does get drunk and is sent to the house of correction so often, to hold up his head among men.

"If I go to Boston every day and sell tape from morning till night," says the merchant (which we will admit is not a beautiful action), "some time or other I shall be able to buy the best of fuel without stint." Yes, but not the pleasure of picking it up by the riverside, which, I may say, is of more value than the warmth it yields, for it but keeps the vital heat in us that we may repeat such pleasing exercises. It warms us twice, and the first warmth is the most wholesome and memorable, compared with which the other is mere coke. It is to give no account of my employment to say that I cut wood to keep me from freezing, or cultivate beans to keep me from starving. Oh, no, the greatest value of these labors is received before the wood is teamed home, or the beans are harvested (or winnowed from it). Goodwin stands on the solid earth. The earth looks solider under him, and for such as he no *political* economies, with *their* profit and loss, supply and demand, need ever be written, for, they will need to use no policy. As for the complex ways of living, I love them not, however much I practice them. In as many places as possible, I will get my feet down to the earth. There is no secret in his trade, more than in the sun's. It is no mystery how he gets his living; no, not even when he steals it. But there is less double-dealing in his living than in your trade.

Goodwin is a most constant fisherman. He must well know the taste of pickerel by this time. He will fish, I would not venture to say how many days in succession. When I can remember to have seen him fishing almost daily for some time, if it rains, I am surprised on looking out to see him slowly wending his way to the river in his oilcloth coat, with his basket and pole. I saw him the other day fishing in the middle of the stream, the day after I had seen him fishing on the shore, while by a kind of magic I sailed by him; and he said he was catching minnow for bait in the winter. When I was twenty rods off, he held up a pickerel that weighed two and a half pounds, which he had forgot to show me before, and the next morning, as he afterward told me, he caught one that weighed three pounds. If it is ever necessary to appoint a committee on fish ponds and pickerel, let him be one of them. Surely he is tenacious of life, hard to scale.

JOURNAL / OCTOBER 26, 1853

Why is [it] that we look upon the Indian as the man of the woods? There are races half civilized, and barbarous even, that dwell in towns, but the Indians we associate in our minds with the wilderness.

*   *   *

How watchful we must be to keep the crystal well that we were made, clear!—that it be not made turbid by our contact with the world, so that it will not reflect objects. What other liberty is there worth having if we have not freedom and peace in our minds—if our inmost and most private man is but a sour and turbid pool? Often we are so jarred by chagrins in dealing with the world that we cannot reflect. Everything beautiful impresses us as sufficient to itself. Many men who have had much intercourse with the world and not borne the trial well affect me as all resistance, all bur and rind, without any gentleman, or tender and innocent core, left. They have become hedgehogs.

Ah! the world is too much with us, and our whole soul is stained by what it works in, like the dyer's hand. A man had better starve at once than lose his innocence in the process of getting his bread. This is the pool of Bethsaida [sic] which must be stilled and become smooth before we can enter to be healed. If within the old man there is not a young man—within the sophisticated, one unsophisticated—then he is but one of the devil's angels.

JOURNAL / NOVEMBER 1, 1853

About three weeks ago my indignation was roused by hearing that one of my townsmen, notorious for meanness, was endeavoring to get and keep a premium of four dollars which a poor Irish laborer whom he hired had gained by fifteen minutes' spading at our Agricultural Fair. Tonight a free colored woman is lodging at our house, whose errand to the North is to get money to buy her husband, who is a slave to one Moore in Norfolk, Virginia. She persuaded Moore, though not a kind master, to buy him that he might not be sold further South. Moore paid six hundred dollars for him but asks her eight hundred. My most natural reflection was that he was even meaner than my townsman. As mean as a slaveholder!

JOURNAL / NOVEMBER 12, 1853

I cannot but regard it as a kindness in those who have the steering of me that, by the want of pecuniary wealth, I have been nailed down to this my native region so long and steadily, and made to study and love this spot of earth more and more. What would signify in comparison a thin and diffused love and knowledge of the whole earth instead, got by wandering? The traveler's is but a barren and comfortless condition. Wealth will not buy a man a home in nature—house nor farm there. The man of business does not by his business earn a residence in nature, but is denaturalized rather. What is a farm, house and land, office or shop, but a settlement in nature under the most favorable conditions? It is insignificant, and a merely negative good fortune, to be provided with thick garments against cold and wet themselves, and to clothe them with our sympathy. The rich man buys woolens and furs, and sits naked and shivering still in spirit, besieged by cold and wet. But the poor Lord of Creation, cold and wet he makes to warm him, and be his garments.

JOURNAL / NOVEMBER 20, 1853

I once came near speculating in cranberries. Being put to it to raise the wind to pay for *A Week on the Concord and Merrimack Rivers,* and having occasion to go to New York to peddle some pencils which I had made, as I passed through Boston I went to Quincy Market and inquired the price of cranberries. The dealers took me down cellar, asked if I wanted wet or dry, and showed me them. I gave them to understand that I might want an indefinite quantity. It made a slight sensation among them, and for aught I know, raised the price of the berry for a time. I then visited various New York packets and was told what would be the freight, on deck and in the hold, and one skipper was very anxious for my freight. When I got to New York, I again visited the markets as a purchaser, and "the best of Eastern cranberries" were offered me by the barrel at a cheaper rate than I could buy them in Boston. I was obliged to manufacture a thousand dollars' worth of pencils and slowly dispose of and finally sacrifice them, in order to pay an assumed debt of a hundred dollars.

JOURNAL / DECEMBER 22, 1853

I have offered myself much more earnestly as a lecturer than a surveyor. Yet I do not get any employment as a lecturer; was not invited to lecture once last winter, and only once (without pay) this winter. But I can get surveying enough, which a hundred others in this country can do as well as I, though it is not boasting much to say a hundred others in New England cannot lecture as well as I on my themes. But they who do not make the highest demand on you shall rue it. It is because they make a low demand on themselves. All the while that they use only your humbler faculties, your higher unemployed faculties, like an invisible scimitar, are cutting them in twain. Woe be to the generation that lets any higher faculty in its midst go unemployed! That is to deny God and know him not, and he, accordingly, will know not of them.

JOURNAL / DECEMBER 26, 1853

Was overtaken by an Irishman seeking work. I asked him if he could chop wood. He said he was not long in this country; that he could cut one side of a tree well enough, but he had not learned to change hands and cut the other without going around it—what we call crossing the carf. They get very small wages at this season of the year; almost give up the ghost in the effort to keep soul and body together. He left me on the run to find a new master.

JOURNAL / FEBRUARY 18, 1854

I read some of the speeches in Congress about the Nebraska Bill—a thing the like of which I have not done for a year. What trifling upon a serious subject! while honest men are sawing wood for them outside. Your Congress halls have an alehouse odor—a place for stale jokes and vulgar wit. It compels me to think of my fellow creatures as apes and baboons. . . .

JOURNAL / APRIL 27, 1854

It is only the irresolute and idle who have no leisure for their proper pursuit. Be preoccupied with this, devoted to it, and no accident can befall you, no idle engagements distract you. No man ever had the opportunity to postpone a high calling to a disagreeable *duty*. Misfortunes occur only when a man is false to his Genius. You cannot hear music and noise at the same time. We avoid all the calamities that may occur in a lower sphere by abiding perpetually in a higher. Most men are engaged in business the greater part of their lives, because the soul abhors a vacuum, and they have not discovered any continuous employment for man's nobler faculties. Accordingly they do not pine, because they are not greatly disappointed. A little relaxation in your exertion, a little idleness, will let in sickness and death into your own body, or your family and their attendant duties and distractions. Every human being is the artificer of his own fate in these respects. The well have no time to be sick. Events, circumstances, etc., have their origin in ourselves. They spring from seeds which we have sown. Though I may call it a European War, it is only a phase or trait in my biography that I wot of. The most foreign scrap of news which the journals report to me—from Turkey or Japan—is but a hue of my inmost thought.

JOURNAL / APRIL 16, 1854

When I meet one of my neighbors these days who is ridiculously stately, being offended, I say in my mind: "Farewell! I will wait till you get your manners off. Why make politeness of so much consequence, when you are ready to assassinate with a word? I do not like any better to be assassinated with a rapier than to be knocked down with a bludgeon. You are so grand that I cannot get within ten feet of you." Why will men so try to impose on one another? Why not be simple, and pass for what they are worth only? O such thin skins, such crockery, as I have to deal with! Do they not know that I can laugh? Some who have so much dignity that they cannot be contradicted! Perhaps somebody will introduce me one day, and then we may have some intercourse. I meet with several who cannot afford to be simple and true men, but personate, so to speak, their own ideal of themselves, trying to make the manners supply the place of the man. They are puffballs filled with dust and ashes.

JOURNAL / JUNE 1, 1854

Now I see gentlemen and ladies sitting at anchor in boats on the lakes in the calm afternoons, under parasols, making use of nature, not always accumulating money. The farmer hoeing is wont to look with scorn and pride on a man sitting in a motionless boat with a whole half-day, but he does not realize that the object of his own labor is perhaps merely to add another dollar to his heap, nor through what coarseness and inhumanity to his family and servants he often accomplishes this. He has an Irishman or a Canadian working for him by the month; and what, probably, is the lesson that he is teaching him by precept and example? Will it make that laborer more of a man? this earth more like heaven?

JOURNAL / JUNE 18, 1854

What we want is not mainly to colonize Nebraska with free men, but to colonize Massachusetts with free men—to be free ourselves. As the enterprise of a few individuals, that is brave and practical; but as the enterprise of the State, it is cowardice and imbecility. What odds where we squat, or how much ground we cover? It is not the soil that we would make free, but men.

As for asking the South to grant us the trial by jury in the case of runaway slaves, it is as if, seeing a righteous man sent to hell, we should run together and petition the devil first to grant him a trial by jury, forgetting that there is another power to be petitioned, that there is another law and other precedents.

✶　　✶　　✶

Men may talk about measures till all is blue and smells of brimstone, and then go home and sit down and expect their measures to do their duty for them. The only measure is integrity and manhood.

✶　　✶　　✶

It is not any such free-soil party as I have seen, but a free-man party—*i.e.* a party of free men—that is wanted. It is not any politicians, even the truest and soundest, but, strange as it may sound, even godly men, as Cromwell discovered, who are wanted to fight this battle—men not of policy but of probity. Politicians! I have looked into the eyes of two or three of them, but I saw nothing there to satisfy me. They will vote for my man tomorrow if I will vote for theirs today. They will whirl round and round, not only horizontally like weathercocks, but vertically also.

My advice to the State is simply this: to dissolve her union with the slaveholder instantly. She can find no respectable law or precedent which sanctions its continuance. And to each inhabitant of Massachusetts, to dissolve his union with the State as long as she hesitates to do her duty.

Mrs. Mowatt, the actress, describes a fancy ball in Paris, given by an American millionaire, at which "one lady . . . wore so many diamonds (said to be valued at two hundred thousand dollars) that she was escorted in her carriage by gendarmes, for fear of robbery." This illustrates the close connection between luxury and robbery, but commonly the gendarmes are farther off.

WHERE I LIVED,
AND WHAT I LIVED FOR
1854

*Thoreau went to live at Walden Pond on July 4, 1845, moving into
the cabin he had built on Emerson's land. He wanted to simplify his
life and cut down his expenses while writing a memorial account of
his vacation trip with his brother,* A Week on the Concord and
Merrimack Rivers. *It now seems clear that shortly after settling in,
he got the idea of writing another book,* Walden. *In February 1847
(six months before he left Walden) the Concord Lyceum heard him
give two lectures on the purpose of life which were early versions
of the beginning of his book. He felt confident that* Walden *would
be ready for the press shortly after* A Week, *but the public's indifference to his first book led to the postponement of the second for
another five years. In the interval, Thoreau worked his way through
at least seven drafts of* Walden, *emerging in 1854 with the classic
the world has now enjoyed in a great variety of editions and transla-
tions.*

Chapter Two of Walden, *"Where I Lived, And What I Lived
For," tells why he undertook his experiment. Later in* Walden
*Thoreau reveals that he left the pond not only because he had
written* A Week *and most of* Walden, *but because he had several
more lives to live. "I learned this, at least, by my experiment," he
said; "that if one advances confidently in the direction of his dreams,
and endeavors to live the life which he has imagined, he will meet
with a success unexpected in common hours. He will put some things
behind, will pass an invisible boundary; new, universal, and more
liberal laws will begin to establish themselves around and within*

*him; or the old laws be expanded and interpreted in his favor in a
more liberal sense, and he will live with the license of a higher order
of beings. In proportion as he simplifies his life, the laws of the universe will appear less complex, and solitude will not be solitude, nor
poverty poverty, nor weakness weakness. If you have built castles in
the air, your work need not be lost; that is where they should be.
Now put the foundations under them."*

*The chapter printed here may convey the essence of Thoreau's
experience at Walden, but no one can dispense with a reading of the
whole book. It is many things at once—natural history, escape literature, a critique of modern civilization, a spiritual autobiography. And
it is also one of the best books written by an American. (M.M.)*

At a certain season of our life we are accustomed to consider
every spot as the possible site of a house. I have thus surveyed
the country on every side within a dozen miles of where I live.
In imagination I have bought all the farms in succession, for all
were to be bought, and I knew their price. I walked over each
farmer's premises, tasted his wild apples, discoursed on husbandry
with him, took his farm at his price, at any price, mortgaging it
to him in my mind; even put a higher price on it—took everything but a deed of it—took his word for his deed, for I dearly
love to talk—cultivated it, and him, too, to some extent, I trust,
and withdrew when I had enjoyed it long enough, leaving him
to carry it on. This experience entitled me to be regarded as a
sort of real-estate broker by my friends. Wherever I sat, there I
might live, and the landscape radiated from me accordingly.
What is a house but a sedes, a seat?—better if a country seat.
I discovered many a site for a house not likely to be soon improved, which some might have thought too far from the village,
but to my eyes the village was too far from it. Well, there I
might live, I said; and there I did live, for an hour, a summer and
a winter life; saw how I could let the years run off, buffet the
winter through, and see the spring come in. The future inhabitants of this region, wherever they may place their houses, may
be sure that they have been anticipated. An afternoon sufficed
to lay out the land into orchard, wood lot, and pasture, and to

decide what fine oaks or pines should be left to stand before the door, and whence each blasted tree could be seen to the best advantage; and then I let it lie, _fallow_ perchance, for a man is rich in proportion to the number of things which he can afford to let alone.

My imagination carried me so far that I even had the refusal of several farms—the refusal was all I wanted—but I never got my fingers burned by actual possession. The nearest that I came to actual possession was when I bought the Hollowell place, and had begun to sort my seeds, and collected materials with which to make a wheelbarrow to carry it on or off with; but before the owner gave me a deed of it, his wife—every man has such a wife—changed her mind and wished to keep it, and he offered me ten dollars to release him. Now, to speak the truth, I had but ten cents in the world, and it surpassed my arithmetic to tell, if I was that man who had ten cents, or who had a farm, or ten dollars, or all together. However, I let him keep the ten dollars and the farm, too, for I had carried it far enough; or rather, to be generous, I sold him the farm for just what I gave for it, and, as he was not a rich man, made him a present of ten dollars, and still had my ten cents, and seeds, and materials for a wheelbarrow left. I found thus that I had been a rich man without any damage to my poverty. But I retained the landscape, and I have since annually carried off what it yielded without a wheelbarrow. With respect to landscapes:

> I am monarch of all I survey,
> My right there is none to dispute.

I have frequently seen a poet withdraw, having enjoyed the most valuable part of a farm, while the crusty farmer supposed that he had got a few wild apples only. Why, the owner does not know it for many years when a poet has put his farm in rhyme, the most admirable kind of invisible fence, has fairly impounded it, milked it, skimmed it, and got all the cream, and left the farmer only the skimmed milk.

The real attractions of the Hollowell farm, to me, were: its complete retirement, being about two miles from the village, half a mile from the nearest neighbor, and separated from the highway by a broad field; its bounding on the river, which the owner said protected it by its fogs from frosts in the spring, though that was nothing to me; the gray color and ruinous state of the house and barn, and the dilapidated fences, which put such an interval between me and the last occupant; the hollow and lichen-covered apple trees, gnawed by rabbits, showing what kind of neighbors I should have; but above all, the recollection I had of it from my earliest voyages up the river, when the house was concealed behind a dense grove of red maples, through which I heard the house-dog bark. I was in haste to buy it before the proprietor finished getting out some rocks, cutting down the hollow apple trees, and grubbing up some young birches which had sprung up in the pasture, or, in short, had made any more of his improvements. To enjoy these advantages I was ready to carry it on; like Atlas, to take the world on my shoulders—I never heard what compensation he received for that—and do all those things which had no other motive or excuse but that I might pay for it and be unmolested in my possession of it; for I knew all the while that it would yield the most abundant crop of the kind I wanted, if I could only afford to let it alone. But it turned out as I have said.

All that I could say, then, with respect to farming on a large scale—I have always cultivated a garden—was, that I had had my seeds ready. Many think that seeds improve with age. I have no doubt that time discriminates between the good and the bad; and when at last I shall plant, I shall be less likely to be disappointed. But I would say to my fellows, once for all, As long as possible live free and uncommitted. It makes but little difference whether you are committed to a farm or the county jail.

Old Cato, whose *De Re Rustica* is my "Cultivator," says—and the only translation I have seen makes sheer nonsense of the passage—"When you think of getting a farm, turn it thus in your mind, not to buy greedily; nor spare your pains to look at it, and do not think it enough to go round it once. The oftener you go there, the more it will please you, if it is good." I think I shall not buy greedily, but go round and round it as long as I live, and be buried in it first, that it may please me the more at last.

The present was my next experiment of this kind, which I

purpose to describe more at length, for convenience putting the experience of two years into one. As I have said, I do not propose to write an ode to dejection, but to brag as lustily as chanticleer in the morning, standing on his roost, if only to wake my neighbors up.

When first I took up my abode in the woods, that is, began to spend my nights as well as days there, which, by accident, was on Independence Day, or the Fourth of July, 1845, my house was not finished for winter, but was merely a defense against the rain, without plastering or chimney, the walls being of rough, weather-stained boards, with wide chinks, which made it cool at night. The upright white hewn studs and freshly planed door and window casings gave it a clean and airy look, especially in the morning, when its timbers were saturated with dew, so that I fancied that by noon some sweet gum would exude from them. To my imagination it retained throughout the day more or less of this auroral character, reminding me of a certain house on a mountain which I had visited a year before. This was an airy and unplastered cabin, fit to entertain a traveling god, and where a goddess might trail her garments. The winds which passed over my dwelling were such as sweep over the ridges of mountains, bearing the broken strains, or celestial parts only, of terrestrial music. The morning wind forever blows, the poem of creation is uninterrupted; but few are the ears that hear it. Olympus is but the outside of the earth everywhere.

The only house I had been the owner of before, if I except a boat, was a tent, which I used occasionally when making excursions in the summer, and this is still rolled up in my garret; but the boat, after passing from hand to hand, has gone down the stream of time. With this more substantial shelter about me, I had made some progress toward settling in the world. This frame, so slightly clad, was a sort of crystallization around me, and reacted on the builder. It was suggestive somewhat as a picture in outlines. I did not need to go outdoors to take the air, for the atmosphere within had lost none of its freshness. It was not so much within-doors as behind a door where I sat, even in the rainiest weather. The Harivansha says, "An abode without birds is like a meat without seasoning." Such was not my abode, for I found myself suddenly neighbor to the birds; not by having imprisoned one, but having caged myself near them. I was not only nearer to some of those which commonly frequent the garden and the orchard, but to those wilder and more thrilling songsters of the forest which never, or rarely, serenade a villager—the wood thrush, the veery, the scarlet tanager, the field sparrow, the whippoorwill, and many others.

I was seated by the shore of a small pond, about a mile and a half south of the village of Concord and somewhat higher than it, in the midst of an extensive wood between that town and Lincoln, and about two miles south of that our only field known to fame, Concord battleground; but I was so low in the woods that the opposite shore, half a mile off, like the rest, covered with wood, was my most distant horizon. For the first week, whenever I looked out on the pond it impressed me like a tarn high *mountain lake* up on the side of a mountain, its bottom far above the surface of other lakes, and, as the sun arose, I saw it throwing off its nightly clothing of mist, and here and there, by degrees, its soft ripples or its smooth reflecting surface was revealed, while the mists, like ghosts, were stealthily withdrawing in every direction into the woods, as at the breaking up of some nocturnal conventicle. The very dew seemed to hang upon the trees later into the day than usual, as on the sides of mountains.

This small lake was of most value as a neighbor in the intervals of a gentle rainstorm in August, when, both air and water being perfectly still, but the sky overcast, mid-afternoon had all the serenity of evening, and the wood thrush sang around, and was heard from shore to shore. A lake like this is never smoother than at such a time; and the clear portion of the air above it being shallow and darkened by clouds, the water, full of light and reflections, becomes a lower heaven itself, so much the more important. From a hilltop near by, where the wood had been recently cut off, there was a pleasing vista southward across the pond, through a wide indentation in the hills which form the shore there, where their opposite sides loping toward each other suggested a stream flowing out in that direction through a wooded valley, but stream there was none. That way I looked between and over the near green hills to some distant and higher ones in

97

the horizon, tinged with blue. Indeed, by standing on tiptoe I could catch a glimpse of some of the peaks of the still bluer and more distant mountain ranges in the northwest, those true-blue coins from heaven's own mint, and also of some portion of the village. But in other directions, even from this point, I could not see over or beyond the woods which surrounded me. It is well to have some water in your neighborhood, to give buoyancy to and float the earth. One value even of the smallest well is that when you look into it, you see that earth is not continent but insular. This is as important as that it keeps butter cool. When I looked across the pond from this peak toward the Sudbury meadows, which in time of flood I distinguished elevated perhaps by a mirage in their seething valley, like a coin in a basin, all the earth beyond the pond appeared like a thin crust insulated and floated even by this small sheet of intervening water, and I was reminded that this on which I dwelt was but dry land.

Though the view from my door was still more contracted, I did not feel crowded or confined in the least. There was pasture enough for my imagination. The low shrub-oak plateau to which the opposite shore arose stretched away toward the prairies of the West and the steppes of Tartary, affording ample room for all the roving families of men. "There are none happy in the world but beings who enjoy freely a vast horizon," said Damodara when his herds required new and larger pastures.

Both place and time were changed, and I dwelt nearer to those parts of the universe and to those eras in history which had most attracted me. Where I lived was as far off as many a region viewed nightly by astronomers. We are wont to imagine rare and delectable places in some remote and more celestial corner of the system, behind the constellation of Cassiopeia's Chair, far from noise and disturbance. I discovered that my house actually had its site in such a withdrawn, but forever new and unprofaned, part of the universe. If it were worth the while to settle in those parts near to the Pleiades or the Hyades, to Aldebaran or Altair, then I was really there, or at an equal remoteness from the life which I had left behind, dwindled and twinkling with as fine a ray to my nearest neighbor, and to be seen only in moonless nights by him. Such was that part of creation where I had squatted.

> There was a shepherd that did live,
>   And held his thoughts as high
> As were the mounts whereon his flocks
>   Did hourly feed him by.

What should we think of the shepherd's life if his flocks always wandered to higher pastures than his thoughts?

Every morning was a cheerful invitation to make my life of equal simplicity, and I may say innocence, with Nature herself. I have been as sincere a worshiper of Aurora as the Greeks. I got up early and bathed in the pond; that was a religious exercise, and one of the best things which I did. They say that characters were engraven on the bathing tub of King Tching-thang to this effect: "Renew thyself completely each day; do it again, and again, and forever again." I can understand that. Morning brings back the heroic ages. I was as much affected by the faint hum of a mosquito making its invisible and unimaginable tour through my apartment at earliest dawn, when I was sitting with door and windows open, as I could be by any trumpet that ever sang of fame. It was Homer's requiem; itself an Iliad and Odyssey in the air, singing its own wrath and wanderings. There was something cosmical about it; a standing advertisement, till forbidden, of the everlasting vigor and fertility of the world. The morning, which is the most memorable season of the day, is the awakening hour. Then there is least somnolence in us; and for an hour, at least, some part of us awakes which slumbers all the rest of the day and night. Little is to be expected of that day, if it can be called a day, to which we are not awakened by our Genius, but by the mechanical nudgings of some servitor, are not awakened by our own newly acquired force and aspirations from within, accompanied by the undulations of celestial music, instead of factory bells, and a fragrance filling the air—to a higher life than we fell asleep from; and thus the darkness bear its fruit, and prove itself to be good, no less than the light. That man who does not believe that each day contains an earlier, more sacred, and

99

auroral hour than he has yet profaned, has despaired of life, and is pursuing a descending and darkening way. After a partial cessation of his sensuous life, the soul of man, or its organs rather, are reinvigorated each day, and his Genius tries again what noble life it can make. All memorable events, I should say, transpire in morning time and in a morning atmosphere. The Vedas say, "All intelligences awake with the morning." Poetry and art, and the fairest and most memorable of the actions of men, date from such an hour. All poets and heroes, like Memnon, are the children of Aurora, and emit their music at sunrise. To him whose elastic and vigorous thought keeps pace with the sun, the day is a perpetual morning. It matters not what the clocks say or the attitudes and labors of men. Morning is when I am awake and there is a dawn in me. Moral reform is the effort to throw off sleep. Why is it that men give so poor an account of their day if they have not been slumbering? They are not such poor calculators. If they had not been overcome with drowsiness, they would have performed something. The millions are awake enough for physical labor; but only one in a million is awake enough for effective intellectual exertion, only one in a hundred millions to a poetic or divine life. To be awake is to be alive. I have never yet met a man who was quite awake. How could I have looked him in the face?

We must learn to rewaken and keep ourselves awake, not by mechanical aids, but by an infinite expectation of the dawn, which does not forsake us in our soundest sleep. I know of no more encouraging fact than the unquestionable ability of man to elevate his life by a conscious endeavor. It is something to be able to paint a particular picture, or to carve a statue, and so to make a few objects beautiful; but it is far more glorious to carve and paint the very atmosphere and medium through which we look, which morally we can do. To affect the quality of the day, that is the highest of arts. Every man is tasked to make his life, even in its details, worthy of the contemplation of his most elevated and critical hour. If we refused, or rather used up, such paltry information as we get, the oracles would distinctly inform us how this might be done.

I went to the woods because I wished to live deliberately, to front only the essential facts of life, and see if I could not learn what it had to teach, and not, when I came to die, discover that I had not lived. I did not wish to live what was not life, living is so dear; nor did I wish to practice resignation, unless it was quite necessary. I wanted to live deep and suck out all the marrow of life, to live so sturdily and Spartan-like as to put to rout all that was not life, to cut a broad swath and shave close, to drive life into a corner, and reduce it to its lowest terms, and, if it proved to be mean, why then to get the whole and genuine meanness of it, and publish its meanness to the world; or if it were sublime, to know it by experience, and be able to give a true account of it in my next excursion. For most men, it appears to me, are in a strange uncertainty about it, whether it is of the devil or of God, and have somewhat hastily concluded that is the chief end of man here to "glorify God and enjoy him forever."

Still we live meanly, like ants; though the fable tells us that we were long ago changed into men; like pygmies we fight with cranes; it is error upon error, and clout upon clout, and our best virtue has for its occasion a superfluous and evitable wretchedness. Our life is frittered away by detail. An honest man has hardly need to count more than his ten fingers, or in extreme cases he may add his ten toes, and lump the rest. Simplicity, simplicity, simplicity! I say, let your affairs be as two or three, and not a hundred or a thousand; instead of a million, count half a dozen, and keep your accounts on your thumbnail. In the midst of this chopping sea of civilized life, such are the clouds and storms and quicksands and thousand-and-one items to be allowed for, that a man has to live, if he would not founder and go to the bottom and not make his port at all, by dead reckoning, and he must be a great calculator indeed who succeeds. Simplify, simplify. Instead of three meals a day, if it be necessary, eat but one; instead of a hundred dishes, five; and reduce other things in proportion. Our life is like a German confederacy, made up of petty states, with its boundary forever fluctuating, so that even a German cannot tell you how it is bounded at any moment. The nation itself, with all its so-called internal improvements, which, by the way, are all external and superficial, is just such an unwieldy and overgrown establishment, cluttered with furniture and tripped up by its own traps, ruined by luxury and heedless expense, by want of calculation and a worthy aim, as the million households in the land; and the only cure for it, as for them, is in a rigid economy, a stern and more than Spartan simplicity of life and elevation of purpose. It lives too fast. Men think that it is essential that the Nation have commerce, and export ice, and talk through a telegraph, and ride thirty miles an hour, without a doubt, whether they do or not; but whether we should live like baboons or like men, is a little uncertain. If we do not get our sleepers, and forge rails, and devote days and nights to the work, but go to tinkering upon our lives to improve them, who will build railroads? And if railroads are not built, how shall we get to heaven in season? But if we stay at home and mind our business, who will want railroads? We do not ride on the railroad; it rides upon us. Did you ever think what those sleepers are that underlie the railroad? Each one is a man, an Irishman or a Yankee man. The rails are laid on them, and they are covered with sand, and the cars run smoothly over them. They are sound sleepers, I assure you. And every few years a new lot is laid down and run over; so that, if some have the pleasure of riding on a rail, others have the misfortune to be ridden upon. And when they run over a man that is walking in his sleep, a supernumerary sleeper in the wrong position, and wake him up, they suddenly stop the cars, and make a hue and cry about it, as if this were an exception. I am glad to know that it takes a gang of men for every five miles to keep the sleepers down and level in their beds as it is, for this is a sign that they may sometime get up again.

Why should we live with such hurry and waste of life? We are determined to be starved before we are hungry. Men say that a stitch in time saves nine, and so they take a thousand stitches today to save nine tomorrow. As for work, we haven't any of any consequence. We have the Saint Vitus' dance, and cannot possibly keep our heads still. If I should only give a few pulls at the parish bell rope, as for a fire, that is, without setting the bell, there is hardly a man on his farm in the outskirts of Concord, notwithstanding that press of engagements which was his excuse so many times this morning, nor a boy, nor a woman,

102

I might almost say, but would forsake all and follow that sound, not mainly to save property from the flames, but, if we will confess the truth, much more to see it burn, since burn it must, and we, be it known, did not set it on fire—or to see it put out, and have a hand in it, if that is done as handsomely; yes, even if it were the parish church itself. Hardly a man takes a half hour's nap after dinner, but when he wakes he holds up his head and asks, "What's the news?" as if the rest of mankind had stood his sentinels. Some give directions to be waked every half hour, doubtless for no other purpose; and then, to pay for it, they tell what they have dreamed. After a night's sleep the news is as indispensable as the breakfast. "Pray tell me anything new that has happened to a man anywhere on this globe"—and he reads it over his coffee and rolls, that a man has had his eyes gouged out this morning on the Wachito River; never dreaming the while that he lives in the dark unfathomed mammoth cave of this world, and has but the rudiment of an eye himself.

For my part, I could easily do without the post office. I think that there are very few important communications made through it. To speak critically, I never received more than one or two letters in my life—I wrote this some years ago—that were worth the postage. The penny post is, commonly, an institution through which you seriously offer a man that penny for his thoughts which is so often safely offered in jest. And I am sure that I never read any memorable news in a newspaper. If we read of one man robbed, or murdered, or killed by accident, or one house burned, or one vessel wrecked, or one steamboat blown up, or one cow run over on the Western Railroad, or one mad dog killed, or one lot of grasshoppers in the winter—we never need read of another. One is enough. If you are acquainted with the principle, what do you care for a myriad instances and applications? To a philosopher all news, as it is called, is gossip, and they who edit and read it are old women over their tea. Yet not a few are greedy after this gossip. There was such a rush, as I hear, the other day at one of the offices to learn the foreign news by the last arrival, that several large squares of plate glass belonging to the establishment were broken by the pressure—news which I seriously think a ready wit might write a twelvemonth, or twelve years, beforehand with sufficient accuracy. As for Spain, for instance, if you know how to throw in Don Carlos and the Infanta, and Don Pedro and Seville and Granada, from time to time in the right proportions—they may have changed the names a little since I saw the papers—and serve up a bullfight when other entertainments fail, it will be true to the letter, and give us as good an idea of the exact state or ruin of things in Spain as the most succinct and lucid reports under this head in the newspapers. And as for England, almost the last significant scrap of news from that quarter was the revolution of 1649; and if you have learned the history of her crops for an average year, you never need attend to that thing again, unless your speculations are of a merely pecuniary character. If one may judge who rarely looks into the newspapers, nothing new does ever happen in foreign parts, a French revolution not excepted.

What news! how much more important to know what that is which was never old! "Kieou-he-yu (great dignitary of the state of Wei) sent a man to Khoung-tseu to know his news. Khoung-tseu caused the messenger to be seated near him, and questioned him in these terms: What is your master doing? The messenger answered with respect: My master desires to diminish the number of his faults, but he cannot come to the end of them. The messenger being gone, the philosopher remarked: What a worthy messenger! What a worthy messenger!" The preacher, instead of vexing the ears of drowsy farmers on their day of rest at the end of the week—for Sunday is the fit conclusion of an ill-spent week, and not the fresh and brave beginning of a new one—with this one other draggle-tail of a sermon, should shout with thundering voice, "Pause! Avast! Why so seeming fast, but deadly slow?"

Shams and delusions are esteemed for soundest truths, while reality is fabulous. If men would steadily observe realities only, and not allow themselves to be deluded, life, to compare it with such things as we know, would be like a fairy tale and the Arabian Nights' Entertainments. If we respected only what is inevitable and has a right to be, music and poetry would resound along the streets. When we are unhurried and wise, we perceive that only great and worthy things have any permanent and absolute ex-

104

istence, that petty fears and petty pleasures are but the shadow of the reality. This is always exhilarating and sublime. By closing the eyes and slumbering, and consenting to be deceived by shows, men establish and confirm their daily life of routine and habit everywhere, which still is built on purely illusory foundations. Children, who play life, discern its true law and relations more clearly than men, who fail to live it worthily, but who think that they are wiser by experience, that is, by failure. I have read in a Hindu book, that "there was a king's son, who, being expelled in infancy from his native city, was brought up by a forester, and growing up to maturity in that state, imagined himself to belong to the barbarous race with which he lived. One of his father's ministers having discovered him, revealed to him what he was, and the misconception of his character was removed, and he knew himself to be a prince. So soul," continues the Hindu philosopher, "from the circumstances in which it is placed, mistakes its own character, until the truth is revealed to it by some holy teacher, and then it knows itself to be Brahma." I perceive that we inhabitants of New England live this mean life that we do because our vision does not penetrate the surface of things. We think that that is which appears to be. If a man should walk through this town and see only the reality, where, think you, would the "Mill dam" go to? If he should give us an account of the realities he beheld there, we should not recognize the place in his description. Look at a meetinghouse, or a court-house, or a jail, or a shop, or a dwelling house, and say what that thing really is before a true gaze, and they would all go to pieces in your account of them. Men esteem truth remote, in the out-skirts of the system, behind the farthest star, before Adam and after the last man. In eternity there is indeed something true and sublime. But all these times and places and occasions are now and here. God himself culminates in the present moment, and will never be more divine in the lapse of all the ages. And we are enabled to apprehend at all what is sublime and noble only by the perpetual instilling and drenching of the reality that surrounds us. The universe constantly and obediently answers to our conceptions; whether we travel fast or slow, the track is laid for us. Let us spend our lives in conceiving then. The poet or the artist never yet had so fair and noble a design but some of his posterity at least could accomplish it.

Let us spend one day as deliberately as Nature, and not be thrown off the track by every nutshell and mosquito's wing that falls on the rails. Let us rise early and fast, or·break fast, gently and without perturbation; let company come and let company go, let the bells ring and the children cry—determined to make a day of it. Why should we knock under and go with the stream? Let us not be upset and overwhelmed in that terrible rapid and whirlpool called a dinner, situated in the meridian shallows. Weather this danger and you are safe, for the rest of the way is down hill. With unrelaxed nerves, with morning vigor, sail by it, looking another way, tied to the mast like Ulysses. If the engine whistles, let it whistle till it is hoarse for its pains. If the bell rings, why should we run? We will consider what kind of music they are like. Let us settle ourselves, and work and wedge our feet downward through the mud and slush of opinion, and prejudice, and tradition, and delusion, and appearance, that alluvion which covers the globe, through Paris and London, through New York and Boston and Concord, through Church and State, through poetry and philosophy and religion, till we come to a hard bottom and rocks in place, which we can call reality, and say, This is, and no mistake; and then begin, having a *point d'appui*, below freshet and frost and fire, a place where you might found a wall or a state, or set a lamppost safely, or perhaps a gauge, not a Nilometer, but a realometer, that future ages might know how deep a freshet of shams and appearances had gathered from time to time. If you stand right fronting and face to face to a fact, you will see the sun glimmer on both its surfaces, as if it were a scimitar, and feel its sweet edge dividing you through the heart and marrow, and so you will happily conclude your mortal career. Be it life or death, we crave only reality. If we are really dying, let us hear the rattle in our throats and feel cold in the extremities; if we are alive, let us go about our business.

Time is but the stream I go afishing in. I drink at it; but while I drink, I see the sandy bottom and detect how shallow it is. Its thin current slides away, but eternity remains. I would drink

106

deeper; fish in the sky, whose bottom is pebbly with stars. I cannot count one. I know not the first letter of the alphabet. I have always been regretting that I was not as wise as the day I was born. The intellect is a cleaver; it discerns and rifts its way into the secret of things. I do not wish to be any more busy with my hands than is necessary. My head is hands and feet. I feel all my best faculties concentrated in it. My instinct tells me that my head is an organ for burrowing, as some creatures use their snout and forepaw, and with it I would mine and burrow my way through these hills. I think that the richest vein is somewhere hereabouts; so by the divining rod and thin rising vapors I judge; and here I will begin to mine.

SLAVERY IN MASSACHUSETTS
1854

Five years after the obscure printing of "Civil Disobedience" another political speech of Thoreau's was published, this time, however, in the most widely read newspaper in America. The essay was "Slavery in Massachusetts"; the newspaper, Horace Greeley's New York Tribune. The occasion was the annual Fourth of July celebration of the Massachusetts Anti-Slavery Society, attended by three thousand people in a picnic grove in Framingham. Here it was that William Lloyd Garrison publicly burned a copy of the Constitution as a symbol of his protest against an instrument that protected slavery. From the same platform Thoreau delivered a lecture which came largely from entries made in his Journal *in response to fugitive-slave rescue cases.*

The passage of the Fugitive Slave Law in 1850 had pushed many Northern moderates towards the abolitionists. "A filthy enactment," Emerson said; "I will not obey it, by God!" Thousands of others felt the law compelling the return of runaway slaves to their masters was a violation of the "higher law" of man's conscience, and therefore not to be obeyed. When fugitives sought refuge in the North, many citizens gave moral or direct support to the men and women who dared harbor them.

In February 1851 Concord abolitionists helped the Virginia slave Shadrach escape his pursuers. In April Thomas Sims of Georgia reached Boston as a stowaway, but was shipped back into bondage by the slave-catchers, on order of the Federal official, Ellis Gray Loring. A Concord minister led the witnesses on the wharf in a prayer for the fugitive. In October Henry Williams, fleeing before his master's agents, reached Concord and was put safely aboard a

108

train for Canada by Thoreau. Syracuse, Philadelphia, New York,
Cincinnati, Wisconsin—their names blazed in the press as local citizens
took clubs, battering rams, and rifles to protect a fugitive's new-
found freedom. "Forcible resistance to the black bill was now obedi-
ence to God," one Negro witness wrote.

Speaking at Framingham, Thoreau advocated violation of the Fugi-
tive Slave Law and the boycott of newspapers which did not oppose
the law's enforcement. His words were burning, harsh—as significant
to moral decision now as then.

On July 21, 1854, the Liberator *published the speech. On August*
2, the New York Tribune *carried it to the largest audience Thoreau*
was to reach in his lifetime. (M.M.)

I lately attended a meeting of the citizens of Concord, expecting, as one among many, to speak on the subject of slavery in
Massachusetts; but I was surprised and disappointed to find that
what had called my townsmen together was the destiny of Nebraska, and not of Massachusetts, and that what I had to say
would be entirely out of order. I had thought that the house was
on fire, and not the prairie; but though several of the citizens of
Massachusetts are now in prison for attempting to rescue a slave
from her own clutches, not one of the speakers at that meeting
expressed regret for it, not one even referred to it. It was only
the disposition of some wild lands a thousand miles off which
appeared to concern them. The inhabitants of Concord are not
prepared to stand by one of their own bridges, but talk only of
taking up a position on the highlands beyond the Yellowstone
River. Our Buttricks and Davises and Hosmers are retreating
thither, and I fear that they will leave no Lexington Common
between them and the enemy. There is not one slave in Nebraska;
there are perhaps a million slaves in Massachusetts.

They who have been bred in the school of politics fail now
and always to face the facts. Their measures are half measures
and makeshifts merely. They put off the day of settlement indefinitely, and meanwhile the debt accumulates. Though the
Fugitive Slave Law had not been the subject of discussion on that
occasion, it was at length faintly resolved by my townsmen, at

an adjourned meeting, as I learn, that the compromise compact of 1820 having been repudiated by one of the parties, "therefore, . . . the Fugitive Slave Law of 1850 must be repealed." But this is not the reason why an iniquitous law should be repealed. The fact which the politician faces is merely that there is less honor among thieves than was supposed, and not the fact that they are thieves.

As I had no opportunity to express my thoughts at that meeting, will you allow me to do so here?

Again it happens that the Boston Courthouse is full of armed men, holding prisoner and trying a man, to find out if he is not really a slave. Does any one think that justice or God awaits Mr. Loring's decision? For him to sit there deciding still, when this question is already decided from eternity to eternity, and the unlettered slave himself and the multitude around have long since heard and assented to the decision, is simply to make himself ridiculous. We may be tempted to ask from whom he received his commission, and who he is that received it; what novel statutes he obeys, and what precedents are to him of authority. Such an arbiter's very existence is an impertinence. We do not ask him to make up his mind, but to make up his pack.

I listen to hear the voice of a Governor, Commander-in-Chief of the forces of Massachusetts. I hear only the creaking of crickets and the hum of insects which now fill the summer air. The Governor's exploit is to review the troops on muster days. I have seen him on horseback, with his hat off, listening to a chaplain's prayer. It chances that that is all I have ever seen of a Governor. I think that I could manage to get along without one. If he is not of the least use to prevent my being kidnaped, pray of what important use is he likely to be to me? When freedom is most endangered, he dwells in the deepest obscurity. A distinguished clergyman told me that he chose the profession of a clergyman because it afforded the most leisure for literary pursuits. I would recommend to him the profession of a Governor.

Three years ago, also, when the Sims tragedy was acted, I said to myself, There is such an officer, if not such a man, as the Governor of Massachusetts—what has he been about the last fortnight? Has he had as much as he could do to keep on the fence during this moral earthquake? It seemed to me that no keener satire could have been aimed at, no more cutting insult have been offered to that man, than just what happened—the absence of all inquiry after him in that crisis. The worst and the most I chance to know of him is that he did not improve that opportunity to make himself known, and worthily known. He could at least have resigned himself into fame. It appeared to be forgotten that there was such a man or such an office. Yet no doubt he was endeavoring to fill the gubernatorial chair all the while. He was no Governor of mine. He did not govern me.

But at last, in the present case, the Governor was heard from. After he and the United States Government had perfectly succeeded in robbing a poor innocent black man of his liberty for life, and, as far as they could, of his Creator's likeness in his breast, he made a speech to his accomplices, at a congratulatory supper!

I have read a recent law of this State, making it penal for any officer of the "Commonwealth" to "detain or aid in the . . . detention," anywhere within its limits, "of any person, for the reason that he is claimed as a fugitive slave." Also, it was a matter of notoriety that a writ of replevin to take the fugitive out of the custody of the United States marshal could not be served for want of sufficient force to aid the officer.

I had thought that the Governor was, in some sense, the executive officer of the State; that it was his business, as a Governor, to see that the laws of the State were executed; while, as a man, he took care that he did not, by so doing, break the laws of humanity; but when there is any special important use for him, he is useless, or worse than useless, and permits the laws of the State to go unexecuted. Perhaps I do not know what are the duties of a Governor; but if to be a Governor requires to subject one's self to so much ignominy without remedy, if it is to put a restraint upon my manhood, I shall take care never to be Governor of this Commonwealth. It is not profitable reading. They do not always say what is true; and they do not always mean what they say. What I am concerned to know is, that that man's influence and authority were on the side of the slaveholder, and not of the slave—of the guilty, and not of the innocent—of

111

injustice, and not of justice. I never saw him of whom I speak; indeed, I did not know that he was Governor until this event occurred. I heard of him and Anthony Burns at the same time, and thus, undoubtedly, most will hear of him. So far am I from being governed by him. I do not mean that it was anything to his discredit that I had not heard of him, only that I heard what I did. The worst I shall say of him is, that he proved no better than the majority of his constituents would be likely to prove. In my opinion, he was not equal to the occasion.

The whole military force of the State is at the service of a Mr. Suttle, a slaveholder from Virginia, to enable him to catch a man whom he calls his property; but not a soldier is offered to save a citizen of Massachusetts from being kidnaped! Is this what all these soldiers, all this training, have been for these seventy-nine years past? Have they been trained merely to rob Mexico and carry back fugitive slaves to their masters?

These very nights I heard the sound of a drum in our streets. There were men training still; and for what? I could with an effort pardon the cockerels of Concord for crowing still, for they, perchance, had not been beaten that morning; but I could not excuse this rub-a-dub of the "trainers." The slave was carried back by exactly such as these; *i.e.* by the soldier, of whom the best you can say in this connection is that he is a fool made conspicuous by a painted coat.

Three years ago, also, just a week after the authorities of Boston assembled to carry back a perfectly innocent man, and one whom they knew to be innocent, into slavery, the inhabitants of Concord caused the bells to be rung and the cannons to be fired, to celebrate their liberty—and the courage and love of liberty of their ancestors who fought at the bridge. As if those three millions had fought for the right to be free themselves, but to hold in slavery three million others. Nowadays, men wear a fool's cap, and call it a liberty cap. I do not know but there are some who, if they were tied to a whipping post, and could but get one hand free, would use it to ring the bells and fire the cannons to celebrate their liberty. So some of my townsmen took the liberty to ring and fire. That was the extent of their freedom; and when the sound of the bell died away, their liberty died away also; when the powder was all expended, their liberty went off with the smoke.

The joke could be no broader if the inmates of the prisons were to subscribe for all the powder to be used in such salutes, and hire the jailers to do the firing and ringing for them, while they enjoyed it through the grating.

This is what I thought about my neighbors.

Every humane and intelligent inhabitant of Concord, when he or she heard those bells and those cannons, thought not with pride of the events of the nineteenth of April, 1775, but with shame of the events of the twelfth of April, 1851. But now we have half buried that old shame under a new one.

Massachusetts sat waiting Mr. Loring's decision, as if it could in any way affect her own criminality. Her crime, the most conspicuous and fatal crime of all, was permitting him to be the umpire in such a case. It was really the trial of Massachusetts. Every moment that she hesitated to set this man free, every moment that she now hesitates to atone for her crime, she is convicted. The commissioner on her case is God; not Edward G. God, but simple God.

I wish my countrymen to consider that whatever the human law may be, neither an individual nor a nation can ever commit the least act of injustices against the obscurest individual without having to pay the penalty for it. A government which deliberately enacts injustice, and persists in it, will at length even become the laughingstock of the world.

Much has been said about American slavery, but I think that we do not even yet realize what slavery is. If I were seriously to propose to Congress to make mankind into sausages, I have no doubt that most of the members would smile at my proposition, and if any believed me to be in earnest, they would think that I proposed something much worse than Congress had ever done. But if any of them will tell me that to make a man into a sausage would be much worse—would be any worse—than to make him into a slave—than it was to enact the Fugitive Slave Law—I will accuse him of foolishness, of intellectual incapacity, of making a distinction without a difference. The one is just as sensible a proposition as the other.

113

I hear a good deal said about trampling this law under foot. Why, one need not go out of his way to do that. This law rises not to the level of the head or the reason; its natural habitat is in the dirt. It was born and bred, and has its life, only in the dust and mire, on a level with the feet; and he who walks with freedom, and does not with Hindu mercy avoid treading on every venomous reptile, will inevitably tread on it, and so trample it under foot—and Webster, its maker, with it, like the dirt bug and its ball.

Recent events will be valuable as a criticism on the administration of justice in our midst, or, rather, as showing what are the true resources of justice in any community. It has come to this, that the friends of liberty, the friends of the slave, have shuddered when they have understood that his fate was left to the legal tribunals of the country to be decided. Free men have no faith that justice will be awarded in such a case. The judge may decide this way or that; it is a kind of accident, at best. It is evident that he is not a competent authority in so important a case. It is no time, then, to be judging according to his precedents, but to establish a precedent for the future. I would much rather trust to the sentiment of the people. In their vote you would get something of some value, at least, however small; but in the other case, only the trammeled judgment of an individual, of no significance, be it which way it might.

It is to some extent fatal to the courts, when the people are compelled to go behind them. I do not wish to believe that the courts were made for fair weather, and for very civil cases merely; but think of leaving it to any court in the land to decide whether more than three millions of people, in this case a sixth part of a nation, have a right to be freemen or not! But it has been left to the courts of justice, so called—to the Supreme Court of the land—and, as you all know, recognizing no authority but the Constitution, it has decided that the three millions are and shall continue to be slaves. Such judges as these are merely the inspectors of a pick-lock and murderer's tools, to tell him whether they are in working order or not, and there they think that their responsibility ends. There was a prior case on the docket, which they, as judges appointed by God, had no right to skip; which having been justly settled, they would have been saved from this humiliation. It was the case of the murderer himself.

The law will never make men free; it is men who have got to make the law free. They are the lovers of law and order who observe the law when the government breaks it.

Among human beings, the judge whose words seal the fate of a man furthest into eternity is not he who merely pronounces the verdict of the law, but he, whoever he may be, who, from a love of truth, and unprejudiced by any custom or enactment of men, utters a true opinion or sentence concerning him. He it is that sentences him. Whoever can discern truth has received his commission from a higher source than the chiefest justice in the world who can discern only law. He finds himself constituted judge of judge. Strange that it should be necessary to state such simple truths!

I am more and more convinced that, with reference to any public question, it is more important to know what the country thinks of it than what the city thinks. The city does not think much. On any moral question, I would rather have the opinion of Boxboro than of Boston and New York put together. When the former speaks, I feel as if somebody had spoken, as if humanity was yet, and a reasonable being had asserted its rights— as if some unprejudiced men among the country's hills had at length turned their attention to the subject, and by a few sensible words redeemed the reputation of the race. When, in some obscure country town, the farmers come together to a special town meeting, to express their opinion on some subject which is vexing the land, that, I think, is the true Congress, and the most respectable one that is ever assembled in the United States.

It is evident that there are, in this Commonwealth at least, two parties, becoming more and more distinct—the party of the city and the party of the country. I know that the country is mean enough, but I am glad to believe that there is a slight difference in her favor. But as yet she has few if any organs through which to express herself. The editorials which she reads, like the news, come from the seaboard. Let us, the inhabitants of the country, cultivate self-respect. Let us not send to the city for aught more essential than our broadcloths and groceries; or, if we read the opinions of the city, let us entertain opinions of our own.

Among measures to be adopted, I would suggest to make as earnest and vigorous an assault on the press as has already been made, and with effect, on the church. The church has much improved within a few years; but the press is, almost without exception, corrupt. I believe that in this country the press exerts a greater and a more pernicious influence than the church did in its worst period. We are not a religious people, but we are a nation of politicians. We do not care for the Bible, but we do care for the newspaper. At any meeting of politicians—like that at Concord the other evening, for instance—how impertinent it would be to quote from the Bible! how pertinent to quote from a newspaper or from the Constitution! The newspaper is a Bible which we read every morning and every afternoon, standing and sitting, riding and walking. It is a Bible which every man carries in his pocket, which lies on every table and counter, and which the mail, and thousands of missionaries, are continually dispersing. It is, in short, the only book which America has printed, and which America reads. So wide is its influence. The editor is a preacher whom you voluntarily support. Your tax is commonly one cent daily, and it costs nothing for pew hire. But how many of these preachers preach the truth? I repeat the testimony of many an intelligent foreigner, as well as my own convictions, when I say that probably no country was ever ruled by so mean a class of tyrants as, with a few noble exceptions, are the editors of the periodical press in this country. And as they live and rule only by their servility, and appealing to the worse, and not the better, nature of man, the people who read them are in the condition of the dog that returns to his vomit.

The *Liberator* and the *Commonwealth* were the only papers in Boston, as far as I know, which made themselves heard in condemnation of the cowardice and meanness of the authorities of that city, as exhibited in '51. The other journals, almost without exception, by their manner of referring to and speaking of the Fugitive Slave Law, and the carrying back of the slave Sims, insulted the common sense of the country, at least. And, for the most part, they did this, one would say, because they thought so to secure the approbation of their patrons, not being aware that a sounder sentiment prevailed to any extent in the heart of the Commonwealth. I am told that some of them have improved of late; but they are still eminently time serving. Such is the character they have won.

But, thank fortune, this preacher can be even more easily reached by the weapons of the reformer than could the recreant priest. The free men of New England have only to refrain from purchasing and reading these sheets, have only to withhold their cents, to kill a score of them at once. One whom I respect told me that he purchased Mitchell's *Citizen* in the cars, and then threw it out the window. But would not his contempt have been more fatally expressed if he had not bought it?

Are they Americans? are they New Englanders? are they inhabitants of Lexington and Concord and Framingham, who read and support the Boston *Post, Mail, Journal, Advertiser, Courier,* and *Times*? Are these the flags of our Union? I am not a newspaper reader, and may omit to name the worst.

Could slavery suggest a more complete servility than some of these journals exhibit? Is there any dust which their conduct does not lick, and make fouler still with its slime? I do not know whether the Boston *Herald* is still in existence, but I remember to have seen it about the streets when Sims was carried off. Did it not act its part well—serve its master faithfully! How could it have gone lower on its belly? How can a man stoop lower than he is low? do more than put his extremities in the place of the head he has? than make his head his lower extremity? When I have taken up this paper with my cuffs turned up, I have heard the gurgling of the sewer through every column. I have felt that I was handling a paper picked out of the public gutters, a leaf from the gospel of the gambling house, the groggery, and the brothel, harmonizing with the gospel of the Merchants' Exchange.

The majority of the men of the North, and of the South and East and West, are not men of principle. If they vote, they do not send men to Congress on errands of humanity; but while their brothers and sisters are being scourged and hung for loving liberty, while—I might here insert all that slavery implies and is—it is the mismanagement of wood and iron and stone and gold

117

which concerns them. Do what you will, O Government, with my wife and children, my mother and brother, my father and sister, I will obey your commands to the letter. It will indeed grieve me if you hurt them, if you deliver them to overseers to be hunted by hounds or to be whipped to death; but, nevertheless, I will peaceably pursue my chosen calling on this fair earth, until perchance, one day, when I have put on mourning for them dead, I shall have persuaded you to relent. Such is the attitude, such are the words of Massachusetts.

Rather than do thus, I need not say what match I would touch, what system endeavor to blow up; but as I love my life, I would side with the light, and let the dark earth roll from under me, calling my mother and my brother to follow.

I would remind my countrymen that they are to be men first, and Americans only at a late and convenient hour. No matter how valuable law may be to protect your property, even to keep soul and body together, if it do not keep you and humanity together.

I am sorry to say that I doubt if there is a judge in Massachusetts who is prepared to resign his office and get his living innocently whenever it is required of him to pass sentence under a law which is merely contrary to the law of God. I am compelled to see that they put themselves, or rather are by character, in this respect, exactly on a level with the marine who discharges his musket in any direction he is ordered to. They are just as much tools, and as little men. Certainly, they are not the more to be respected, because their master enslaves their understandings and consciences, instead of their bodies.

The judges and lawyers—simply as such, I mean—and all men of expediency, try this case by a very low and incompetent standard. They consider, not whether the Fugitive Slave Law is right, but whether it is what they call constitutional. Is virtue constitutional, or vice? Is equity constitutional, or iniquity? In important moral and vital questions, like this, it is just as impertinent to ask whether a law is constitutional or not, as to ask whether it is profitable or not. They persist in being the servants of the worst of men, and not the servants of humanity. The question is, not whether you or your grandfather, seventy years

118

ago, did not enter into an agreement to serve the devil, and that service is not accordingly now due; but whether you will not now, for once and at last, serve God—in spite of your own past recreancy, or that of your ancestor—by obeying that eternal and only just CONSTITUTION, which He, and not any Jefferson or Adams, has written in your being.

The amount of it is, if the majority vote the devil to be God, the minority will live and behave accordingly, and obey the successful candidate, trusting that, some time or other, by some speaker's casting-vote, perhaps, they may reinstate God. This is the highest principle I can get out or invent for my neighbors. These men act as if they believed that they could safely slide down a hill a little way—or a good way—and would surely come to a place, by and by, where they could begin to slide up again. This is expediency, or choosing that course which offers the slightest obstacles to the feet, that is, a downhill one. But there is no such thing as accomplishing a righteous reform by the use of "expediency." There is no such thing as sliding uphill. In morals the only sliders are backsliders.

Thus we steadily worship Mammon, both school and state and church, and on the seventh day curse God with a tintamarre from one end of the Union to the other.

Will mankind never learn that policy is not morality—that it never secures any moral right, but considers merely what is expedient? chooses the available candidate—who is invariably the devil—and what right have his constituents to be surprised, because the devil does not behave like an angel of light? What is wanted is men, not of policy, but of probity—who recognize a higher law than the Constitution or the decision of the majority. The fate of the country does not depend on how you vote at the polls—the worst man is as strong as the best at that game; it does not depend on what kind of paper you drop into the ballot box once a year, but on what kind of man you drop from your chamber into the street every morning.

What should concern Massachusetts is not the Nebraska Bill, nor the Fugitive Slave Bill, but her own slaveholding and servility. Let the State dissolve her union with the slaveholder. She may wriggle and hesitate, and ask leave to read the Constitution

119

once more; but she can find no respectable law or precedent which sanctions the continuance of such a union for an instant.

Let each inhabitant of the State dissolve his union with her, as long as she delays to do her duty.

The events of the past month teach me to distrust Fame. I see that she does not finely discriminate, but coarsely hurrahs. She considers not the simple heroism of an action, but only as it is connected with its apparent consequences. She praises till she is hoarse the easy exploit of the Boston Tea Party, but will be comparatively silent about the braver and more distinterestedly heroic attack on the Boston Courthouse, simply because it was unsuccessful!

Covered with disgrace, the State has sat down coolly to try for their lives and liberties the men who attempted to do its duty for it. And this is called justice! They who have shown that they can behave particularly well may perchance be put under bonds for their good behavior. They whom truth requires at present to plead guilty are, of all the inhabitants of the State, pre-eminently innocent. While the Governor, and the Mayor, and countless officers of the Commonwealth are at large, the champions of liberty are imprisoned.

Only they are guiltless who commit the crime of contempt of such a court. It behooves every man to see that his influence is on the side of justice, and let the courts make their own characters. My sympathies in this case are wholly with the accused, and wholly against their accusers and judges. Justice is sweet and musical; but injustice is harsh and discordant. The judge still sits grinding at his organ, but it yields no music, and we hear only the sound of the handle. He believes that all the music resides in the handle, and the crowd toss him their coppers the same as before.

Do you suppose that that Massachusetts which is now doing these things—which hesitates to crown these men, some of whose lawyers, and even judges, perchance, may be driven to take refuge in some poor quibble, that they may not wholly outrage their instinctive sense of justice—do you suppose that she is anything but base and servile? that she is the champion of liberty?

Show me a free state, and a court truly of justice, and I will fight for them, if need be; but show me Massachusetts, and I refuse her my allegiance, and express contempt for her courts.

The effect of a good government is to make life more valuable; of a bad one, to make it less valuable. We can afford that railroad and all merely material stock should lose some of its value, for that only compels us to live more simply and economically; but suppose that the value of life itself should be diminished! How can we make a less demand on man and nature, how live more economically in respect to virtue and all noble qualities, than we do? I have lived for the last month—and I think that every man in Massachusetts capable of the sentiment of patriotism must have had a similar experience—with the sense of having suffered a vast and indefinite loss. I did not know at first what ailed me. At last it occurred to me that what I had lost was a country. I had never respected the government near to which I lived, but I had foolishly thought that I might manage to live here, minding my private affairs, and forget it. For my part, my old and worthiest pursuits have lost I cannot say how much of their attraction, and I feel that my investment in life here is worth many per cent less since Massachusetts last deliberately sent back an innocent man, Anthony Burns, to slavery. I dwelt before, perhaps, in the illusion that my life passed somewhere only between heaven and hell, but now I cannot persuade myself that I do not dwell wholly within hell. The site of that political organization called Massachusetts is to me morally covered with volcanic scoriae and cinders, such as Milton describes in the infernal regions. If there is any hell more unprincipled than our rulers, and we, the ruled, I feel curious to see it. Life itself being worth less, all things with it, which minister to it, are worth less. Suppose you have a small library, with pictures to adorn the walls—a garden laid out around—and contemplate scientific and literary pursuits, and discover all at once that your villa, with all its contents, is located in hell, and that the justice of the peace has a cloven foot and a forked tail—do not these things suddenly lose their value in your eyes?

I feel that, to some extent, the State has fatally interfered with my lawful business. It has not only interrupted me in my passage through Court Street on errands of trade, but it has interrupted me and every man on his onward and upward path, on which he had trusted soon to leave Court Street far behind. What right had it to remind me of Court Street? I have found that hollow which even I had relied on for solid.

I am surprised to see men going about their business as if nothing had happened. I say to myself, "Unfortunates! they have not heard the news." I am surprised that the man whom I just met on horseback should be so earnest to overtake his newly bought cows running away—since all property is insecure, and if they do not run away again, they may be taken away from him when he gets them. Fool! does he not know that his seed-corn is worth less this year—that all beneficent harvests fail as you approach the empire of hell? No prudent man will build a stone house under these circumstances, or engage in any peaceful enterprise which it requires a long time to accomplish. Art is as long as ever, but life is more interrupted and less available for a man's proper pursuits. It is not an era of repose. We have used up all our inherited freedom. If we would save our lives, we must fight for them.

I walk toward one of our ponds; but what signifies the beauty of nature when men are base? We walk to lakes to see our serenity reflected in them; when we are not serene, we go not to them. Who can be serene in a country where both the rulers and the ruled are without principle? The remembrance of my country spoils my walk. My thoughts are murder to the State, and involuntarily go plotting against her.

But it chanced the other day that I scented a white water lily, and a season I had waited for had arrived. It is the emblem of purity. It bursts up so pure and fair to the eye, and so sweet to the scent, as if to show us what purity and sweetness reside in, and can be extracted from, the slime and muck of earth. I think I have plucked the first one that has opened for a mile. What confirmation of our hopes is in the fragrance of this flower! I shall not so soon despair of the world for it, notwithstanding slavery, and the cowardice and want of principle of Northern men. It suggests what kind of laws have prevailed longest and widest, and still prevail, and that the time may come when man's deeds will smell as sweet. Such is the odor which the plant emits. If nature can compound this fragrance still annually, I shall believe her still young and full of vigor, her integrity and genius unimpaired, and that there is virtue even in man, too, who is fitted to perceive and love it. It reminds me that Nature has been partner to no Missouri Compromise. I scent no compromise in the fragrance of the water lily. It is not a Nymphoea Douglasii. In it, the sweet, and pure, and innocent are wholly sundered from the obscene and baleful. I do not scent in this the time-serving irresolution of a Massachusetts Governor, nor of a Boston Mayor. So behave that the odor of your actions may enhance the general sweetness of the atmosphere, that when we behold or scent a flower, we may not be reminded how inconsistent your deeds are with it; for all odor is but one form of advertisement of a moral quality, and if fair actions had not been performed, the lily would not smell sweet. The foul slime stands for the sloth and vice of man, the decay of humanity; the fragrant flower that springs from it, for the purity and courage which are immortal.

Slavery and servility have produced no sweet-scented flower annually, to charm the senses of men, for they have no real life: they are merely a decaying and a death, offensive to all healthy nostrils. We do not complain that they live, but that they do not get buried. Let the living bury them; even they are good for manure.

JOURNAL AND LETTERS
1855–1856

JOURNAL / JANUARY 26, 1855

One is educated to believe, and would rejoice if the rising generation should find no occasion to doubt, that the State and the Church are on the side of morality, that the voice of the people is the voice of God. Harvard College was partly built by a lottery. My father tells me he bought a ticket in it. Perhaps she thus laid the foundation of her Divinity School. Thus she teaches by example. New England is flooded with the "Official Schemes of the Maryland State Lotteries," and in this that State is no less unprincipled than in her slaveholding. Maryland, and every fool who buys a ticket of her, is bound straight to the bottomless pit. The State of Maryland is a moral fungus. Her offense is rank; it smells to heaven. Knowing that she is doing the devil's work, and that her customers are ashamed to be known as such, she advertises, as in the case of private diseases, that "the strictest confidence will be observed." "Consolidated" Deviltry!

JOURNAL / OCTOBER 19, 1855

Talking with Bellew this evening about Fourierism and communities, I said that I suspected any enterprise in which two were engaged together. "But," said he, "it is difficult to make a stick stand unless you slant two or more against it." "Oh, no," answered I, "you may split its lower end into three, or drive it

124

single into the ground, which is the best way; but most men, when they start on a new enterprise, not only figuratively, but really, *pull up stakes*. When the sticks prop one another, none, or only one, stands erect."

JOURNAL / OCTOBER 20, 1855

It is always a recommendation to me to know that a man has ever been poor, has been regularly born into this world, knows the language. I require to be assured of certain philosophers that they have once been barefooted, footsore, have eaten a crust because they had nothing better, and know what sweetness resides in it.

JOURNAL / OCTOBER 26, 1855

I sometimes think that I must go off to some wilderness where I can have a better opportunity to play life—can find more suitable materials to build my house with, and enjoy the pleasure of collecting my fuel in the forest. I have more taste for the wild sports of hunting, fishing, wigwam-building, making garments of skins, and collecting wood wherever you find it, than for butchering, farming, carpentry, working in a factory, or going to a wood market.

JOURNAL / NOVEMBER 5, 1855

I hate the present modes of living and getting a living. Farming and shopkeeping and working at a trade or profession are all odious to me. I should relish getting my living in a simple, primitive fashion. The life which society proposes to me to live is so artificial and complex—bolstered up on many weak supports, and sure to topple down at last—that no man surely can ever be inspired to live it, and only "old fogies" ever praise it. At best some think it their duty to live it. I believe in the infinite joy and satisfaction of helping myself and others to the extent of my ability. But what is the use in trying to live simply, raising what you eat, making what you wear, building what you inhabit, burning what you cut or dig, when those to whom you are allied insanely want and will have a thousand other things which neither you nor they can raise and nobody else, perchance, will pay for? The fellow man to whom you are yoked is a steer that is ever bolting right the other way.

I was suggesting once to a man who was wincing under some of the consequences of our loose and expensive way of living. "But you might raise all your own potatoes, etc., etc." We had often done it at our house and had some to sell. At which he demurring, I said, setting it high, "You could raise twenty bushels even." "But," said he, "I use thirty-five." "How large is your family?" "A wife and three infant children." This was the real family; I need not enumerate those who were hired to *help* eat the potatoes and waste them. So he had to hire a man to raise his potatoes.

Thus men invite the devil in at every angle and then prate about the garden of Eden and the fall of man.

JOURNAL / NOVEMBER 9, 1855

I affect what would commonly be called a mean and miserable way of living. I thoroughly sympathize with all savages and gypsies in so far as they merely assert the original right of man to the productions of Nature and a place in her. The Irishman moves into the town, sets up a shanty on the railroad land, and then gleans the dead wood from the neighboring forest, which would never get to market. But the so-called owner forbids it and complains of him as a trespasser. The highest law gives a thing to him who can use it.

JOURNAL / NOVEMBER 17, 1855

It is interesting to me to talk with Rice, he lives so thoroughly and satisfactorily to himself. He has learned that rare art of living, the every elements of which most professors do not know. His life has been not a failure but a success. Seeing me going to sharpen some plane-irons, and hearing me complain of the want of tools, he said that I ought to have a chest of tools. But I said it was not worth the while. I should not use them enough to pay for them. "You would use them more if you had them," said he. "When I came to do a piece of work, I used to find commonly that I wanted a certain tool, and I make it a rule first always to make that tool. I have spent as much as three thousand dollars thus on my tools." Comparatively speaking, his life is a success; not such a failure as most men's. He gets more out of any enterprise than his neighbors, for he helps himself more and hires less. Whatever pleasure there is in it, he enjoys. By good sense and calculation he has become rich and has invested his property well, yet practices a fair and neat economy, dwells not in untidy luxury. It costs him less to live, and he gets more out of life, than others. To get his living, or keep it, is not a hasty or disagreeable toil. He works slowly but surely, enjoying the sweet of it. He buys a piece of meadow at a profitable rate, works at it in pleasant weather, he and his son, when they are inclined, goes afishing or a-bee-hunting or a-rifle-shooting quite as often, and thus the meadow gets redeemed, and potatoes get planted, perchance, and he is very sure to have a good crop stored in his cellar in the fall, and some to sell. He always has the best of potatoes there. In the same spirit in which he and his son tackle up their Dobbin (he never keeps a fast horse) and go a-spearing or a-fishing through the ice, they also tackle up and go to their Sudbury farm to hoe or harvest a little, and when they return, they bring home a load of stumps in their hay rigging, which impeded their labors, but, perchance, supply them with their winter wood. All the woodchucks they shoot or trap in the beanfield are brought home also. And thus their life is a long sport and they know not what hard times are.

✓ ✓ ✓

I was so warmed in spirit in *getting* my wood that the heat it finally yielded when burned was coldness in comparison. That first is a warmth which you cannot buy.

JOURNAL / JANUARY 3, 1856

It is astonishing how far a merely well-dressed and good-looking man may go without being challenged by any sentinel. What is called good society will bid high for such.

✦   ✦   ✦

The man whom the State has raised to high office, like that of governor, for instance, from some, it may be, honest but less respected calling, cannot return to his former humble but profitable pursuits, his old customers will be so shy of him. His ex-honorableness-ship stands seriously in his way, whether he is a lawyer or a shopkeeper. He can't get ex-honorated. So he becomes a sort of State pauper, an object of charity on its hands, which the State is bound in honor to see through and provide still with offices of similar respectability that he may not come to want. A man who has been President becomes the ex-President, and can't travel or stay at home anywhere but men will persist in paying respect to his ex-ship. It is cruel to remember his deeds so long. When his time is out, why can't they let the poor fellow go?

JOURNAL / JANUARY 24, 1856

I have seen many a collection of stately elms which better deserved to be represented at the General Court than the manikins beneath—than the barroom and victualing cellar and groceries they overshadowed. When I see their magnificent domes, miles away in the horizon, over intervening valleys and forests, they suggest a village, a community, there. But, after all, it is a secondary consideration whether there are human dwellings beneath them; these may have long since passed away. I find that into my idea of the village has entered more of the elm than of the human being. They are worth many a political borough. They constitute a borough. The poor human representative of his party sent out from beneath their shade will not suggest a tithe of the dignity, the true nobleness and comprehensiveness of view, the sturdiness and independence, and the serene beneficence that they do. They look from township to township. A fragment of their bark is worth the backs of all the politicians in the union. They are free-soilers in their own broad sense. They send their roots north and south and east and west into many a conservative's Kansas and Carolina, who does not suspect such underground railroads—they improve the subsoil he has never disturbed—and many times their length, if the support of their principles requires it. They battle with the tempests of a century. See what scars they bear, what limbs they lost before we were born! Yet they never adjourn; they steadily vote for their principles, and send their roots farther and wider from the *same center*. They die at their posts, and they leave a tough butt for the choppers to exercise themselves about, and a stump which serves for their monument. They attend no caucus, they make no compromise, they use no policy. Their one principle is growth. They combine a true radicalism with a true conservatism. Their radicalism is not cutting away of roots, but an infinite multiplication and extension of them under all surrounding institutions. They take a firmer hold on the earth that they may rise higher into the heavens. Their conservative heartwood, in which no sap longer flows, does not impoverish their growth, but is a firm column to support it; and when their expanding trunks no longer require it, it utterly decays. Their conservatism is a dead but solid heartwood, which is the pivot and firm column of support to all this growth, appropriating nothing to itself, but forever by its support assisting to extend the area of their radicalism. Half a century after they are dead at the core, they are preserved by radical reforms. They do not, like men, from radicals turn conservative. Their conservative part dies out first; their radical and growing part survives. They acquire new States and Territories, while the old dominions decay, and become the habitation of bears and owls and coons.

JOURNAL / FEBRUARY 27, 1856

The papers are talking about the prospect of a war between England and America. Neither side sees how its country can avoid a long and fratricidal war without sacrificing its honor.

Both nations are ready to take a desperate step, to forget the interests of civilization and Christianity and their commercial prosperity and fly at each other's throats. When I see an individual thus beside himself, thus desperate, ready to shoot or be shot, like a blackleg who has little to lose, no serene aims to accomplish, I think he is a candidate for bedlam. What asylum is there for nations to go to? Nations are thus ready to talk of wars and challenge one another because they are made up to such an extent of poor, low-spirited, despairing men, in whose eyes the chance of shooting somebody else without being shot themselves exceeds their actual good fortune. Who, in fact, will be the first to enlist but the most desperate class, they who have lost all hope? And they may at last infect the rest.

JOURNAL / FEBRUARY 28, 1856

How various are the talents of men! From the brook in which one lover of nature has never during all his lifetime detected anything larger than a minnow, another extracts a trout that weighs three pounds, or an otter four feet long. How much more game he will see who carries a gun, *i.e.* who goes to see it! Though you roam the woods all your days, you never will see by chance what he sees who goes to purpose to see it. One gets his living by shooting woodcocks; most never see one in their lives.

JOURNAL / MARCH 10, 1856

Think of the art of printing, what miracles it has accomplished! Covered the very waste paper which flutters under our feet like leaves and is almost as cheap, a stuff now commonly put to the most trivial uses, with thought and poetry! The wood chopper reads the wisdom of ages recorded on the paper that holds his dinner, then lights his pipe with it. When we ask for a scrap of paper for the most trivial use, it may have the confessions of Augustine or the sonnets of Shakespeare, and we not observe it. The student kindles his fire, the editor packs his trunk, the sportsman loads his gun, the traveler wraps his dinner, the

Irishman papers his shanty, the schoolboy peppers the plastering, the belle pins up her hair, with the printed thoughts of men. Surely he who can see so large a portion of earth's surface thus darkened with the record of human thought and experience, and feel no desire to learn to read it, is without curiosity. He who cannot read is worse than deaf and blind, is yet but half alive, is stillborn.

JOURNAL / AUGUST 30, 1856

If you would really take a position outside the street and daily life of men, you must have deliberately planned your course, you must have business which is not your neighbors' business, which they cannot understand. For only absorbing employment prevails, succeeds, takes up space, occupies territory, determines the future of individuals and states, drives Kansas out of your head, and actually and permanently occupies the only desirable and free Kansas against all border ruffians. The attitude of resistance is one of weakness, inasmuch as it only faces an enemy; it has its back to all that is truly attractive. You shall have your affairs, I will have mine. You will spend this afternoon in setting up your neighbor's stove, and be paid for it; I will spend it in gathering a few berries of the *Vaccinium Oxycoccus* which Nature produces here, before it is too late, and *be paid for it also* after another fashion.

It is in vain to dream of a wildness distant from ourselves. There is none such. . . . I shall never find in the wilds of Labrador any greater wildness than in some recess in Concord, *i.e.* than I import into it. A little more manhood or virtue will make the surface of the globe anywhere thrillingly novel and wild.

JOURNAL / SEPTEMBER 2, 1856

Captain Hubbard said on Sunday that he had plowed up an Indian gouge, but how little impression that had made on him compared with the rotting of his cranberries or the loss of meadow grass! It seemed to me that it made an inadequate impression compared with many trivial events. Suppose he had plowed up five dollars!

✓   ✓   ✓

My father asked John Legross if he took an interest in politics and did his duty to his country at this crisis. He said he did. He went into the woodshed and read the newspaper Sundays. Such is the dawn of the literary taste, the first seed of literature that is planted in the new country. His grandson may be the author of a Bhagavad-Gita.

JOURNAL / OCTOBER 5, 1856

It is well to find your employment and amusement in simple and homely things. These wear best and yield most. I think I would rather watch the motions of these cows in their pasture for a day, which I now see all headed one way and slowly advancing—watch them and project their course carefully on a chart, and report all their behavior faithfully—than wander to Europe or Asia and watch other motions there; for it is only ourselves that we report in either case, and perchance we shall report a more restless and worthless self in the latter case than in the first.

LETTER TO THOMAS CHOLMONDELEY / OCTOBER 20, 1856

While war [Crimean War] has given place to peace on your side, perhaps a more serious war still is breaking out here. I seem to hear its distant mutterings, though it may be long before the bolt will fall in our midst. There has not been anything which you could call union between the North and South in this country for many years, and there cannot be so long as slavery is in the way. I only wish that Northern—that any men—were better material, or that I for one had more skill to deal with them; that the North had more spirit and would settle the question at once, and here instead of struggling feebly and protractedly away off on the plains of Kansas. They are on the eve of a Presidential election, as perhaps you know, and all good people are praying that of the three candidates, Frémont may be the man; but in my opinion the issue is quite doubtful. As far as I have observed, the worst man stands the best chance in this country. But as for politics, what I most admire nowadays is not the regular governments but the irregular primitive ones, like the Vigilance Committee in California and even the free-state men in Kansas. They are the most divine.

LETTER TO H. G. O. BLAKE / NOVEMBER 19, 1856

We visited Whitman the next morning (A. had already seen him), and were much interested and provoked. He is apparently the greatest democrat the world has seen. Kings and aristocracy go by the board at once, as they have long deserved to. A remarkably strong though coarse nature, of a sweet disposition, and much prized by his friends. Though peculiar and rough in his exterior, his skin [all over (?)] red, he is essentially a gentleman. I am still somewhat in a quandary about him—feel that he is essentially strange to me, at any rate; but I am surprised by the sight of him. He is very broad, but, as I have said, not fine. He said that I misapprehended him. I am not quite sure that I do. He told us that he loved to ride up and down Broadway all day on an omnibus, sitting beside the driver, listening to the roar of the carts, and sometimes gesticulating and declaiming Homer at the top of his voice. He has long been an editor and writer for the newspapers—was editor of the New Orleans *Crescent* once; but now has no employment but to read and write in the forenoon, and walk in the afternoon, like all the rest of the scribbling gentry.

JOURNAL / DECEMBER 2, 1856

Sam Melvin's lank bluish-white black-spotted hound, and Melvin and his gun near, going home at eve. He follows hunting, praise be to him, as regularly in our tame fields as the farmers follow farming. Persistent Genius! How I respect him and thank him for him (*sic*)! I trust the Lord will provide us with another Melvin when he is gone. How good in him to follow his own bent, and not continue at the Sabbath-school all his days! What a wealth he thus becomes in the neighborhood! Few know how to take the census. I thank my stars for Melvin. I think of him with gratitude when I am going to sleep, grateful that he exists —that Melvin who is such a trial to his mother. Yet he is agreeable to me as a tinge of russet on the hillside. I would fain give thanks morning and evening for my blessings. Awkward, gawky, loose-hung, dragging his legs after him. He is my contemporary and neighbor. He is one tribe, I am another, and we are not at war.

JOURNAL / DECEMBER 3, 1856

How I love the simple, reserved countrymen, my neighbors, who mind their own business and let me alone, who never waylaid nor shot at me, to my knowledge, when I crossed their fields, though each one has a gun in his house! For nearly twoscore years I have known, at a distance, these long-suffering men, whom I never spoke to, who never spoke to me, and now feel a certain tenderness for them, as if this long probation were but the prelude to an eternal friendship. What a long trial we have withstood, and how much more admirable we are to each other, perchance, than if we had been bedfellows! I am not only grateful because Veias, and Homer, and Christ, and Shakespeare have lived, but I am grateful for Minott, and Rice, and Melvin, and Goodwin, and Puffer even. I see Melvin all alone filling his sphere, in russet suit, which no others could fill or suggest. He takes up as much room in nature as the most famous.

LETTER TO H. G. O. BLAKE / DECEMBER 6, 1856

I am grateful for what I am and have. My thanksgiving is perpetual. It is surprising how contented one can be with nothing definite—only a sense of existence. Well, anything for variety. I am ready to try this for the next one thousand years, and exhaust it. How sweet to think of! My extremities well charred, and my intellectual part too, so that there is no danger of worm or rot for a long while. My breath is sweet to me. O how I laugh when I think of my vague indefinite riches. No run on my bank can drain it—for my wealth is not possession but enjoyment.

JOURNAL / DECEMBER 5, 1856

My themes shall not be far-fetched. I will tell of homely every-day phenomena and adventures. Friends! Society! It seems to me that I have an abundance of it, there is so much that I rejoice and sympathize with, and men, too, that I never speak to but only know and think of. What you call bareness and poverty is to me simplicity. God could not be unkind to me if he should try. I love the winter, with its imprisonment and its cold, for it compels the prisoner to try new fields and resources. I love to have the river closed up for a season and a pause put to my boating, to be obliged to get my boat in. I shall launch it again in the spring with so much more pleasure. This is an advantage in point of abstinence and moderation compared with the seaside boating, where the boat ever lies on the shore. I love best to have each thing in its season only, and enjoy doing without it at all other times. It is the greatest of all advantages to enjoy no advantage at all. I find it invariably true, the poorer I am, the richer I am. What you consider my disadvantage, I consider my advantage. While you are pleased to get knowledge and culture in many ways, I am delighted to think that I am getting rid of them. I have never got over my surprise that I should have been born into the most estimable place in all the world, and in the very nick of time, too.

LETTER TO H. G. O. BLAKE / DECEMBER 7, 1856

That Walt Whitman, of whom I wrote to you, is the most interesting fact to me at present. I have just read his second edition (which he gave me), and it has done me more good than any reading for a long time. Perhaps I remember best the poem of Walt Whitman an American and the Sun Down Poem. There are two or three pieces in the book which are disagreeable, to say the least, simply sensual. He does not celebrate love at all. It is as if the beasts spoke. I think that men have not been ashamed of themselves without reason. No doubt, there have always been dens where such deeds were unblushingly recited, and it is no merit to compete with their inhabitants. But even on this side, he has spoken more truth than any American or modern that I know. I have found his poem exhilarating, encouraging. As for its sensuality—and it may turn out to be less sensual than it appeared—I do not so much wish that those parts were not written, as that men and women were so pure that they could read them without harm, that is, without understanding them. One woman told me that no woman could read it, as if a man could read what a woman could not. Of course Walt Whitman can communicate to us no experience, and if we are shocked, whose experience is it that we are reminded of?

On the whole it sounds to me very brave and American after whatever deductions. I do not believe that all the sermons so called that have been preached in this land put together are equal to it for preaching. . . .

We ought to rejoice greatly in him. He occasionally suggests something a little more than human. You can't confound him with the other inhabitants of Brooklyn or New York. How they must shudder when they read him! He is awfully good.

To be sure I sometimes feel a little imposed on. By his heartiness and broad generalities he puts me into a liberal frame of mind prepared to see wonders—as it were, sets me upon a hill or in the midst of a plain—stirs me well up, and then—throws in a thousand of brick. Though rude and sometimes ineffectual, it is a great primitive poem—an alarum or trumpet note ringing through the American camp. Wonderfully like the Orientals, too, considering that when I asked him if he had read them, he answered, "No: tell me about them."

I did not get far in conversation with him—two more being present—and among the few things which I chanced to say, I remember that one was, in answer to him as representing America, that I did not think much of America or of politics, and so on, which may have been somewhat of a damper to him.

Since I have seen him, I find that I am not disturbed by any brag or egoism in his book. He may turn out the least of a braggart of all, having a better right to be confident.

He is a great fellow.

JOURNAL / DECEMBER 10, 1856

Yesterday I walked under the murderous Lincoln Bridge, where at least ten men have been swept dead from the cars within as many years. I looked to see if their heads had indented the bridge, if there were sturdy blows given as well as received, and if their brains lay about. But I could see neither the one nor the other. The bridge is quite uninjured, even, and straight, not even the paint worn off or discolored. The ground is clean, the snow spotless, and the place looks as innocent as a bank whereon the wild thyme grows. It does its work in an artistic manner. We have another bridge of exactly the same character on the other side of the town, which has killed one, at least, to my knowledge. Surely the approaches to our town, are well guarded. These are our modern Dragons of Wantley. Buccaneers of the Fitchburg Railroad, they lie in wait at the narrow passes and decimate the employees. The Company has signed a bond to give up one employee at this pass annually. The Vermont mother commits her son to their charge, and when she asks for him, again the Directors say: "I am not your son's keeper. Go look beneath the ribs of the Lincoln Bridge." It is a monster which would not have minded Perseus with his Medusa's head. If he could be held back only four feet from where he now crouches, all travelers might pass in safety and laugh him to scorn. This would require but a little resolution in our Legislature, but it is preferred to pay tribute still. I felt a curiosity to see this famous bridge, naturally far greater than my curiosity to see the gallows on which Smith was hung, which was burned in the old courthouse, for the exploits of this bridge are ten times as memorable. Here they are killed without priest, and the gallows bears an ill name, and I think deservedly. Lincoln Bridge, long as it has been in our midst and busy as it has been, no legislature, nobody, indeed, has ever seriously complained of, unless it was some bereaved mother, who was naturally prejudiced against it. To my surprise,

I found no difficulty in getting a sight of it. It stands right out in broad daylight in the midst of the fields. No sentinels, no spiked fence, no crowd about it, and you have to pay no fee for looking at it. It is perfectly simple and easy to construct, and does its work silently. The days of the gallows are numbered. The next time this county has a Smith to dispose of, they have only to hire him out to the Fitchburg Railroad Company. Let the priest accompany him to the freight train, pray with him, and take leave of him there. Another advantage I have hinted at, an advantage to the morals of the community, that, strange as it may seem, no crowd ever assembles at this spot; there are no morbidly curious persons, no hardened reprobates, no masculine women, no anatomists there.

Does it not make life more serious? I feel as if these were stirring times, as good as the days of the Crusaders, the Northmen, or the Buccaneers.

JOURNAL / DECEMBER 30, 1856

What an evidence it is, after all, of civilization, or of a capacity for improvement, that savages like our Indians, who in their protracted wars stealthily slay men, women, and children without mercy, with delight, who delight to burn, torture, and devour one another, proving themselves more inhuman in these respects even than beasts—what a wonderful evidence it is, I say, of their capacity for improvement that even they can enter into the most formal compact or treaty of peace, burying the hatchet, etc., etc., and treating with each other with as much consideration as the most enlightened states. You would say that they had a genius for diplomacy as well as for war. Consider that Iroquois, torturing his captive, roasting him before a slow fire, biting off the fingers of him alive, and finally eating the heart of him dead, betraying not the slightest evidence of humanity; and now behold him in the council chamber, where he meets the representatives of the hostile nation to treat of peace, conducting with such perfect dignity and decorum, betraying such a sense of justness. These savages are equal to us civilized men in their treaties, and, I fear, not essentially worse in their wars.

JOURNAL AND LETTERS
1857–1859

JOURNAL / JANUARY 11, 1857

There was wit and even poetry in the Negro's answer to the man who tried to persuade him that the slaves would not be obliged to work in heaven. "Oh, you g' way, Massa. I know better. If dere 's no work for cullud folks up dar, dey 'll *make* some fur 'em, and if dere 's nuffin better to do, dey 'll make 'em *shub de clouds along.* You can't fool this chile, Massa."

JOURNAL / JANUARY 18, 1857

We sometimes think that the inferior animals act foolishly, but are there any greater fools than mankind? Consider how so many, perhaps most, races—Chinese, Japanese, Arabs, Mussulmen generally, Russians—treat the traveler; what fears and prejudices he has to contend with. So many million believing that he has come [to] do them some harm. Let a traveler set out to go round the world, visiting every race, and he shall meet with such treatment at their hands that he will be obliged to pronounce them incorrigible fools. Even in Virginia a naturalist who was seen crawling through a meadow catching frogs, etc., was seized and carried before the authorities.

139

JOURNAL / FEBRUARY 8, 1857

Again and again I congratulate myself on my so-called poverty. I was almost disappointed yesterday to find thirty dollars in my desk which I did not know that I possessed, though now I should be sorry to lose it. The week that I go away to lecture, however much I may get for it, is unspeakably cheapened. The preceding and succeeding days are a mere sloping down and up from it.

In the society of many men, or in the midst of what is called success, I find my life of no account, and my spirits rapidly fall. I would rather be the barrenest pasture lying fallow than cursed with the compliments of kings, than be the sulphurous and accursed desert where Babylon once stood. But when I have only a rustling oak leaf, or the faint metallic cheep of a tree sparrow, for variety in my winter walk, my life becomes continent and sweet as the kernel of a nut. I would rather hear a single shrub-oak leaf at the end of a wintry glade rustle of its own accord at my approach, than receive a shipload of stars and garters from the strange kings and peoples of the earth.

JOURNAL / MAY 3, 1857

Up and down the town, men and boys that are under subjection are polishing their shoes and brushing their go-to-meeting clothes. I, a descendant of Northmen who worshiped Thor, spend my time worshiping neither Thor nor Christ; a descendant of Northmen who sacrificed men and horses, sacrifice neither men nor horses. I care not for Thor nor for the Jews. I sympathize not today with those who go to church in newest clothes and sit quietly in straight-backed pews. I sympathize rather with the boy who has none to look after him, who borrows a boat and paddle and in common clothes sets out to explore these temporary vernal lakes. I meet such a boy paddling along under a sunny bank, with bare feet and his pants rolled up above his knees, ready to leap into the water at a moment's warning. Better for him to read *Robinson Crusoe* than Baxter's *Saints' Rest*.

JOURNAL / MAY 10, 1857

How rarely I meet with a man who can be free, even in thought! We live according to rule. Some men are bedridden; all, world-ridden. I take my neighbor, an intellectual man, out into the woods and invite him to take a new and absolute view of things, to empty clean out of his thoughts all institutions of men and start again; but he can't do it, he sticks to his traditions and crotchets. He thinks that governments, colleges, newspapers, etc., are from everlasting to everlasting.

JOURNAL / MAY 29, 1857

With all this opportunity, this comedy and tragedy, how near all men come to doing nothing! It is strange that they did not make us more intense and emphatic, that they do not goad us into some action. Generally, with all our desires and restlessness, we are no more likely to embark in any enterprise than a tree is to walk to a more favorable locality. The seaboard swarms with adventurous and rowdy fellows, but how unaccountably they train and are held in check! They are as likely to be policemen as anything. It exhausts their wits and energy merely to get their living, and they can do no more. The Americans are very busy and adventurous sailors, but all in somebody's employ—as hired men. I have not heard of one setting out in his own bark, if only to run down our own coast on a voyage of adventure or observation, on his own account.

JOURNAL / JUNE 21, 1857

When Mr. Pool, the Doorkeeper of the House of Representatives—if that is his name and title—who makes out a list of the Representatives and their professions, asked him his business, he answered, "Fisherman." At which Pool was disturbed and said that no representative had ever called himself a fisherman before. It would not do to print it so. And so Atwood is put down as "Master Mariner"!! So much for American democracy. I reminded him that Fisherman had been a title of honor with a large party ever since the Christian era at least. When next we have occasion to speak of the apostles, I suppose we should call them "Master Mariners"!

JOURNAL / AUGUST 10, 1857

How meanly and miserably we live for the most part! We escape fate continually by the skin of our teeth, as the saying is. We are practically desperate. But as every man, in respect to material wealth, aims to become independent or wealthy, so, in respect to our spirits and imagination, we should have some spare capital and superfluous vigor, have some margin and leeway in which to move. What kind of gift is life unless we have spirits to enjoy it and taste its true flavor? if, in respect to spirits, we are to be forever cramped and in debt? In our ordinary estate we have not, so to speak, quite enough air to breathe, and this poverty qualifies our piety; but we should have more than enough and breathe it carelessly. Poverty is the rule. We should first of all be full of vigor like a strong horse, and beside have the free and adventurous spirit of his driver; *i.e.* we should have such a reserve of elasticity and strength that we may at any time be able to put ourselves at the top of our speed and go beyond our ordinary limits, just as the invalid hires a horse. Have the gods sent us into this world—to this *muster*—to do chores, hold horses, and the like, and not given us any spending money?

The poor and sick man keeps a horse, often a hostler; but the well man is a horse to himself, is horsed on himself; he feels his own oats. Look at the other's shanks. How spindling! like the timber of his gig! First a sound and healthy life, and then spirits to live it with.

JOURNAL / SEPTEMBER 30, 1857

What poor crack-brains we are! easily upset and unable to take care of ourselves! If there were a precipice at our doors, some would be found jumping off today for fear that, if they survived, they might jump off tomorrow. . . .

JOURNAL / OCTOBER 13, 1857

It is indeed a golden autumn. These ten days are enough to make the reputation of any climate. A tradition of these days might be handed down to posterity. They deserve a notice in history, in the history of Concord. All kinds of crudities have a chance to get ripe this year. Was there ever such an autumn? And yet there was never such a panic and hard times in the commercial world. The merchants and banks are suspending and failing all the country over, but not the sandbanks, solid and warm, and streaked with bloody blackberry vines. You may run upon them as much as you please[1]—even as the crickets do, and find their account in it. They are the stockholders in these banks, and I hear them creaking their content. You may see them on change any warmer hour. In these banks, too, and such as these, are my funds deposited, a fund of health and enjoyment. Their (the crickets) prosperity and happiness and, I trust, mine do not depend on whether the New York banks suspend or no. We do not rely on such slender security as the thin paper of the Suffolk Bank. To put your trust in such a bank is to be swallowed up and undergo suffocation. Invest, I say, in these country banks. Let your capital be simplicity and contentment. Withered golden-rod (*Solidago nemoralis*) is no failure, like a broken bank, and yet in its most golden season nobody counterfeits it. Nature needs no counterfeit-detector. I have no compassion for, nor sympathy with, this miserable state of things. Banks built of granite, after some Grecian or Roman style, with their porticoes and their safes of iron, are not so permanent, and cannot give me so good security for capital invested in them, as the heads of withered hardhack in the meadow. I do not suspect the solvency of these. I know who is their president and cashier.

LETTER TO H. G. O. BLAKE / NOVEMBER 16, 1857

They make a great ado nowadays about hard times; but I think that the community generally, ministers and all, take a wrong view of the matter, though some of the ministers preach-

[1] You cannot break them. If you should slump, 'tis to a finer sand.

ing according to a formula may pretend to take a right one. This general failure, both private and public, is rather occasion for rejoicing, as reminding us whom we have at the helm—that justice is always done. If our merchants did not most of them fail, and the banks too, my faith in the old laws of the world would be staggered. The statement that ninety-six in a hundred doing such business surely break down is perhaps the sweetest fact that statistics have revealed—exhilarating as the fragrance of sallows in spring. Does it not say somewhere, "The Lord reigneth, let the earth rejoice"? If thousands are thrown out of employment, it suggests that they were not well employed. Why don't they take the hint? It is not enough to be industrious; so are the ants. What are you industrious about?

The merchants and company have long laughed at transcendentalism, higher laws, etc., crying, "None of your moonshine," as if they were anchored to something not only definite, but sure and permanent. If there was any institution which was presumed to rest on a solid and secure basis, and more than any other represented this boasted common sense, prudence, and practical talent, it was the bank; and now those very banks are found to be mere reeds shaken by the wind. Scarcely one in the land has kept its promise. It would seem as if you only need live forty years in any age of this world, to see its most promising government become the government of Kansas, and banks nowhere. Not merely the Brook Farm and Fourierite communities, but now the community generally has failed. But there is the moonshine still, serene, beneficent, and unchanged. Hard times, I say, have this value, among others, that they show us what such promises are worth—where the sure banks are.

JOURNAL / DECEMBER 8, 1857

Staples says he came to Concord some twenty-four years ago, a poor boy with a dollar and three cents in his pocket, and he spent the three cents for a drink at Bigelow's tavern, and now he's worth "twenty hundred dollars clear." He remembers many who inherited wealth whom he can buy out today. I told him that he had done better than I in a pecuniary respect, for I had only earned my living. "Well," said he, "that's all I've done, and I don't know as I've got much better clothes than you." I was particularly poorly clad then, in the woods; my hat, pants, boots, rubbers, and gloves would not have brought fourpence, and I told the Irishman that it wasn't everybody could afford to have a fringe round his legs, as I had, my corduroys not preserving a selvage.

JOURNAL / JANUARY 25, 1858

The creditor is servant to his debtor, especially if he is about paying his due. I am amused to see what airs men take upon themselves when they have money to pay me. No matter how long they have deferred it, they imagine that they are my benefactors or patrons, and send me word graciously that *if I will come to their houses* they will pay me, when it is their business to come to me.

JOURNAL / FEBRUARY 18, 1858

George Minott tells me that he, when young, used often to go to a store by the side of where Bigelow's tavern was and kept by Ephraim Jones—the Goodnow store. That was probably the one kept by my old trader. Told me how Casey, who was a slave to a man—Whitney—who lived where Hawthorne owns—the same house—before the Revolution, ran off one Sunday, was pursued by the neighbors, and hid himself in the river up to his neck till nightfall, just across the Great Meadows. He ran through Gowing's Swamp and came back that night to a Mrs. Cogswell, who lived where Charles Davis does, and got something to eat; then cleared far away, enlisted, and was freed as a soldier after the war. Whitney's boy threw snowballs at him the day before, and finally C., who was chopping in the yard, threw his ax at him, and W. said he was an ugly nigger and must put him in jail. He may have been twenty years old when stolen from Africa; left a wife and one child there. Used to say that he went home to Africa in the night and came back again in the morning; *i.e.* he dreamed of home. Lived to be old. Called Thanksgiving "Tom Kiver."

JOURNAL / FEBRUARY 20, 1858

We hear the names of the worthies of Concord—Squire Cuming and the rest—but the poor slave Casey seems to have lived a more adventurous life than any of them. Squire Cuming probably never had to run for his life on the plains of Concord.

JOURNAL / MARCH 2, 1858

The last new journal thinks that it is very liberal, nay, bold, but it dares not publish a child's thought on important subjects, such as life and death and good books. It requires the sanction of the divines just as surely as the tamest journal does. If it had been published at the time of the famous dispute between Christ and the doctors, it would have published only the opinions of the doctors and suppressed Christ's. There is no need of a law to check the license of the press. It is law enough, and more than enough, to itself. Virtually, the community have come together and agreed what things shall be uttered, have agreed on a platform and to excommunicate him who departs from it, and not one in a thousand dares utter anything else. There are plenty of journals brave enough to say what they think about the government, this being a free one; but I know of none, widely circulated or well conducted, that dares say what it thinks about the Sunday or the Bible. They have been bribed to keep dark. They are in the service of hypocrisy.

JOURNAL / MARCH 20, 1858

If a man do not revive with nature in the spring, how shall he revive when a white-collared priest prays for him?

JOURNAL / APRIL 3, 1858

The gregariousness of men is their most contemptible and discouraging aspect. See how they follow each other like sheep, not knowing why. Day and Martin's blacking was preferred by the last generation, and also is by this. They have not so good a reason for preferring this or that religion as in this case even. Apparently in ancient times several parties were nearly equally matched. They appointed a committee and made a compromise, agreeing to vote or believe so and so, and they still helplessly abide by that. Men are the inveterate foes of all improvement. Generally speaking, they think more of their hen houses than of any desirable heaven. If you aspire to anything better than politics, expect no cooperation from men. They will not further anything good. You must prevail of your own force, as a plant springs and grows by its own vitality.

LETTER TO JAMES RUSSELL LOWELL / JUNE 22, 1858

Dear Sir,

When I received the proof of that portion of my story printed in the July number of your magazine [*Atlantic Monthly*], I was surprised to find that the sentence—"It is as immortal as I am, and perchance will go to as high a heaven, there to tower above me still" (which comes directly after the words "heals my cuts," page 230, tenth line from the top) have been crossed out, and it occurred to me that, after all, it was of some consequence that I should see the proofs; supposing, of course, that my "stet" etc. in the margin would be respected, as I perceive that it was in other cases of comparatively little importance to me. However, I have just noticed that that sentence was, in a very mean and cowardly manner, omitted. I hardly need to say that this is a liberty which I will not permit to be taken with my MS. The editor has, in this case, no more right to omit a sentiment than to insert one, or put words into my mouth. I do not ask anybody to adopt my opinions, but I do expect that when they ask for them to print, they will print them, or obtain my consent to their alteration or omission. I should not read many books if I thought that they had been thus expurgated. I feel this treatment to be an insult, though not intended as such, for it is to presume that I can be hired to suppress my opinions.

I do not mean to charge you with this omission, for I cannot believe that you knew anything about it, but there must be a responsible editor somewhere, and you, to whom I entrusted my MS. are the only party that I know in this matter. I therefore write to ask if you sanction this omission, and if there are any other sentiments to be omitted in the remainder of my article. If you do not sanction it—or whether you do or not—will you do me the justice to print that sentence, as an omitted one, indicating its place, in the August number?

I am not willing to be associated in any way, unnecessarily, with parties who will confess themselves so bigoted and timid as this implies. I could excuse a man who was afraid of an uplifted fist, but if one habitually manifests fear at the utterance of a sincere thought, I must think that his life is a kind of nightmare continued into broad daylight. It is hard to conceive of one so completely derivative. Is this the avowed character of the *Atlantic Monthly*? I should like an early reply.

JOURNAL / AUGUST 6, 1858

I hear of pickers ordered out of the huckleberry fields, and I see stakes set up with written notices forbidding any to pick there. Some let their fields, or allow so much for the picking. *Sic transit gloria ruris.* We are not grateful enough that we have lived part of our lives before these evil days came. What becomes of the true value of country life? What if you must go to market for it? Shall things come to such a pass that the butcher commonly brings round huckleberries in his cart? It is as if the hangman were to perform the marriage ceremony, or were to preside at the communion table. Such is the inevitable tendency of our civilization—to reduce huckleberries to a level with beefsteak. The butcher's item on the door is now "calf's head and huckleberries." I suspect that the inhabitants of England and of the Continent of Europe have thus lost their natural rights with the increase of population and of monopolies. The wild fruits of the earth disappear before civilization, or are only to be found in large markets. The whole country becomes, as it were, a town or beaten common, and the fruits left are a few hips and haws.

JOURNAL / AUGUST 9, 1858

It is surprising what a tissue of trifles and crudities make the daily news. For one event of interest there are nine hundred and ninety-nine insignificant, but about the same stress is laid on the last as on the first. The newspapers have just told me that the transatlantic telegraph cable is laid. That is important, but they instantly proceed to inform me how the news was received in every large town in the United States—how many guns they fired, or how high they jumped—in New York, and Milwaukee, and Sheboygan; and the boys and girls, old and young, at the corners of the streets are reading it all with glistening eyes, down to the very last scrap, not omitting what they did at New Rochelle and Evansville. And all the speeches are reported, and some think of collecting them into a volume!!!

It is surprising to what extent the world is ruled by cliques. They who constitute, or at least lead, New England or New York society, in the eyes of the world, are but a clique, a few "men of the ages" and of the town, who work best in the harness provided for them. The institutions of almost all kinds are thus of a sectarian or party character. Newspapers, magazines, colleges, and all forms of government and religion express the superficial activity of a few, the mass either conforming or not attending. The newspapers have just got over that eating-fullness or dropsy which takes place with the annual commencements and addresses before the Philomathean or Alpha Beta Gamma societies. Neither they who make these addresses nor they who attend to them are representative of the latest age. The boys think that these annual recurrences are part and parcel of the annual revolution of the system. There are also regattas and fireworks and "surprise parties" and horseshows. So that I am glad when I see or hear of a man anywhere who does not know of these things nor recognizes these particular fuglers. I was pleased to hear the other day that there were two men in Tamworth, N.H., who had been fishing for trout there ever since May; but it was a serious drawback to be told that they sent their fish to Boston and so catered for the few. The editors of newspapers, the popular clergy, politicians and orators of the day and office-holders, though they may be thought to be of very different politics and religion, are essentially one and homogeneous, inasmuch as they are only the various ingredients of the froth which ever floats on the surface of society.

LETTER TO GEORGE WILLIAM CURTIS / AUGUST 18, 1858

As for the Presidency—I cannot speak for my neighbors, but, for my own part, I am politically so benighted (or belighted?) that I do not know what Seward's qualifications are. I know, however, that no one in whom I could feel much interest would stand any chance of being elected. But the nail which is hard to drive is hard to draw.

JOURNAL / OCTOBER 4, 1858

See B—— a-fishing notwithstanding the wind. A man runs down, fails, loses self-respect, and goes a-fishing, though he were never seen on the river before. Yet methinks his "misfortune" is good for him, and he is more mellow and humane. Perhaps he begins to perceive more clearly that the object of life is something else than acquiring property, and he really stands in a truer relation to his fellow men than when he commanded a false respect of them. There he stands at length, perchance better employed than ever, holding communion with nature and himself and coming to understand his real position and relation to men in this world. It is better than a poor debtors' prison, better than most successful money-getting.

JOURNAL / OCTOBER 18, 1858

The large sugar maples on the common are now at the height of their beauty. One, the earliest to change, is partly bare. This turned so early and so deep a scarlet that some thought it was surely going to die. Also that one at the head of the Turnpike reveals its character now as far as you can see it. Yet about ten days ago all but one of these was quite green, and I thought they would not acquire any bright tints. A delicate but warmer than golden yellow is the prevailing color, with scarlet cheeks. They are great regular oval masses of yellow and scarlet. All the sunny warmth of the season seems to be absorbed in their leaves. There is an auction on the common, but its red flag is hard to be discerned amid this blaze of color. The lowest and inmost leaves next the bole are of the most delicate yellow and green, as usual, like the complexion of young men brought up in the house.

Little did the fathers of the town anticipate this brilliant success when they caused to be imported from farther in the country some straight poles with the tops cut off, which they called sugar maple trees—and a neighboring merchant's clerk, as I remember, by way of jest, planted beans about them. Yet these which were then jestingly called bean poles are these days far the most beautiful objects noticeable in our streets. They are worth all and more than they have cost—though one of the selectmen did take the cold which occasioned his death in setting them out—if only because they have filled the open eyes of children with their rich color so unstintedly so many autumns. We will not ask them to yield us sugar in the spring while they yield us so fair a prospect in the autumn. Wealth may be the inheritance of few in the houses, but it is equally distributed on the Common. All children alike can revel in this golden harvest. These trees, throughout the street, are at least equal to an annual festival and holiday, or a week of such—not requiring any special police to keep the peace—and poor indeed must be that New England village's October which has not the maple in its streets. This October festival cost no powder nor ringing of bells, but every tree is a liberty pole on which a thousand bright flags are run up. Hundreds of children's eyes are steadily drinking in this color, and by these teachers even the truants are caught and educated the moment they step abroad. It is as if some cheap and innocent gala day were celebrated in our town every autumn —a week or two of such days.

What meant the fathers by establishing this *living* institution before the church—this institution which needs no repairing nor repainting, which is continually "enlarged and repaired" by its growth? Surely trees should be set in our streets with a view to their October splendor. Do you not think it will make some odds to these children that they were brought up under the maples? Indeed, neither the truant nor the studious are at present taught colors in the schools. These are instead of the bright colors in apothecary shops and city windows. It is a pity we have not more red maples and some hickories in the streets as well. Our paintbox is very imperfectly filled. Instead of, or besides, supplying paintboxes, I would supply these natural colors to the young.

I know of one man at least, called an excellent and peculiarly successful farmer, who has thoroughly repaired his house and built a new barn with a barn cellar, such as every farmer seems fated to have, who has not a single tree or shrub of any kind about his house or within a considerable distance of it.

No annual training or muster of soldiery, no celebration with its scarfs and banners, could import into the town a hundredth part of the annual splendor of our October. We have only to set the trees, or let them stand, and Nature will find the colored drapery—flags of all her nations, some of whose private signals hardly the botanist can read. Let us have a good many maples and hickories and scarlet oaks, then, I say.

Blaze away! Shall that dirty roll of bunting in the gunhouse be all the colors a village can display? A village is not complete unless it has these trees to mark the season in it. They are as important as a town clock. Such a village will not be found to work well. It has a screw loose; an essential part is wanting. Let us have willows for spring, elms for summer, maples and walnuts and tupelos for autumn, evergreens for winter, and oaks for all seasons. What is a gallery in a house to a gallery in the streets! I think that there is not a picture gallery in the country which would be worth so much to us as is the western view under the elms of our main street. They are the frame to a picture, and we are not in the dilemma of the Irishman who, having bought a costly gilt picture frame at an auction, found himself obliged to buy a picture at private sale to put into it, for our picture is already painted with each sunset behind it. An avenue of elms as large as our largest, and three miles long, would seem to lead to some admirable place, though only Concord were at the end of it. Such a street as I have described would be to the traveler, especially in October, an ever-changing panorama.

A village needs these innocent stimulants of bright and cheery prospects to keep off melancholy and superstition. Show me two villages, one embowered in trees and blazing with all the glories of October; the other a merely trivial and treeless waste, and I shall be sure that in the latter will be found the most desperate and hardest drinkers. What if we were to take half as much pains in protecting them as we do in setting them out—not stupidly tie our horses to our dahlia stems? They are cheap preachers, permanently settled, which preach their half-century, and century, aye, and century-and-a-half sermons, with continually increasing influence and unction, ministering to many generations of men, and the least we can do is to supply them with suitable colleagues as they grow infirm.

JOURNAL / OCTOBER 19, 1858

Barrett's apprentice, it seems, makes trays of black birch and of red maple, in a dark room under the mill. I was pleased to see this work done here. A wooden tray is so handsome. You could count the circles of growth on the end of the tray, and the dark heart of the tree was seen at each end above, producing a semi-circular ornament. It was a satisfaction to be reminded that we may so easily make our own trenchers as well as fill them. To see the tree reappear on the table, instead of going to the fire or some equally coarse use, is some compensation for having it cut down. The wooden tray is still in demand to chop meat in, at least. If taken from the bench to the kitchen, they are pretty sure to crack, being made green. They should be placed to season for three months on the beams in a barn, said the miller. . . .

I was the more pleased with the sight of the trays because the tools used were so simple, and they were made by hand, not by machinery. They may make equally good pails, and cheaper as well as faster, at the pail factory with the home-made ones, but that interests me less, because the man is turned partly into a machine there himself. In this case the workman's relation to his work is more poetic, he also shows more dexterity and is more of a man. You come away from the great factory saddened, as if the chief end of man were to make pails; but in the case of the countryman who makes a few by hand, rainy days, the relative importance of human life and of pails is preserved, and you come away thinking of the simple and helpful life of the man—you do not turn pale at the thought—and would fain go to making pails yourself. We admire more the man who can use an ax or adz skillfully than him who can merely tend a machine. When labor is reduced to turning a crank, it is no longer amusing nor truly profitable; but let this business become very profitable in a pecuniary sense, and so be "driven," as the phrase is, and carried on on a large scale, and the man is sunk in it, while only the pail or tray floats; we are interested in it only in the same way as the proprietor or company is.

JOURNAL / NOVEMBER 1, 1858

As the afternoons grow shorter, and the early evening drives us home to complete our chores, we are reminded of the shortness of life, and become more pensive, at least in this twilight of the year. We are prompted to make haste and finish our work before the night comes. I leaned over a rail in the twilight on the Walden road, waiting for the evening mail to be distributed, when such thoughts visited me. I seemed to recognize the November evening as a familiar thing come round again, and yet I could hardly tell whether I had ever known it or only divined it. The November twilights just begun! It appeared like a part with which I was perfectly familiar just coming into view, and I foresaw how it would look and roll along, and prepared to be pleased. Just such a piece of art merely, though infinitely sweet and grand, did it appear to me, and just as little were any active duties required of me. We are independent on all that we see. The hangman whom I have *seen* cannot hang me. The earth which I have *seen* cannot bury me. Such doubleness and distance does sight prove. Only the rich and such as are troubled with ennui are implicated in the maze of phenomena. You cannot see anything until you are clear of it. The long railroad causeway through the meadows west of me, the still twilight in which hardly a cricket was heard,* the dark bank of clouds in the horizon long after sunset, the villagers crowding to the post office, and the hastening home to supper by candlelight, had I not seen all this before! What new sweet was I to extract from it? Truly they mean that we shall learn our lesson well. Nature gets thumbed like an old spelling book. The almshouse and Frederick were still as last November. I was no nearer, methinks, nor farther off from my friends. Yet I sat the bench with perfect contentment, unwilling to exchange the familiar vision that was to be unrolled for any treasure or heaven that could be imagined. Sure to keep just so far apart in our orbits still, in obedience to the laws of attraction and repulsion, affording each other only steady but indispensable starlight. It was as if I was promised the greatest novelty the world has ever seen or shall see, though the utmost possible novelty would be the difference between me and myself a year ago. This alone encouraged me, and was my fuel for the approaching winter. That we may behold the panorama with this slight improvement or change, this is what we sustain life for with so much effort from year to year.

And yet there is no more tempting novelty than this new November. No going to Europe or another world is to be named with it. Give me the old familiar walk, post office and all, with this ever-new self, with this infinite expectation and faith which does not know when it is beaten. We'll go nutting once more. We'll pluck the nut of the world, and crack it in the winter evenings. Theatres and all other sightseeing are puppet shows in comparison. I will take another walk to the cliff, another row on the river, another skate on the meadow, be out in the first snow, and associate with the winter birds. Here I am at home. In the bare and bleached crust of the earth I recognize my friend.

One actual Frederick that you know is worth a million only read of. Pray, am I altogether a bachelor, or am I a widower, that I should go away and leave my bride? This Morrow that is ever knocking with irresistible force at our door, there is no such guest as that; I will stay at home and receive company.

* Probably too cool for any these evenings; only in the afternoon.

I want nothing new, if I can have but a tithe of the old secured to me. I will spurn all wealth beside. Think of the consummate folly of attempting to go away from *here!* When the constant endeavor should be to get nearer and nearer *here.* Here are all the friends I ever had or shall have, and as friendly as ever. Why, I never had any quarrel with a friend but it was just as sweet as unanimity could be. I do not think we budge an inch forward or backward in relation to our friends. How many things can you go away from? They see the comet from the northwest coast just as plainly as we do, and the same stars through its tail. Take the shortest way round and stay at home. A man dwells in his native valley like a corolla in its calyx, like an acorn in its cup. *Here,* of course, is all that you love, all that you expect, all that you are. Here is your bride-elect, as close to you as she can be got. Here is all the best and all the worst you can imagine. What more do you want? Bear here-away then! Foolish people imagine that what they imagine is somewhere else. The stuff is not made in any factory but their own.

JOURNAL / NOVEMBER 16, 1858

Preaching? Lecturing? Who are ye that ask for these things? What do ye want to hear, ye puling infants? A trumpet sound that would train you up to mankind, or a nurse's lullaby? The preachers and lecturers deal with men of straw, as they are men of straw themselves. Why, a free-spoken man, of sound lungs, cannot draw a long breath without causing your rotten institutions to come toppling down by the vacuum he makes. Your church is a baby-house made of blocks, and so of the state. It would be a relief to breathe one's self occasionally among men. If there were any magnanimity in us, any grandeur of soul, anything but sects and parties undertaking to patronize God and keep the mind within bounds, how often we might encourage and provoke one another by a free expression! I will not consent to walk with my mouth muzzled, not till I am rabid, until there is danger that I shall bite the unoffending and that my bite will produce hydrophobia.

Freedom of speech! It hath not entered into your hearts to

conceive what those words mean. It is not leave given me by your sect to say this or that; it is when leave is given to your sect to withdraw. The church, the state, the school, the magazine, think they are liberal and free! It is the freedom of a prison yard. I ask only that one fourth part of my honest thoughts be spoken aloud. What is it you tolerate, you church today? Not truth, but a lifelong hypocrisy. Let us have institutions framed not out of our rottenness, but out of our soundness. This factitious piety is like stale gingerbread. I would like to suggest what a pack of fools and cowards we mankind are. They want me to agree not to breathe too hard in the neighborhood of their paper castles. If I should draw a long breath in the neighborhood of these institutions, their weak and flabby sides would fall out, for my own inspiration would exhaust the air about them. The church! it is eminently the timid institution, and the heads and pillars of it are constitutionally and by principle the greatest cowards in the community. The voice that goes up from the monthly concerts is not so brave and so cheering as that which rises from the frog ponds of the land. The best "preachers," so called, are an effeminate class; their bravest thoughts wear petticoats. If they have any manhood, they are sure to forsake the ministry, though they were to turn their attention to baseball. Look at your editors of popular magazines. I have dealt with two or three the most liberal of them. They are afraid to print a whole sentence, a *round* sentence, a free-spoken sentence. They want to get thirty thousand subscribers, and they will do anything to get them. They consult the D.D.'s and all the letters of the alphabet before printing a sentence. I have been into many of these cowardly New England towns where they *profess* Christianity—invited to speak, perchance—where they were trembling in their shoes at the thought of the things you might say, as if they knew their weak side— that they were weak on all sides. The devil they have covenanted with is a timid devil. If they would let their sores alone, they might heal, and they could to the wars again like men; but instead of that they get together in meetinghouse cellars, rip off the bandages, and poultice them with sermons.

One of our New England towns is sealed up hermetically like a molasses-hogshead—such is its sweet Christianity—only a little of the sweet trickling out at the cracks enough to daub you. The few more liberal-minded or indifferent inhabitants are the flies that buzz about it. It is Christianity bunged up. I see awful eyes looking out through a bull's-eye at the bung-hole. It is doubtful if they can fellowship with me.

The farther you go up country, I think the worse it is, the more benighted they are. On the one side you will find a barroom which holds the "scoffers," so called, on the other, a vestry where is a monthly concert of prayer. There is just as little to cheer you in one of these companies as the other. It may be often the truth and righteousness of the barroom that saves the town. There is nothing to redeem the bigotry and moral cowardice of New Englanders in my eyes. You may find a cape which runs six miles into the sea that has not a man of moral courage upon it. What is called faith is an immense prejudice. Like the Hindus and Russians[?] and Sandwich Islanders (that were), they are the creatures of an institution. They do not think; they adhere like oysters to what their fathers and grandfathers adhered to. How often is it that the shoemaker, by thinking over his last, can think as valuable a thought as he makes a valuable shoe?

I have been into the town, being invited to speak to the inhabitants, not valuing, not having read even, the assembly's catechism, and I try to stimulate them by reporting the best of my experience. I see the craven priest looking round for a hole to escape at, alarmed because it was he that invited me thither, and an awful silence pervades the audience. They think they will never get me there again. But the seed has not all fallen in stony and shallow ground.

✓　　　✓　　　✓

It is no compliment to be invited to lecture before the rich institutes and lyceums. The settled lecturers are as tame as the settled ministers. The audiences do not want to hear any prophets; they do not wish to be stimulated and instructed, but entertained. They, their wives and daughters, go the Lyceum to suck a sugar plum. The little of medicine they get is disguised with sugar. It is never the reformer they hear there, but a faint and timid echo of him only. They seek a pastime merely. Their

greatest guns and sons of thunder are only wooden guns and
great-grandsons of thunder, who give them smooth words well
pronounced from manuscripts well punctuated—they who have
stolen the little fire they have from prophets whom the audience
would quake to hear. They ask for orators that will entertain
them and leave them where they found them. The most successful lecturing on Washington, or whatnot, is an awful scratch-
ing of backs to the tune, it may be, of fifty thousand dollars.
Sluggards that want to have a lullaby sung to them! Such
manikins as I have described are they, alas, who have made the
greatest stir (and what a shallow stir) in the Church and Lyceum,
and in Congress. They want a medicine that will not interfere
with their daily meals.

There is the Lowell Institute with its restrictions, requiring a
certain faith in the lecturers. How can any free-thinking man
accept its terms? It is as if you were to resolve that you would
not eat oysters that were not of a particular faith—that, for
instance, did not believe the Thirty-Nine Articles—for the faith
that is in an oyster is just as valuable as the faith referred to in
Mr. Lowell's will. These popular lecturers, our preachers, and
magazines are for women and children *in the bad sense.*

The curators have on their lists the names of the men who
came before the Philomathean Institute in the next large town
and did no harm; left things *in statu quo,* so that all slept the
better for it; only confirmed the audience in their previous bad-
ness; spoke a good word for God; gave the clergy, the heavy
set, a lift; told the youngsters to be good boys. A man may have
a good deal to say who has not any desk to thump on, who does
not thunder in bad air.

They want all of a man but his truth and independence and
manhood.

One who spoke to their condition would of course make them
wince, and they would retaliate, *i.e.* kick him out, or stop their
ears.

JOURNAL / DECEMBER 26, 1858

Call at a farmer's this Sunday afternoon, where I surprise the
well-to-do masters of the house lounging in very ragged clothes

(for which they think it necessary to apologize), and one of them is busy laying the supper table (at which he invites me to sit down at last), bringing up cold meat from the cellar and a lump of butter on the end of his knife, and making the tea by the time his mother gets home from church. Thus sincere and homely, as I am glad to know, is the actual life of these New England men, wearing rags indoors there which would disgrace a beggar (and are not beggars and paupers they who *could be* disgraced so?) and doing the indispensable work, however humble. How much better and more humane it was than if they had imported and set among their penates a headless torso from the ruins of Ireland! I am glad to find that our New England life has a genuine humane core to it; that inside, after all, there is so little pretense and brag. Better than that, methinks, is the hard drinking and quarreling which we must allow is not uncommon there. The middle-aged son sits there in the old unpainted house in a ragged coat, and helps his old mother about her work when the field does not demand him.

JOURNAL / FEBRUARY 3, 1859

Some have spoken slightingly of the Indians, as a race possessing so little skill and wit, so low in the scale of humanity, and so brutish that they hardly deserved to be remembered—using only the terms "miserable," "wretched," "pitiful," and the like. In writing their histories of this country they have so hastily disposed of this refuse of humanity (as they might have called it) which littered and defiled the shore and the interior. But even the indigenous animals are inexhaustibly interesting to us. How much more, then, the indigenous man of America! If wild men, so much more like ourselves than they are unlike, have inhabited these shores before us, we wish to know particularly what manner of men they were, how they lived here, their relation to nature, their arts and their customs, their fancies and superstitions. They paddled over these waters, they wandered in these woods, and they had their fancies and beliefs connected with the sea and the forest, which concern us quite as much as the fables of Oriental nations do. It frequently happens that the historian, though he professes more humanity than the trapper, mountain man, or gold digger, who shoots one as a wild beast, really exhibits and practices a similar inhumanity to him, wielding a pen instead of a rifle.

One tells you with more contempt than pity that the Indian had no religion, holding up both hands, and this to all the shallow-brained and bigoted seems to mean something important, but it is commonly a distinction without a difference. Pray, how much more religion has the historian? If Henry Ward Beecher knows so much more about God than another, if he has made some discovery of truth in this direction, I would thank him to publish it in *Silliman's Journal*, with as few flourishes as possible.

It is the spirit of humanity, that which animates both so-called savages and civilized nations, working through a man, and not the man expressing himself, that interests us most. The thought of a so-called savage tribe is generally far more just than that of a single civilized man.

JOURNAL / FEBRUARY 23, 1859

What an army of nonproducers society *produces*—ladies generally (old and young) and gentlemen *of leisure*, so called! Many think themselves well employed as charitable dispensers of wealth which somebody else earned, and these who produce nothing, being of the most luxurious habits, are precisely they who want the most, and complain loudest when they do not get what they want. They who are literally paupers maintained at the public expense are the most importunate and insatiable beggars. They cling like the glutton to a living man and suck his vitals up. To every locomotive man there are three or four deadheads clinging to him, as if they conferred a great favor on society by living upon it. Meanwhile they fill the churches, and die and revive from time to time. They have nothing to do but sin, and repent of their sins. How can you expect such bloodsuckers to be happy?

JOURNAL / APRIL 8, 1859

What a pitiful business is the fur trade, which has been pursued now for so many ages, for so many years by famous companies

which enjoy a profitable monopoly and control a large portion of
the earth's surface, unweariedly pursuing and ferreting out small
animals by the aid of all the loafing class tempted by rum and
money, that you may rob some little fellow creature of its coat
to adorn or thicken your own, that you may get a fashionable
covering in which to hide your head, or a suitable robe in which
to dispense justice to your fellow men! Regarded from the philosopher's point of view, it is precisely on a level with rag and
bone picking in the streets of the cities. The Indian led a more
respectable life before he was tempted to debase himself so much
by the white man. Think how many musquash and weasel skins
the Hudson's Bay Company pile up annually in their warehouses,
leaving the bare red carcasses on the banks of the streams throughout all British America—and this it is, chiefly, which makes it
British America. It is the place where Great Britain goes amous-
ing. We have heard much of the wonderful intelligence of the
beaver, but that regard for the beaver is all a pretense, and we
would give more for a beaver hat than to preserve the intelligence of the whole race of beavers.

When we see men and boys spend their time shooting and
trapping musquash and mink, we cannot but have a poorer
opinion of them, unless we thought meanly of them before. Yet
the world is imposed on by the fame of the Hudson's Bay and
Northwest Fur companies, who are only so many partners more
or less in the same sort of business, with thousands of just such
loafing men and boys in their service to abet them. On the one
side is the Hudson's Bay Company, on the other the company of
scavengers who clear the sewers of Paris of their vermin. There
is a good excuse for smoking out or poisoning rats which infest
the house, but when they are as far off as Hudson's Bay, I think
that we had better let them alone. To such an extent do time and
distance, and our imaginations, consecrate at last not only the
most ordinary but even vilest pursuits. The efforts of legislation
from time to time to stem the torrent are significant as showing
that there is some sense and conscience left, but they are insignificant in their effects. We will fine Abner if he shoots a singing
bird, but encourage the army of Abners that compose the Hudson's Bay Company.

One of the most remarkable sources of profit opened to the Yankee within a year is the traffic in skunk skins. I learn from the newspapers—as from other sources (vide *Journal of Commerce* in *Tribune* for April 5, 1859)—that "the traffic in skunk skins has suddenly become a most important branch of the fur trade, and the skins of an animal which three years ago were deemed of no value whatever, are now in the greatest demand." "The principal markets are Russia and Turkey, though some are sent to Germany, where they are sold at a large profit." Furs to Russia! "The black skins are valued the most, and during the past winter the market price has been as high as one dollar per skin, while mottled skins brought only seventy cents." "Upward of fifty thousand of these skins have been shipped from this city [New York] alone within the past two months." Many of them "are designed for the Leipsic sales, Leipsic being next to Novgorod, in Russia, the most important fur entrepot in Europe. The first intimation received in this market of the value of this new description of fur came from the Hudson's Bay Company, which, having shipped a few to London at a venture, found the returns so profitable that they immediately prosecuted the business on an extensive scale." "The heaviest collections are made in the Middle and Eastern States, in some parts of which the mania for capturing these animals seems to have equaled the Western Pike's Peak gold excitement, men, women, and children turning out en masse for that purpose." And beside, "our fur dealers also receive a considerable sum for the *fat* of these animals!!"

Almost all smile, or otherwise express their contempt, when they hear of this or the rat-catching of Paris, but what is the difference between catching and skinning the skunk and the mink? It is only in the name. When you pass the palace of one of the managers of the Hudson's Bay Company, you are reminded that so much he got for his rat skins. In such a snarl and contamination do we live that it is almost impossible to keep one's skirts clean. Our sugar and cotton are stolen from the slave, and if we jump out of the fire, it is wont to be into the frying pan at least. It will not do to be thoughtless with regard to any of our valuables or property. When you get to Europe, you will meet the most tender-hearted and delicately bred lady, perhaps

163

the president of the Antislavery Society, or of that for the encouragement of humanity to animals, marching or presiding with the scales from a tortoise's back—obtained by laying live coals on it to make them curl up—stuck in her hair, rat skin fitting as close to her fingers as erst to the rat, and, for her cloak, trimmings perchance adorned with the spoils of a hundred skunks—rendered inodorous, we trust. Poor misguided woman! Could she not wear other armor in the war of humanity?

When a new country like North America is discovered, a few feeble efforts are made to Christianize the natives before they are all exterminated, but they are not found to pay, in any sense. But the energetic traders of the discovering country organize themselves, or rather inevitably crystallize, into a vast rat-catching society, tempt the natives to become mere vermin hunters and rum drinkers, reserving half a continent for the field of their labors. Savage meets savage, and the white man's only distinction is that he is the chief.

She says to the turtle basking on the shore of a distant isle, "I want your scales to adorn my head" (though fire be used to raise them); she whispers to the rats in the wall, "I want your skins to cover my delicate fingers"; and, meeting an army of a hundred skunks in her morning walk, she says, "worthless vermin, strip off your cloaks this instant, and let me have them to adorn my robe with"; and she comes home with her hands muffled in the pelt of a gray wolf that ventured abroad to find food for its young that day.

When the question of the protection of birds comes up, the legislatures regard only a low use and never a high use; the best-disposed legislators employ one, perchance, only to examine their crops and see how many grubs or cherries they contain, and never to study their dispositions, or the beauty of their plumage, or listen and report on the sweetness of their song. The legislature will preserve a bird professedly not because it is a beautiful creature, but because it is a good scavenger or the like. This, at least, is the defense set up. It is as if the question were whether some celebrated singer of the human race—some Jenny Lind or another—did more harm or good, should be destroyed, or not, and therefore a committee should be appointed, not to listen to her singing at all, but to examine the contents of her stomach and see if she devoured anything which was injurious to the farmers and gardeners, or which they cannot spare.

JOURNAL / MAY 2, 1859

I feel no desire to go to California or Pike's Peak, but I often think at night with inexpressible satisfaction and yearning of the *arrowheadiferous* sands of Concord.

JOURNAL / SEPTEMBER 18, 1859

Dr. Bartlett handed me a paper today, desiring me to subscribe for a statue to Horace Mann. I declined, and said that I thought a man ought not any more to take up room in the world after he was dead. We shall lose one advantage of a man's dying if we are to have a statue of him forthwith. This is probably meant to be an opposition statue to that of Webster. At this rate they will crowd the streets with them. A man will have to add a clause to his will, "No statue to be made of me." It is very offensive to my imagination to see the dying stiffen into statues at this rate. We should wait till their bones begin to crumble— and then avoid too near a likeness to the living.

JOURNAL / OCTOBER 15, 1859

Each town should have a park, or rather a primitive forest, of five hundred or a thousand acres, where a stick should never be cut for fuel, a common possession forever, for instruction and recreation. We hear of cow-commons and ministerial lots, but we want *men*-commons and lay lots, inalienable forever. Let us keep the New World *new*, preserve all the advantages of living in the country. There is meadow and pasture and wood lot for the town's poor. Why not a forest and huckleberry field for the town's rich? All Walden Wood might have been preserved for our park forever, with Walden in its midst, and the Easterbrooks Country, an unoccupied area of some four square miles, might have been our huckleberry field. If any owners of these tracts are about to leave the world without natural heirs who need or deserve to be specially remembered, they will do wisely to abandon their possession to all, and not will them to some individual who perhaps has enough already. As some give to Harvard College or another institution, why might not another give a forest or huckleberry field to Concord? A tówn is an institution which deserves to be remembered. We boast of our system of education, but why stop at schoolmasters and schoolhouses? We are all schoolmasters, and our schoolhouse is the universe. To attend chiefly to the desk or schoolhouse while we neglect the scenery in which it is placed is absurd. If we do not look out we shall find our fine schoolhouse standing in a cow-yard at last.

JOURNAL / NOVEMBER 12, 1859

There was a remarkable sunset, I think the twenty-fifth of October. The sunset sky reached quite from west to east, and it was the most varied in its forms and colors of any that I remember to have seen. At one time the clouds were most softly and delicately rippled, like the ripple marks on sand. But it was hard for me to see its beauty then, when my mind was filled with Captain Brown. So great a wrong as his fate implied overshadowed all beauty in the world.

JOURNAL / DECEMBER 3, 1859

Talking with Walcott and Staples today, they declared that John Brown did wrong. When I said that I thought he was right, they agreed in asserting that he did wrong because he threw his life away, and that no man had a right to undertake anything which he knew would cost him his life. I inquired if Christ did not foresee that he would be crucified if he preached such doctrines as he did, but they both, though as if it was their only escape, asserted that they did not believe that he did. Upon which a third party threw in, "You do not think that he had so much foresight as Brown." Of course, they as good as said that if Christ *had* foreseen that he would be crucified, he would have "backed out." Such are the principles and the logic of the mass of men.

✸   ✸   ✸

X was betrayed by his eyes, which had a glaring film over them and no serene depth into which you could look. Inquired particularly the way to Emerson's and the distance, and when I told him, said he knew it as well as if he saw it. Wished to turn and proceed to his house. Told me one or two things which he asked me not to tell S. Said, "I know I am insane"—and I knew it, too. Also called it "nervous excitement." At length, when I made a certain remark, he said, "I don't know but you are Emerson; are you? You look somewhat like him." He said as much two or three times, and added once, "But then Emerson wouldn't lie." Finally put his questions to me, of Fate, etc., etc., as if I were Emerson. Getting to the woods, I remarked upon them, and he mentioned my name, but never to the end suspected who his companion was. Then "proceeded to business"—"since the time was short"—and put to me the questions he was going to put to Emerson. His insanity exhibited itself chiefly by his incessant excited talk, scarcely allowing me to interrupt him, but once or twice apologizing for his behavior. What he said was for the most part connected and sensible enough.

JOURNAL / DECEMBER 4, 1859

Talk about slavery! It is not the peculiar institution of the South. It exists wherever men are bought and sold, wherever a man allows himself to be made a mere thing or a tool, and surrenders his inalienable rights of reason and conscience. Indeed, this slavery is more complete than that which enslaves the body alone. It exists in the Northern States, and I am reminded by what I find in the newspapers that it exists in Canada. I never yet met with, or heard of, a judge who was not a slave of this kind, and so the finest and most unfailing weapon of injustice. He fetches a slightly higher price than the black man only because he is a more valuable slave.

It appears that a colored man killed his would-be kidnaper in Missouri and fled to Canada. The bloodhounds have tracked him to Toronto and now demand him of her judges. From all that I can learn, they are playing their parts like judges. They are servile, while the poor fugitive in their jail is free in spirit at least.

JOURNAL / DECEMBER 31, 1859

How vain to try to teach youth, or anybody, truths! They can only learn them after their own fashion, and when they get ready. I do not mean by this to condemn our system of education, but to show what it amounts to. A hundred boys at college are drilled in physics and metaphysics, languages, etc. There *may* be one or two in each hundred, prematurely old perchance, who approaches the subject from a similar point of view to his teachers, but as for the rest, and the most promising, it is like agricultural chemistry to so many Indians. They get a valuable drilling, it *may* be, but they do not learn what you profess to teach. They at most only learn where the arsenal is, in case they should ever want to use any of its weapons. The young men, being young, necessarily listen to the lecturer in history, just as they do the singing of a bird. They expect to be affected by something he may say. It is a kind of poetic pabulum and imagery that they get. Nothing comes quite amiss to their mill.

A PLEA FOR CAPTAIN JOHN BROWN
1859

One day in 1857, at lunch at his own family table, Thoreau discovered his "minority of one"—a man of principle who carried out the purpose of his life till the trap was sprung on his scaffold. John Brown had come to Concord to raise support for his secret plans to carry the war against slavery into the South. He talked about the troubles in Kansas at the town hall that night, and the next evening Thoreau met him again, this time at Emerson's. He was deeply moved by the old Puritan who had never studied the humanities at Harvard, but had publicly practiced Humanity in Kansas.

Two years later the astounding news of Brown's raid on Harpers Ferry was flashed to the world. For three days Thoreau wrote in his Journal *the fiery words ignited by Brown's bold deed. On October 30, 1859, he summoned the villagers to the town hall to hear what he had to say about the meaning of Brown's action. When some warned him it was untimely to defend a man even Republicans and abolitionists were calling mad, he coolly said he wanted no one's advice.*

"A Plea for Captain John Brown" was probably the first public defense. No apology, it acclaimed the greatness of Brown. To Thoreau the raid was "the best news that America has ever heard," and its leader was "a transcendentalist above all, a man of ideas and principles," superior even to the men of Concord Bridge. They had bravely faced their country's foes, while "he had the courage to face his country herself when she was in the wrong."

Thoreau repeated his speech on November 1 in Theodore Parker's Temple in Boston, and two days later in Worcester. A few newspapers reported his remarks, but his effort to have the speech issued

as a pamphlet to aid Brown's family failed to find a publisher bold
enough. In 1860 the "Plea" was included in James Redpath's book
Echoes of Harper's Ferry. *It has been called by many one of the*
greatest speeches in America's history. (M.M.)

I trust that you will pardon me for being here. I do not wish
to force my thoughts upon you, but I feel forced myself. Little
as I know of Captain Brown, I would fain do my part to correct the tone and the statements of the newspapers, and of my
countrymen generally, respecting his character and actions. It
costs us nothing to be just. We can at least express our sympathy
with, and admiration of, him and his companions, and that is
what I now propose to do.

First, as to his history. I will endeavor to omit, as much as
possible, what you have already read. I need not describe his
person to you, for probably most of you have seen and will not
soon forget him. I am told that his grandfather, John Brown, was
an officer in the Revolution; that he himself was born in Connecticut about the beginning of this century, but early went with
his father to Ohio. I heard him say that his father was a con-
tractor who furnished beef to the army there, in the War of
1812; that he accompanied him to the camp, and assisted him in
that employment, seeing a good deal of military life—more, perhaps, than if he had been a soldier; for he was often present at
the councils of the officers. Especially, he learned by experience
how armies are supplied and maintained in the field—a work
which, he observed, requires at least as much experience and
skill as to lead them in battle. He said that few persons had any
conception of the cost, even the pecuniary cost, of firing a single
bullet in war. He saw enough, at any rate, to disgust him with a
military life; indeed, to excite in him a great abhorrence of it; so
much so, that though he was tempted by the offer of some petty
office in the army when he was about eighteen, he not only declined that, but he also refused to train when warned, and was
fined for it. He then resolved that he would never have anything
to do with any war, unless it were a war for liberty.

When the troubles in Kansas began, he sent several of his

sons thither to strengthen the party of the Free State men, fitting them out with such weapons as he had; telling them that if the troubles should increase, and there should be need of him, he would follow, to assist them with his hand and counsel. This, as you all know, he soon after did; and it was through his agency, far more than any other's, that Kansas was made free.

For a part of his life he was a surveyor, and at one time he was engaged in wool-growing, and he went to Europe as an agent about that business. There, as everywhere, he had his eyes about him, and made many original observations. He said, for instance, that he saw why the soil of England was so rich, and that of Germany (I think it was) so poor, and he thought of writing to some of the crowned heads about it. It was because in England the peasantry live on the soil which they cultivate, but in Germany they are gathered into villages at night. It is a pity that he did not make a book of his observations.

I should say that he was an old-fashioned man in his respect for the Constitution, and his faith in the permanence of this Union. Slavery he deemed to be wholly opposed to these, and he was its determined foe.

He was by descent and birth a New England farmer, a man of great common sense, deliberate and practical as that class is, and tenfold more so. He was like the best of those who stood at Concord Bridge once, on Lexington Common, and on Bunker Hill, only he was firmer and higher-principled than any that I have chanced to hear of as there. It was no abolition lecturer that converted him. Ethan Allen and Stark, with whom he may in some respects be compared, were rangers in a lower and less important field. They could bravely face their country's foes, but he had the courage to face his country herself when she was in the wrong. A Western writer says, to account for his escape from so many perils, that he was concealed under a "rural exterior"; as if, in that prairie land, a hero should, by good rights, wear a citizen's dress only.

He did not go to the college called Harvard, good old alma mater as she is. He was not fed on the pap that is there furnished. As he phrased it, "I know no more of grammar than one of your calves." But he went to the great university of the West, where he sedulously pursued the study of Liberty, for which he had early betrayed a fondness, and having taken many degrees, he finally commenced the public practice of Humanity in Kansas, as you all know. Such were *his humanities*, and not any study of grammar. He would have left a Greek accent slanting the wrong way, and righted up a falling man.

He was one of that class of whom we hear a great deal, but, for the most part, see nothing at all—the Puritans. It would be in vain to kill him. He died lately in the time of Cromwell, but he reappeared here. Why should he not? Some of the Puritan stock are said to have come over and settled in New England. They were a class that did something else than celebrate their forefathers' day, and eat parched corn in remembrance of that time. They were neither Democrats nor Republicans, but men of simple habits, straightforward, prayerful; not thinking much of rulers who did not fear God, not making many compromises, nor seeking after available candidates.

"In his camp," as one has recently written, and as I have myself heard him state, "he permitted no profanity; no man of loose morals was suffered to remain there, unless, indeed, as a prisoner of war. 'I would rather,' said he, 'have the smallpox, yellow fever, and cholera, all together in my camp, than a man without principle. . . . It is a mistake, sir, that our people make, when they think that bullies are the best fighters, or that they are the fit men to oppose these Southerners. Give me men of good principles—God-fearing men—men who respect themselves, and with a dozen of them I will oppose any hundred such men as these Buford ruffians.' " He said that if one offered himself to be a soldier under him, who was forward to tell what he could or would do if he could only get sight of the enemy, he had but little confidence in him.

He was never able to find more than a score or so of recruits whom he would accept, and only about a dozen, among them his sons, in whom he had perfect faith. When he was here, some years ago, he showed to a few a little manuscript book—his "orderly book," I think he called it—containing the names of his company in Kansas, and the rules by which they bound themselves; and he stated that several of them had already sealed the contract with their blood. When someone remarked that, with the addition of a chaplain, it would have been a perfect Cromwellian troop, he observed that he would have been glad to add a chaplain to the list, if he could have found one who could fill that office worthily. It is easy enough to find one for the United States Army. I believe that he had prayers in his camp morning and evening, nevertheless.

He was a man of Spartan habits, and at sixty was scrupulous about his diet at your table, excusing himself by saying that he must eat sparingly and fare hard, as became a soldier, or one who was fitting himself for difficult enterprises, a life of exposure.

A man of rare common sense and directness of speech, as of action; a transcendentalist above all, a man of ideas and principles —that was what distinguished him. Not yielding to a whim or transient impulse, but carrying out the purpose of a life. I noticed that he did not overstate anything, but spoke within bounds. I remember particularly how, in his speech here, he referred to what his family had suffered in Kansas, without ever giving the least vent to his pent-up fire. It was a volcano with an ordinary chimney flue. Also referring to the deeds of certain Border Ruffians, he said, rapidly paring away his speech, like an experienced soldier, keeping a reserve of force and meaning, "They had a perfect right to be hung." He was not in the least a rhetorician, was not talking to Buncombe or his constituents anywhere, had no need to invent anything but to tell the simple truth, and communicate his own resolution; therefore he appeared incomparably strong, and eloquence in Congress and elsewhere seemed to me at a discount. It was like the speeches of Cromwell compared with those of an ordinary king.

As for his tact and prudence, I will merely say that at a time when scarcely a man from the Free States was able to reach Kansas by any direct route, at least without having his arms taken from him, he, carrying what imperfect guns and other weapons he could collect, openly and slowly drove an ox cart through Missouri, apparently in the capacity of a surveyor, with his surveying compass exposed in it, and so passed unsuspected, and had ample opportunity to learn the designs of the enemy. For some time after his arrival he still followed the same profession. When, for instance, he saw a knot of the ruffians on the prairie, discussing, of course, the single topic which then occupied their minds, he would, perhaps, take his compass and one of his sons, and proceed to run an imaginary line right through the very spot on which that conclave had assembled, and when he came up to them, he would naturally pause and have some talk with them, learning their news, and, at last, all their plans perfectly; and having thus completed his real survey he would resume his imaginary one, and run on his line till he was out of sight.

When I expressed surprise that he could live in Kansas at all with a price set upon his head and so large a number, including the authorities, exasperated against him, he accounted for it by saying, "It is perfectly well understood that I will not be taken." Much of the time for some years he has had to skulk in swamps, suffering from poverty and from sickness which was the consequence of exposure, befriended only by Indians and a few whites. But though it might be known that he was lurking in a particular swamp, his foes commonly did not care to go in after him. He could even come out into a town where there were more Border Ruffians than Free State men, and transact some business, without delaying long, and yet not be molested; for, said he, "no little handful of men were willing to undertake it, and a large body could not be got together in season."

As for his recent failure, we do not know the facts about it. It was evidently far from being a wild and desperate attempt. His enemy Mr. Vallandigham is compelled to say that "it was among the best planned and executed conspiracies that ever failed."

Not to mention his other successes, was it a failure, or did it show a want of good management, to deliver from bondage a dozen human beings, and walk off with them by broad daylight, for weeks if not months, at a leisurely pace, through one State after another, for half the length of the North, conspicuous to all parties, with a price set upon his head, going into a courtroom on his way and telling what he had done, thus convincing Missouri that it was not profitable to try to hold slaves in his neighborhood?—and this, not because the government menials were lenient, but because they were afraid of him.

Yet he did not attribute his success, foolishly, to "his star," or to any magic. He said, truly, that the reason why such greatly superior numbers quailed before him was, as one of his prisoners confessed, because they lacked a cause—a kind of armor which he and his party never lacked. When the time came, few men were found willing to lay down their lives in defense of what they knew to be wrong; they did not like that this should be their last act in this world.

But to make haste to his last act, and its effects.

The newspapers seem to ignore, or perhaps are really ignorant, of the fact that there are at least as many as two or three individuals to a town throughout the North who think much as the present speaker does about him and his enterprise. I do not hesitate to say that they are an important and growing party. We aspire to be something more than stupid and timid chattels, pretending to read history and our Bibles but desecrating every house and every day we breathe in. Perhaps anxious politicians may prove that only seventeen white men and five Negroes were concerned in the late enterprise; but their very anxiety to prove this might suggest to themselves that all is not told. Why do they still dodge the truth? They are so anxious because of a dim consciousness of the fact, which they do not distinctly face, that at least a million of the free inhabitants of the United States would have rejoiced if it had succeeded. They at most only criticize the tactics. Though we wear no crape, the thought of that man's position and probable fate is spoiling many a man's day here at the North for other thinking. If any one who has seen him here can pursue successfully any other train of thought, I do not know what he is made of. If there is any such who gets his usual allowance of sleep, I will warrant him to fatten easily under any circumstances which do not touch his body or purse. I put a piece of paper and a pencil under my pillow, and when I could not sleep I wrote in the dark.

On the whole, my respect for my fellow men, except as one may outweigh a million, is not being increased these days. I have noticed the cold-blooded way in which newspaper writers and men generally speak of this event, as if an ordinary malefactor, though one of unusual "pluck"—as the Governor of Virginia is reported to have said, using the language of the cockpit, "the gamest man he ever saw"—had been caught, and were about to be hung. He was not dreaming of his foes when the Governor thought he looked so brave. It turns what sweetness I have to gall, to hear, or hear of, the remarks of some of my neighbors. When we heard at first that he was dead, one of my townsmen observed that "he died as the fool dieth"; which, pardon me, for an instant suggested a likeness in him dying to my neighbor living. Others, craven-hearted, said disparagingly, that "he threw his life away" because he resisted the government. Which way have they thrown their lives, pray?—such as would praise a man for attacking singly an ordinary band of thieves or murderers. I hear another ask, Yankee-like, "What will he gain by it?"—as if he expected to fill his pockets by this enterprise. Such a one has no idea of gain but in this worldly sense. If it does not lead to a "surprise" party, if he does not get a new pair of boots or a vote of thanks, it must be a failure. "But he won't gain anything by it." Well, no, I don't suppose he could get four-and-sixpence a day for being hung, take the year round; but then he stands a chance to save a considerable part of his soul—and such a soul!— when you do not. No doubt you can get more in your market for a quart of milk than for a quart of blood, but that is not the market that heroes carry their blood to.

Such do not know that like the seed is the fruit, and that, in the moral world, when good seed is planted, good fruit is inevitable, and does not depend on our watering and cultivating; that when you plant, or bury, a hero in this field, a crop of heroes is sure to spring up. This is a seed of such force and vitality that it does not ask our leave to germinate.

The momentary charge at Balaklava, in obedience to a blundering command, proving what a perfect machine the soldier is, has, properly enough, been celebrated by a poet laureate; but the steady, and for the most part successful, charge of this man, for some years, against the legions of Slavery, in obedience to an infinitely higher command, is as much more memorable than that as an intelligent and conscientious man is superior to a machine. Do you think that that will go unsung?

"Served him right"—"A dangerous man"—"He is undoubtedly

insane." So they proceed to live their sane, and wise, and altogether admirable lives, reading their Plutarch a little, but chiefly
pausing at that feat of Putnam, who was let down into a wolf's
den; and in this wise they nourish themselves for brave and
patriotic deeds some time or other. The Tract Society could afford to print that story of Putnam. You might open the district
schools with the reading of it, for there is nothing about Slavery
or the Church in it; unless it occurs to the reader that some
pastors are wolves in sheep's clothing. "The American Board of
Commissioners for Foreign Missions," even, might dare to protest
against that wolf. I have heard of boards, and of American boards,
but it chances that I never heard of this particular lumber till
lately. And yet I hear of Northern men, and women, and children, by families, buying a "life membership" in such societies as
these. A life membership in the grave! You can get buried cheaper
than that.

Our foes are in our midst and all about us. There is hardly a
house but is divided against itself, for our foe is the all but universal woodenness of both head and heart, the want of vitality
in man, which is the effect of our vice; and hence are begotten
fear, superstition, bigotry, persecution, and slavery of all kinds.
We are mere figureheads upon a hulk, with livers in the place
of hearts. The curse is the worship of idols, which at length
changes the worshiper into a stone image himself; and the New
Englander is just as much an idolater as the Hindu. This man
was an exception, for he did not set up even a political graven
image between him and his God.

A church that can never have done with excommunicating
Christ while it exists! Away with your broad and flat churches,
and your narrow and tall churches! Take a step forward, and
invent a new style of outhouses. Invent a salt that will save you,
and defend our nostrils.

The modern Christian is a man who has consented to say all
the prayers in the liturgy, provided you will let him go straight
to bed and sleep quietly afterward. All his prayers begin with,
"Now I lay me down to sleep," and he is forever looking forward
to the time when he shall go to his "*long* rest." He has consented
to perform certain old-established charities, too, after a fashion,

177

but he does not wish to hear of any new-fangled ones; he doesn't wish to have any supplementary articles added to the contract, to fit it to the present time. He shows the whites of his eyes on the Sabbath, and the blacks all the rest of the week. The evil is not merely a stagnation of blood, but a stagnation of spirit. Many, no doubt, are well disposed, but sluggish by constitution and by habit, and they cannot conceive of a man who is actuated by higher motives than they are. Accordingly they pronounce this man insane, for they know that they could never act as he does, as long as they are themselves.

We dream of foreign countries, of other times and races of men, placing them at a distance in history or space; but let some significant event like the present occur in our midst, and we discover, often, this distance and this strangeness between us and our nearest neighbors. They are our Austrias, and Chinas, and South Sea islands. Our crowded society becomes well spaced all at once, clean and handsome to the eye—a city of magnificent distances. We discover why it was that we never got beyond compliments and surfaces with them before; we become aware of as many versts between us and them as there are between a wandering Tartar and a Chinese town. The thoughtful man becomes a hermit in the thoroughfares of the market place. Impassable seas suddenly find their level between us, or dumb steppes stretch themselves out there. It is the difference of constitution, of intelligence, and faith, and not streams and mountains, that make the true and impassable boundaries between individuals and between states. None but the like-minded can come plenipotentiary to our court.

I read all the newspapers I could get within a week after this event, and I do not remember in them a single expression of sympathy for these men. I have since seen one noble statement, in a Boston paper, not editorial. Some voluminous sheets decided not to print the full report of Brown's words to the exclusion of other matter. It was as if a publisher should reject the manuscript of the New Testament, and print Wilson's last speech. The same journal which contained this pregnant news was chiefly filled, in parallel columns, with the reports of the political conventions that were being held. But the descent to them was too steep.

They should have been spared this contrast—been printed in an extra, at least. To turn from the voices and deeds of earnest men to the *cackling* of political conventions! Office seekers and speech-makers who do not so much as lay an honest egg, but wear their breasts bare upon an egg of chalk! Their great game is the game of straws, or rather that universal aboriginal game of the platter, at which the Indians cried, *hub, bub!* Exclude the reports of religious and political conventions, and publish the words of a living man.

But I object not so much to what they have omitted as to what they have inserted. Even the *Liberator* called it "a misguided, wild, and apparently insane effort." As for the herd of newspapers and magazines, I do not chance to know an editor in the country who will deliberately print anything which he knows will ultimately and permanently reduce the number of his subscribers. They do not believe that it would be expedient. How then can they print truth? If we do not say pleasant things, they argue, nobody will attend to us. And so they do like some traveling auctioneers, who sing an obscene song, in order to draw a crowd around them. Republican editors, obliged to get their sentences ready for the morning edition, and accustomed to look at everything by the twilight of politics, express no admiration, nor true sorrow even, but call these men "deluded fanatics," "mistaken men," "insane," or "crazed." It suggests what a *sane* set of editors we are blessed with, *not* "mistaken men"; who know very well on which side their bread is buttered, at least.

A man does a brave and humane deed, and at once, on all sides, we hear people and parties declaring, "I didn't do it, nor countenance *him* to do it, in any conceivable way. It can't be fairly inferred from my past career." I, for one, am not interested to hear you define your position. I don't know that I ever was or ever shall be. I think it is mere egotism, or impertinent at this time. Ye needn't take so much pains to wash your skirts of him. No intelligent man will ever be convinced that he was any creature of yours. He went and came, as he himself informs us, "under the auspices of John Brown and nobody else." The Republican Party does not perceive how many his *failure* will make to vote more correctly than they would have them. They have

179

counted the votes of Pennsylvania and Company, but they have not correctly counted Captain Brown's vote. He has taken the wind of their sails—the little wind they had—and they may as well lie to and repair.

What though he did not belong to your clique! Though you may not approve of his method or his principles, recognize his magnanimity. Would you not like to claim kindredship with him in that, though in no other thing he is like, or likely, to you? Do you think that you would lose your reputation so? What you lost at the spile, you would gain at the bung.

If they do not mean all this, then they do not speak the truth, and say what they mean. They are simply at their old tricks still. "It was always conceded to him," *says one who calls him crazy,* "that he was a conscientious man, very modest in his demeanor, apparently inoffensive, until the subject of Slavery was introduced, when he would exhibit a feeling of indignation unparalleled."

The slave ship is on her way, crowded with its dying victims; new cargoes are being added in mid-ocean; a small crew of slaveholders, countenanced by a large body of passengers, is smothering four millions under the hatches, and yet the politician asserts that the only proper way by which deliverance is to be obtained is by "the quiet diffusion of the sentiments of humanity," without any "outbreak." As if the sentiments of humanity were ever found unaccompanied by its deeds, and you could disperse them, all finished to order, the pure article, as easily as water with a watering pot, and so lay the dust. What is that that I hear cast overboard? The bodies of the dead that have found deliverance. That is the way we are "diffusing" humanity, and its sentiments with it.

Prominent and influential editors, accustomed to deal with politicians, men of an infinitely lower grade, say, in their ignorance, that he acted "on the principle of revenge." They do not know the man. They must enlarge themselves to conceive of him. I have no doubt that the time will come when they will begin to see him as he was. They have got to conceive of a man of faith and of religious principle, and not a politician or an Indian; of a man who did not wait till he was personally interfered with or thwarted in some harmless business before he gave his life to the cause of the oppressed.

If Walker may be considered the representative of the South, I wish I could say that Brown was the representative of the North. He was a superior man. He did not value his bodily life in comparison with ideal things. He did not recognize unjust human laws, but resisted them as he was bid. For once we are lifted out of the trivialness and dust of politics into the region of truth and manhood. No man in America has ever stood up so persistently and effectively for the dignity of human nature, knowing himself for a man, and the equal of any and all governments. In that sense he was the most American of us all. He needed no babbling lawyer, making false issues, to defend him. He was more than a match for all the judges that American voters, or officeholders of whatever grade, can create. He could not have been tried by a jury of his peers, because his peers did not exist. When a man stands up serenely against the condemnation and vengeance of mankind, rising above them literally *by a whole body*—even though he were of late the vilest murderer, who has settled that matter with himself—the spectacle is a sublime one—didn't ye know it, ye *Liberators*, ye *Tribunes*, ye *Republicans?*—and we become criminal in comparison. Do yourselves the honor to recognize him. He needs none of your respect.

As for the Democratic journals, they are not human enough to affect me at all. I do not feel indignation at anything they may say.

I am aware that I anticipate a little—that he was still, at the last accounts, alive in the hands of his foes; but that being the case, I have all along found myself thinking and speaking of him as physically dead.

I do not believe in erecting statues to those who still live in our hearts, whose bones have not yet crumbled in the earth around us, but I would rather see the statue of Captain Brown in the Massachusetts Statehouse yard than that of any other man whom I know. I rejoice that I live in this age, that I am his contemporary.

What a contrast, when we turn to that political party which is so anxiously shuffling him and his plot out of its way, and looking

181

around for some available slaveholder, perhaps, to be its candidate, at least for one who will execute the Fugitive Slave Law, and all those other unjust laws which he took up arms to annul!

Insane! A father and six sons, and one son-in-law, and several more men besides—as many at least as twelve disciples—all struck with insanity at once; while the sane tyrant holds with a firmer grip than ever his four millions of slaves, and a thousand sane editors, his abettors, are saving their country and their bacon! Just as insane were his efforts in Kansas. Ask the tyrant who is his most dangerous foe, the sane man or the insane? Do the thousands who know him best, who have rejoiced at his deeds in Kansas, and have afforded him material aid there, think him insane? Such a use of this word is a mere trope with most who persist in using it, and I have no doubt that many of the rest have already in silence retracted their words.

Read his admirable answers to Mason and others. How they are dwarfed and defeated by the contrast! On the one side, half-brutish, half-timid questioning; on the other, truth, clear as lightning, crashing into their obscene temples. They are made to stand with Pilate, and Gessler, and the Inquisition. How ineffectual their speech and action! and what a void their silence! They are but helpless tools in this great work. It was no human power that gathered them about this preacher.

What have Massachusetts and the North sent a few sane representatives to Congress for, of late years?—to declare with effect what kind of sentiments? All their speeches put together and boiled down—and probably they themselves will confess it—do not match for manly directness and force, and for simple truth, the few casual remarks of crazy John Brown on the floor of the Harpers Ferry enginehouse—that man whom you are about to hang, to send to the other world, though not to represent you there. No, he was not our representative in any sense. He was too fair a specimen of a man to represent the like of us. Who, then, were his constituents? If you read his words understandingly, you will find out. In his case there is no idle eloquence, no made, nor maiden speech, no compliments to the oppressor. Truth is his inspirer, and earnestness the polisher of his sentences. He could afford to lose his Sharp's rifles, while he retained his faculty of speech—a Sharp's rifle of infinitely surer and longer range.

And the New York *Herald* reports the conversation verbatim! It does not know of what undying words it is made the vehicle.

I have no respect for the penetration of any man who can read the report of that conversation and still call the principal in it insane. It has the ring of a saner sanity than an ordinary discipline and habits of life, than an ordinary organization, secure. Take any sentence of it—"Any questions that I can honorably answer, I will; not otherwise. So far as I am myself concerned, I have told everything truthfully. I value my word, sir." The few who talk about his vindictive spirit, while they really admire his heroism, have no test by which to detect a noble man, no amalgam to combine with his pure gold. They mix their own dross with it.

It is a relief to turn from these slanders to the testimony of his more truthful, but frightened jailers and hangmen. Governor Wise speaks far more justly and appreciatingly of him than any Northern editor, or politician, or public personage, that I chance to have heard from. I know that you can afford to hear him again on this subject. He says: "They are themselves mistaken who take him to be a madman. . . . He is cool, collected, and indomitable, and it is but just to him to say that he was humane to his prisoners. . . . And he inspired me with great trust in his integrity as a man of truth. He is a fanatic, vain and garrulous" (I leave that part to Mr. Wise), "but firm, truthful, and intelligent. His men, too, who survive, are like him. . . . Colonel Washington says that he was the coolest and firmest man he ever saw in defying danger and death. With one son dead by his side, and another shot through, he felt the pulse of his dying son with one hand, and held his rifle with the other, and commanded his men with the utmost composure, encouraging them to be firm, and to sell their lives as dear as they could. Of the three white prisoners, Brown, Stevens, and Coppoc, it was hard to say which was most firm."

Almost the first Northern men whom the slaveholder has learned to respect!

The testimony of Mr. Vallandigham, though less valuable, is of the same purport, that "it is vain to underrate either the man or his conspiracy. . . . He is the farthest possible removed from the ordinary ruffian, fanatic, or madman."

"All is quiet at Harpers Ferry," say the journals. What is the character of that calm which follows when the law and the slave-holder prevail? I regard this event as a touchstone designed to bring out, with glaring distinctness, the character of this government. We needed to be thus assisted to see it by the light of history. It needed to see itself. When a government puts forth its strength on the side of injustice, as ours to maintain slavery and kill the liberators of the slave, it reveals itself a merely brute force, or worse, a demoniacal force. It is the head of the Plug-Uglies. It is more manifest than ever that tyranny rules. I see this government to be effectually allied with France and Austria in oppressing mankind. There sits a tyrant holding fettered four millions of slaves; here comes their heroic liberator. This most hypocritical and diabolical government looks up from its seat on the grasping four millions, and inquires with an assumption of innocence: "What do you assault me for? Am I not an honest man? Cease agitation on this subject, or I will make a slave of you, too, or else hang you."

We talk about a *representative* government; but what a monster of a government is that where the noblest faculties of the mind, and the *whole* heart, are not *represented!* A semihuman tiger or ox, stalking over the earth, with its heart taken out and the top of its brain shot away. Heroes have fought well on their stumps when their legs were shot off, but I never heard of any good done by such a government as that.

The only government that I recognize—and it matters not how few are at the head of it, or how small its army—is that power that establishes justice in the land, never that which establishes injustice. What shall we think of a government to which all the truly brave and just men in the land are enemies, standing be-tween it and those whom it oppresses? A government that pretends to be Christian and crucifies a million Christs every day!

Treason! Where does such treason take its rise? I cannot help thinking of you as you deserve, ye governments. Can you dry up the fountains of thought? High treason, when it is resistance to tyranny here below, has its origin in, and is first committed by, the power that makes and forever re-creates man. When you have caught and hung all these human rebels, you have accomplished nothing but your own guilt, for you have not struck at the fountainhead. You presume to contend with a foe against whom West Point cadets and rifled cannon *point* not. Can all the art of the cannon founder tempt matter to turn against its maker? Is the form in which the founder thinks he casts it more essential than the constitution of it and of himself?

The United States have a coffle of four millions of slaves. They are determined to keep them in this condition; and Massachusetts is one of the confederated overseers to prevent their escape. Such are not all the inhabitants of Massachusetts, but such are they who rule and are obeyed here. It was Massachusetts, as well as Virginia, that put down this insurrection at Harpers Ferry. She sent the marines there, and she will have *to pay the penalty of her sin.*

Suppose that there is a society in this State that out of its own purse and magnanimity saves all the fugitive slaves that run to us, and protects our colored fellow citizens, and leaves the other work to the government, so called. Is not that government fast losing its occupation, and becoming contemptible to mankind? If private men are obliged to perform the offices of government, to protect the weak and dispense justice, then the government becomes only a hired man, or clerk, to perform menial or indifferent services. Of course, that is but the shadow of a government whose existence necessitates a Vigilant Committee. What should we think of the Oriental Cadi even, behind whom worked in secret a Vigilant Committee? But such is the character of our Northern States generally; each has its Vigilant Committee. And, to a certain extent, these crazy governments recognize and accept this relation. They say, virtually, "We'll be glad to work for you on these terms, only don't make a noise about it." And thus the government, its salary being insured, withdraws into the back shop, taking the Constitution with it, and bestows most of its labor on repairing that. When I hear it at work sometimes, as I go by, it reminds me, at best, of those farmers who in winter contrive to turn a penny by following the coopering business. And what kind of spirit is their barrel made to hold? They speculate in stocks, and bore holes in mountains, but they are not competent to lay out even a decent highway. The only *free* road, the Underground Railroad, is owned and managed by the Vigilant Committee. *They* have tunneled under the whole breadth of the land. Such a government is losing its power and respectability as surely as water runs out of a leaky vessel, and is held by one that can contain it.

I hear many condemn these men because they were so few. When were the good and the brave ever in a majority? Would you have had him wait till that time came?—till you and I came over to him? The very fact that he had no rabble or troop of hirelings about him would alone distinguish him from ordinary heroes. His company was small indeed, because few could be found worthy to pass muster. Each one who there laid down his life for the poor and oppressed was a picked man, culled out of many thousands, if not millions; apparently a man of principle, of rare courage, and devoted humanity; ready to sacrifice his life at any moment for the benefit of his fellow man. It may be doubted if there were as many more their equals in these respects in all the country—I speak of his followers only—for their leader, no doubt, scoured the land far and wide, seeking to swell his troop. These alone were ready to step between the oppressor and the oppressed. Surely they were the very best men you could select to be hung. That was the greatest compliment which this country could pay them. They were ripe for her gallows. She has tried a long time, she has hung a good many, but never found the right one before.

When I think of him, and his six sons, and his son-in-law, not to enumerate the others, enlisted for this fight, proceeding coolly, reverently, humanely to work, for months if not years, sleeping and waking upon it, summering and wintering the thought without expecting any reward but a good conscience, while almost all America stood ranked on the other side—I say again that it affects me as a sublime spectacle. If he had had any journal advocating *"his cause,"* any organ, as the phrase is, monotonously and wearisomely, playing the same old tune, and then passing round

186

the hat, it would have been fatal to his efficiency. If he had acted in any way so as to be let alone by the government, he might have been suspected. It was the fact that the tyrant must give place to him, or he to the tyrant, that distinguished him from all the reformers of the day that I know.

It was his peculiar doctrine that a man has a perfect right to interfere by force with the slaveholder in order to rescue the slave. I agree with him. They who are continually shocked by slavery have some right to be shocked by the violent death of the slaveholder, but no others. Such will be more shocked by his life than by his death. I shall not be forward to think him mistaken in his method who quickest succeeds to liberate the slave. I speak for the slave when I say that I prefer the philanthropy of Captain Brown to that philanthropy which neither shoots me nor liberates me. At any rate, I do not think it is quite sane for one to spend his whole life in talking or writing about this matter, unless he is continuously inspired, and I have not done so. A man may have other affairs to attend to. I do not wish to kill nor to be killed, but I can foresee circumstances in which both these things would be by me unavoidable. We preserve the so-called peace of our community by deeds of petty violence every day. Look at the policeman's billy and handcuffs! Look at the jail! Look at the gallows! Look at the chaplain of the regiment! We are hoping only to live safely on the outskirts of *this* provisional army. So we defend ourselves and our hen roosts, and maintain slavery. I know that the mass of my countrymen think that the only righteous use that can be made of Sharp's rifles and revolvers is to fight duels with them, when we are insulted by other nations, or to hunt Indians, or shoot fugitive slaves with them, or the like. I think that for once the Sharp's rifles and the revolvers were employed in a righteous cause. The tools were in the hands of one who could use them.

The same indignation that is said to have cleared the temple once will clear it again. The question is not about the weapon, but the spirit in which you use it. No man has appeared in America, as yet, who loved his fellow man so well, and treated him so tenderly. He lived for him. He took up his life and he laid it down for him. What sort of violence is that which is encouraged, not by soldiers, but by peaceable citizens, not so much by laymen as by ministers of the Gospel, not so much by the fighting sects as by the Quakers, and not so much by Quaker men as by Quaker women?

This event advertises me that there is such a fact as death— the possibility of a man's dying. It seems as if no man had ever died in America before; for in order to die you must first have lived. I don't believe in the horses, and palls, and funerals that they have had. There was no death in the case, because there had been no life; they merely rotted or sloughed off, pretty much as they had rotted or sloughed along. No temple's veil was rent, only a hole dug somewhere. Let the dead bury their dead. The best of them fairly ran down like a clock. Franklin—Washington —they were let off without dying; they were merely missing one day. I hear a good many pretend that they are going to die; or that they have died, for aught that I know. Nonsense! I'll defy them to do it. They haven't got life enough in them. They'll deliquesce like fungi, and keep a hundred eulogists mopping the spot where they left off. Only half a dozen or so have died since the world began. Do you think that you are going to die, sir? No! there's no hope of you. You haven't got your lesson yet. You've got to stay after school. We make a needless ado about capital punishment—taking lives when there is no life to take. *Memento mori!* We don't understand that sublime sentence which some worthy got sculptured on his gravestone once. We've interpreted it in a groveling and sniveling sense; we've wholly forgotten how to die.

But be sure you do die nevertheless. Do your work, and finish it. If you know how to begin, you will know when to end.

These men, in teaching us how to die, have at the same time taught us how to live. If this man's acts and words do not create a revival, it will be the severest possible satire on the acts and words that do. It is the best news that America has ever heard. It has already quickened the feeble pulse of the North, and infused more and more generous blood into her veins and heart than any number of years of what is called commercial and political prosperity could. How many a man who was lately contemplating suicide has now something to live for!

One writer says that Brown's peculiar monomania made him to be "dreaded by the Missourians as a supernatural being." Sure enough, a hero in the midst of us cowards is always so dreaded. He is just that thing. He shows himself superior to nature. He has a spark of divinity in him.

> Unless above himself he can
> Erect himself, how poor a thing is man!

Newspaper editors argue also that it is a proof of his insanity that he thought he was appointed to do this work which he did—that he did not suspect himself for a moment! They talk as if it were impossible that a man could be "divinely appointed" in these days to do any work whatever; as if vows and religion were out of date as connected with any man's daily work; as if the agent to abolish slavery could only be somebody appointed by the President, or by some political party. They talk as if a man's death were a failure, and his continued life, be it of whatever character, were a success.

When I reflect to what a cause this man devoted himself, and how religiously, and then reflect to what cause his judges and all who condemn him so angrily and fluently devote themselves, I see that they are as far apart as the heavens and earth are asunder.

The amount of it is, our "*leading men*" are a harmless kind of folk, and they know *well enough* that *they* were not divinely appointed, but elected by the votes of their party.

Who is it whose safety requires that Captain Brown be hung? Is it indispensable to any Northern man? Is there no resource but to cast this man also to the Minotaur? If you do not wish it, say so distinctly. While these things are being done, beauty stands veiled and music is a screeching lie. Think of him—of his rare qualities!—such a man as it takes ages to make, and ages to understand; no mock hero, nor the representative of any party. A man such as the sun may not rise upon again in this benighted land. To whose making went the costliest material, the finest adamant; sent to be the redeemer of those in captivity; and the only use to which you can put him is to hang him at the end of a rope! You who pretend to care for Christ crucified, con-

189

sider what you are about to do to him who offered himself to be the saviour of four millions of men.

Any man knows when he is justified, and all the wits in the world cannot enlighten him on that point. The murderer always knows that he is justly punished; but when a government takes the life of a man without the consent of his conscience, it is an audacious government, and is taking a step towards its own dissolution. Is it not possible that an individual may be right and a government wrong? Are laws to be enforced simply because they were made? or declared by any number of men to be good, if they are *not* good? Is there any necessity for a man's being a tool to perform a deed of which his better nature disapproves? Is it the intention of lawmakers that *good* men shall be hung ever? Are judges to interpret the law according to the letter, and not the spirit? What right have *you* to enter into a compact with yourself that you *will* do thus or so, against the light within you? Is it for *you* to *make up* your mind—to form any resolution whatever—and not accept the convictions that are forced upon you, and which ever pass your understanding? I do not believe in lawyers, in that mode of attacking or defending a man, because you descend to meet the judge on his own ground, and, in cases of the highest importance, it is of no consequence whether a man breaks a human law or not. Let lawyers decide trivial cases. Businessmen may arrange that among themselves. If they were the interpreters of the everlasting laws which rightfully bind man, that would be another thing. A counterfeiting law-factory, standing half in a slave land and half in a free! What kind of laws for free men can you expect from that?

I am here to plead his cause with you. I plead not for his life, but for his character—his immortal life; and so it becomes your cause wholly, and is not his in the least. Some eighteen hundred years ago Christ was crucified; this morning, perchance, Captain Brown was hung. These are the two ends of a chain which is not without its links. He is not Old Brown any longer; he is an angel of light.

I see now that it was necessary that the bravest and humanest man in all the country should be hung. Perhaps he saw it himself. I *almost fear* that I may yet hear of his deliverance, doubting if a prolonged life, if any life, can do as much good as his death.

"Misguided!" "Garrulous!" "Insane!" "Vindictive!" So ye write in your easy chairs, and thus he wounded responds from the floor of the armory, clear as a cloudless sky, true as the voice of nature is: "No man sent me here; it was my own prompting and that of my Maker. I acknowledge no master in human form."

And in what a sweet and noble strain he proceeds, addressing his captors, who stand over him: "I think, my friends, you are guilty of a great wrong against God and humanity, and it would be perfectly right for any one to interfere with you, so far as to free those you willfully and wickedly hold in bondage."

And, referring to his movement: "It is, in my opinion, the greatest service a man can render to God."

"I pity the poor in bondage that have none to help them; that is why I am here; not to gratify any personal animosity, revenge, or vindictive spirit. It is my sympathy with the oppressed and the wronged, that are as good as you, and as precious in the sight of God."

You don't know your testament when you see it.

"I want you to understand that I respect the rights of the poorest and weakest of colored people, oppressed by the slave power, just as much as I do those of the most wealthy and powerful."

"I wish to say, furthermore, that you had better, all you people at the South, prepare yourselves for a settlement of that question, that must come up for settlement sooner than you are prepared for it. The sooner you are prepared the better. You may dispose of me very easily. I am nearly disposed of now; but this question is still to be settled—this Negro question, I mean; the end of that is not yet."

I foresee the time when the painter will paint that scene, no longer going to Rome for a subject; the poet will sing it; the historian record it; and, with the Landing of the Pilgrims and the Declaration of Independence, it will be the ornament of some future national gallery, when at least the present form of slavery shall be no more here. We shall then be at liberty to weep for Captain Brown. Then, and not till then, we will take our revenge.

191

THE LAST DAYS OF JOHN BROWN
1860

On December 2, 1859, the day of John Brown's hanging, Emerson, Alcott, and Thoreau took part in memorial services held in Concord. Thoreau's brief address, "After the Death of John Brown," was a tribute to the man's "transcendent moral greatness." The next day, Thoreau helped one of Brown's men, who had evaded capture at Harpers Ferry, to escape to Canada.

Thoreau was invited to speak at the burial services for Brown in North Elba, New York, where the abolitionist's body was finally laid to rest near the family home on July 4, 1860. From Journal entries of November-December, 1859, Thoreau prepared the address, "The Last Days of John Brown." The paper was read for him when he proved too ill to make the journey. (M.M.)

John Brown's career for the last six weeks of his life was meteor-like, flashing through the darkness in which we live. I know of nothing so miraculous in our history.

If any person, in a lecture or conversation at that time, cited any ancient example of heroism, such as Cato or Tell or Winkelried, passing over the recent deeds and words of Brown, it was felt by any intelligent audience of Northern men to be tame and inexcusably far-fetched.

For my own part, I commonly attend more to nature than to man, but any affecting human event may blind our eyes to natural objects. I was so absorbed in him as to be surprised whenever I

192

detected the routine of the natural world surviving still, or met persons going about their affairs indifferent. It appeared strange to me that the "little dipper" should be still diving quietly in the river, as of yore; and it suggested that this bird might continue to dive here when Concord should be no more.

I felt that he, a prisoner in the midst of his enemies and under sentence of death, if consulted as to his next step or resource, could answer more wisely than all his countrymen beside. He best understood his position; he contemplated it most calmly. Comparatively, all other men, North and South, were beside themselves. Our thoughts could not revert to any greater or wiser or better man with whom to contrast him, for he, then and there, was above them all. The man this country was about to hang appeared the greatest and best in it.

Years were not required for a revolution of public opinion; days, nay hours, produced marked changes in this case. Fifty who were ready to say, on going into our meeting in honor of him in Concord, that he ought to be hung, would not say it when they came out. They heard his words read; they saw the earnest faces of the congregation; and perhaps they joined at last in singing the hymn in his praise.

The order of instructors was reversed. I heard that one preacher, who at first was shocked and stood aloof, felt obliged at last, after he was hung, to make him the subject of a sermon, in which, to some extent, he eulogized the man, but said that his act was a failure. An influential class-teacher thought it necessary, after the services, to tell his grown-up pupils that at first he thought as the preacher did then, but now he thought that John Brown was right. But it was understood that his pupils were as much ahead of the teacher as he was ahead of the priest; and I know for a certainty that very little boys at home had already asked their parents, in a tone of surprise, why God did not interfere to save him. In each case the constituted teachers were only half conscious that they were not *leading*, but being *dragged*, with some loss of time and power.

The more conscientious preachers, the Bible men, they who talk about principle, and doing to others as you would that they should do unto you—how could they fail to recognize him, by

far the greatest preacher of them all, with the Bible in his life
and in his acts, the embodiment of principle, who actually carried
out the golden rule? All whose moral sense had been aroused,
who had a calling from on high to preach, sided with him. What
confessions he extracted from the cold and conservative! It is
remarkable, but on the whole it is well, that it did not prove the
occasion for a new sect of *Brownites* being formed in our midst.

They, whether within the Church or out of it, who adhere
to the spirit and let go the letter, and are accordingly called
infidel, were as usual foremost to recognize him. Men have been
hung in the South before for attempting to rescue slaves, and
the North was not much stirred by it. Whence, then, this wonderful difference? We were not so sure of *their* devotion to
principle. We made a subtle distinction, forgot human laws, and
did homage to an idea. The North, I mean the *living* North, was
suddenly all transcendental. It went behind the human law, it
went behind the apparent failure, and recognized eternal justice
and glory. Commonly, men live according to a formula, and are
satisfied if the order of law is observed, but in this instance they,
if to some extent, returned to original perceptions, and there was
a slight revival of old religion. They saw that what was called
order was confusion, what was called justice, injustice, and that
the best was deemed worst. This attitude suggested a more intelligent and generous spirit than that which actuated our forefathers, and the possibility, in the course of ages, of a revolution
in behalf of another and an oppressed people.

Most Northern men, and a few Southern ones, were wonderfully stirred by Brown's behavior and words. They saw and
felt that there had been nothing quite equal to them in their
kind in this country, or in the recent history of the world. But
the minority were unmoved by them. They were only surprised
and provoked by the attitude of their neighbors. They saw that
Brown was brave, and that he believed that he had done right,
but they did not detect any further peculiarity in him. Not being
accustomed to make fine distinctions, or to appreciate magnanimity, they read his letters and speeches as if they read them
not. They were not aware when they approached a heroic statement—they did not know when they *burned*. They did not feel

194

that he spoke with authority, and hence they only remembered that the *law* must be executed. They remembered the old formula, but did not hear the new revelation. The man who does not recognize in Brown's words a wisdom and nobleness, and therefore an authority, superior to our laws, is a modern Democrat. This is the test by which to discover him. He is not willfully but constitutionally blind on this side, and he is consistent with himself. Such has been his past life; no doubt of it. In like manner he has read history and his Bible, and he accepts, or seems to accept, the last only as an established formula, and not because he has been convicted by it. You will not find kindred sentiments in his commonplace-book, if he has one.

When a noble deed is done, who is likely to appreciate it? They who are noble themselves. I was not surprised that certain of my neighbors spoke of John Brown as an ordinary felon, for who are they? They have either much flesh, or much office, or much coarseness of some kind. They are not ethereal natures in any sense. The dark qualities predominate in them. Several of them are decidedly pachydermatous. I say it in sorrow, not in anger. How can a man behold the light who has no answering inward light? They are true to their *sight,* but when they look this way, they *see* nothing, they are blind. For the children of the light to contend with them is as if there should be a contest between eagles and owls. Show me a man who feels bitterly toward John Brown, and let me hear what noble verse he can repeat. He'll be as dumb as if his lips were stone.

It is not every man who can be a Christian, even in a very moderate sense, whatever education you give him. It is a matter of constitution and temperament, after all. He may have to be born again many times. I have known many a man who pretended to be a Christian, in whom it was ridiculous, for he had no genius for it. It is not every man who can be a free man, even.

Editors persevered for a good while in saying that Brown was crazy; but at last they said only that it was "a crazy scheme," and the only evidence brought to prove it was that it cost him his life. I have no doubt that if he had gone with five thousand men, liberated a thousand slaves, killed a hundred or two slave-holders, and had as many more killed on his own side, but not lost his own life, these same editors would have called it by a more respectable name. Yet he has been far more successful than that. He has liberated many thousands of slaves, both North and South. They seem to have known nothing about living or dying for a principle. They all called him crazy then; who calls him crazy now?

All through the excitement occasioned by his remarkable attempt and subsequent behavior the Massachusetts legislature, not taking any steps for the defense of her citizens who were likely to be carried to Virginia as witnesses and exposed to the violence of a slaveholding mob, was wholly absorbed in a liquor-agency question, and indulging in poor jokes on the word "extension." Bad spirits occupied their thoughts. I am sure that no statesman up to the occasion could have attended to that question at all at that time—a very vulgar question to attend to at any time!

When I looked into a liturgy of the Church of England, printed near the end of the last century, in order to find a service applicable to the case of Brown, I found that the only martyr recognized and provided for by it was King Charles I, an eminent scamp. Of all the inhabitants of England and of the world, he was the only one, according to this authority, whom that church had made a martyr and saint of; and for more than a century it had celebrated his martyrdom, so called, by an annual service. What a satire on the Church is that!

Look not to legislatures and churches for your guidance, nor to any soulless *incorporated* bodies, but to *inspirited* or inspired ones.

What avail all your scholarly accomplishments and learning, compared with wisdom and manhood? To omit his other behavior, see what a work this comparatively unread and unlettered man wrote within six weeks. Where is our professor of belles-lettres, or of logic and rhetoric, who can write so well? He wrote in prison, not a history of the world, like Raleigh, but an American book which I think will live longer than that. I do not know of such words, uttered under such circumstances, and so copiously withal, in Roman or English or any history. What a variety of themes he touched on in that short space! There are words in that letter to his wife, respecting the education of his daughters, which deserve to be framed and hung over every mantelpiece in the land. Compare this earnest wisdom with that of Poor Richard.

The death of Irving, which at any other time would have attracted universal attention, having occurred while these things were transpiring, went almost unobserved. I shall have to read of it in the biography of authors.

Literary gentlemen, editors, and critics think that they know how to write because they have studied grammar and rhetoric; but they are egregiously mistaken. The *art* of composition is as simple as the discharge of a bullet from a rifle, and its masterpieces imply an infinitely greater force behind them. This unlettered man's speaking and writing are standard English. Some words and phrases deemed vulgarisms and Americanisms before, he has made standard American; such as, "*It will pay*." It suggests that the one great rule of composition—and if I were a professor of rhetoric I should insist on this—is, to *speak the truth*. This first, this second, this third; pebbles in your mouth or not. This demands earnestness and manhood chiefly.

We seem to have forgotten that the expression "a *liberal* education" originally meant among the Romans one worthy of *free* men; while the learning of trades and professions by which to get your livelihood merely was considered worthy of *slaves* only. But taking a hint from the word, I would go a step further, and say that it is not the man of wealth and leisure simply, though devoted to art, or science, or literature, who, in a true sense, is *liberally* educated, but only the earnest and *free* man. In a slaveholding country like this, there can be no such thing as a *liberal* education tolerated by the State; and those scholars of Austria and France who, however learned they may be, are contented under their tyrannies have received only a *servile* education.

Nothing could his enemies do but it redounded to his infinite advantage—that is, to the advantage of his cause. They did not hang his four followers with him; that scene was still postponed; and so his victory was prolonged and completed. No theatrical manager could have arranged things so wisely to give effect to his behavior and words. And who, think you, *was* the manager?

197

Who placed the slave-woman and her child, whom he stooped to kiss for a symbol, between his prison and the gallows?

We soon saw, as he saw, that he was not to be pardoned or rescued by men. That would have been to disarm him, to restore to him a material weapon, a Sharp's rifle, when he had taken up the sword of the spirit—the sword with which he has really won his greatest and most memorable victories. Now he has not laid aside the sword of the spirit, for he is pure spirit himself, and his sword is pure spirit also.

> He nothing common did or mean
> Upon that memorable scene, . . .
> Nor called the gods with vulgar spite,
> To vindicate his helpless right;
> But bowed his comely head
> Down, as upon a bed.

What a transit was that of his horizontal body alone, but just cut down from the gallows tree! We read that at such a time it passed through Philadelphia, and by Saturday night had reached New York. Thus like a meteor it shot through the Union from the Southern regions toward the North! No such freight had the cars borne since they carried him southward alive.

On the day of his translation, I heard, to be sure, that he was *hung,* but I did not know what that meant; I felt no sorrow on that account; but not for a day or two did I even *hear* that he was *dead,* and not after any number of days shall I believe it. Of all the men who were said to be my contemporaries, it seemed to me that John Brown was the only one who *had not died.* I never hear of a man named Brown now—and I hear of them pretty often—I never hear of any particularly brave and earnest man, but my first thought is of John Brown, and what relation he may be to him. I meet him at every turn. He is more alive than ever he was. He has earned immortality. He is not confined to North Elba nor to Kansas. He is no longer working in secret. He works in public, and in the clearest light that shines on this land.

JOURNAL AND LETTERS
1860–1861

LETTER TO CHARLES SUMNER / JULY 16, 1860

I wish to thank you for your speech on the Barbarism of Slavery, which, I hope and suspect, commences a new era in the history of our Congress, when questions of national importance have come to be considered occasionally from a broadly ethical, and not from a narrowly political point of view alone.

It is refreshing to hear some naked truth, moral or otherwise, uttered there—which can always take care of itself when uttered, and of course belongs to no party. (That was the whole value of Gerrit Smith's presence there, methinks, though he did go to bed early.) Whereas this has only been employed occasionally to perfume the wheel-grease of party or national politics.

JOURNAL / OCTOBER 13, 1860

Truly this is a world of vain delights. We think that men have a substratum of common sense but sometimes are peculiarly frivolous. But consider what a value is seriously and permanently attached to gold and so-called precious stones almost universally. Day and night, summer and winter, sick or well, in war and in peace, men speak of and believe in gold as a great treasure. By a thousand comparisons they prove their devotion to it. If wise men or true philosophers bore any considerable proportion to the whole number of men, gold would be treated with no such distinction. Men seriously and, if possible, religiously believe in and worship gold. They hope to earn golden opinions, to celebrate their golden wedding. They dream of the golden age. Now it is not its intrinsic beauty or value, but its rarity and arbitrarily attached value, that distinguishes gold. You would think it was the reign of shams.

LETTER TO H. G. O. BLAKE / NOVEMBER 4, 1860

Yes, to meet men on an honest and simple footing, meet with rebuffs, suffer from sore feet, as you did, aye and from a sore heart, as perhaps you also did—all that is excellent. What a pity that that young prince [Prince of Wales, later, Edward VII] could not enjoy a little of the legitimate experience of traveling, be dealt with simply and truly though rudely. He might have been invited to some hospitable house in the country, had his bowl of bread and milk set before him, with a clean pinafore, been told that there were the punt and the fishing rod, and he could amuse himself as he chose—might have swung a few birches, dug out a woodchuck, and had a regular good time, and finally been sent to bed with the boys—and so never have been introduced to Mr. [Edward] Everett at all. I have no doubt that this would have been a far more memorable and valuable experience than he got.

JOURNAL / NOVEMBER 29, 1860

Yet, though money can buy no fine fruit whatever, and we are never made truly rich by the possession of it, the value of things generally is commonly estimated by the amount of money they will fetch. A thing is not valuable—e.g. a fine situation for a house—until it is convertible into so much money, that is, can cease to be what it is and become something else which you prefer. So you will see that all prosaic people who possess only the commonest sense, who believe strictly in this kind of wealth, are speculators in fancy stocks and continually cheat themselves, but poets and all disconcerning people, who have an object in life and know what they want, speculate in real values. The mean and low values of anything depend on it[s] convertibility into something else—*i.e.* have nothing to do with its intrinsic value.

This world and our life have practically a similar value only to most. The value of life is what anybody will give you for living. A man has his price at the South, is worth so many dollars, and so he has at the North. Many a man here sets out by saying, I will make so many dollars by such a time, or before I die, and that is his price, as much as if he were knocked off for it by a Southern auctioneer.

We hear a good deal said about moonshine by so-called practical people, and the next day, perchance, we hear of their failure, they having been dealing in fancy stocks; but there really never is any moonshine of this kind in the practice of poets and philosophers; there never are any hard times or failures with them, for they deal with permanent values.

JOURNAL / JANUARY 3, 1861

What are the natural features which make a township handsome? A river, with its waterfalls and meadows, a lake, a hill, a cliff or individual rocks, a forest, and ancient trees standing singly. Such things are beautiful; they have a high use which dollars and cents never represent. If the inhabitants of a town were wise, they would seek to preserve these things, though at a considerable expense; for such things educate far more than any hired teachers or preachers, or any at present recognized system of school education. I do not think him fit to be the founder of a state or even of a town who does not foresee the use of these things, but legislates chiefly for oxen, as it were.

Far the handsomest thing I saw in Boxboro was its noble oak wood. I doubt if there is a finer one in Massachusetts. Let her keep it a century longer, and men will make pilgrimages to it from all parts of the country; and yet it would be very like the rest of New England if Boxboro were ashamed of that woodland.

I have since heard, however, that she is contented to have that forest stand instead of the houses and farms that might supplant (it), because the land pays a much larger tax to the town now than it would then.

I said to myself, if the history of this town is written, the chief stress is probably laid on its parish and there is not a word about this forest in it.

It would be worth the while if in each town there were a committee appointed to see that the beauty of the town received no detriment. If we have the largest boulder in the country, then it should not belong to an individual, nor be made into doorsteps.

As in many countries precious metals belong to the crown, so here more precious natural objects of rare beauty should belong to the public.

Not only the channel but one or both banks of every river should be a public highway. The only use of a river is not to float on it.

Think of a mountaintop in the township—even to the minds of the Indians a sacred place—only accessible through private grounds! a temple, as it were, which you cannot enter except by trespassing and at the risk of letting out or letting in somebody's cattle! in fact the temple itself in this case private property and standing in a man's cow yard—for such is commonly the case!

New Hampshire courts have lately been deciding—as if it was for them to decide—whether the top of Mt. Washington belonged to A or to B; and, it being decided in favor of B, as I hear, he went up one winter with the proper office and took formal possession of it. But I think that the top of Mt. Washington should not be private property; it should be left unappropriated for modesty and reverence's sake, or if only to suggest that earth has higher uses than we put her to. I know it is a mere figure of speech to talk about temples nowadays, when men recognize none, and, indeed, associate the word with heathenism.

It is true we as yet take liberties and go across lots, and steal, or "hook," a good many things, but we naturally take fewer and fewer liberties every year, as we meet with more resistance. In old countries, as England, going across lots is out of the question. You must walk in some beaten path or other, though it may [be] a narrow one. We are tending to the same state of things here, when practically a few will have grounds of their own, but most will have none to walk over but what the few allow them.

Thus we behave like oxen in a flower garden. The true fruit of Nature can only be plucked with a delicate hand not bribed by any earthly reward, and a fluttering heart. No hired man can help us to gather this crop.

How few ever get beyond feeding, clothing, sheltering, and warming themselves in this world, and begin to treat themselves as human beings—as intellectual and moral beings! Most seem not to see any farther—not to see over the ridgepole of their barns—or to be exhausted and accomplish nothing more than a full barn, though it may be accompanied by an empty head. They venture a little, run some risks, when it is a question of a larger crop of corn or potatoes; but they are commonly timid and count their coppers when the question is whether their children shall be educated. He who has the reputation of being the thriftiest farmer and making the best bargains is really the most thriftless and makes the worst. It is safest to invest in knowledge, for the probability is that you can carry that with you wherever you go.

But most men, it seems to me, do not care for Nature and would sell their share in all her beauty, as long as they may live, for a stated sum—many for a glass of rum. Thank God, men cannot as yet fly, and lay waste the sky as well as the earth! We are safe on that side for the present. It is for the very reason that some do not care for those things that we need to continue to protect all from the vandalism of a few.

We cut down the few old oaks which witnessed the transfer of the township from the Indian to the white man, and commence our museum with a cartridge box taken from a British soldier in 1775!

He pauses at the end of his four or five thousand dollars, and then only fears that he has not got enough to carry him through —that is, merely to pay for what he will eat and wear and burn and for his lodging for the rest of his life. But, pray, what does he stay here for? Suicide would be cheaper. Indeed, it would be nobler to found some good institution with the money and then cut your throat. If such is the whole upshot of their living, I think that it would be most profitable for all such to be carried or put through by being discharged from the mouth of a cannon as fast as they attained to years of such discretion.

As boys are sometimes required to show an excuse for being absent from school, so it seems to me that men should show some excuse for being here. Move along; you may come upon the town, sir.

LETTER TO PARKER PILLSBURY / APRIL 10, 1861

As for my prospective reader, I hope that he ignores Fort Sumpter, and Old Abe, and all that, for that is just the most fatal, and indeed the only fatal, weapon you can direct against evil ever; for as long as you know of it, you are *particeps criminis*. What business have you, if you are "an angel of light," to be pondering over the deeds of darkness, reading the New York *Herald* and the like? I do not so much regret the present condition of things in this country (provided I regret it at all) as I do that I ever heard of it. I know one or two who have this year, for the first time, read a President's message; but they do not see that this implies a fall in themselves rather than a rise in the President. Blessed were the days before you read a President's message. Blessed are the young, for they do not read the President's message.

Blessed are they who never read a newspaper, for they shall see Nature, and through her, God.

But alas, I have heard of Sumpter, and Pickens, and even of Buchanan (though I did not read his message).

204

I also read the New York *Tribune*, but then I am reading Herodotus and Strabo, and Blodget's *Climatology*, and *Six Years in the Deserts of North America*, as hard as I can, to counterbalance it.

LIFE WITHOUT PRINCIPLE
1863

The power, the range, the depth of Thoreau's thought, and the beauty with which he expressed it, are plain in the essay "Life Without Principle." It was published in the Atlantic Monthly *in October 1863, seventeen months after Thoreau's death. It goes back to his* Journal *for the years 1851–1855. These entries were formed first into the lecture on getting a living which Thoreau delivered before audiences in New Bedford and Nantucket, and then in Worcester, Concord, Perth Amboy, and probably Philadelphia.*

The year in which the major work on "Life Without Principle" was done was 1854—the same eventful year which stirred Thoreau to the fury of "Slavery in Massachusetts" and which saw the publication of Walden. *In the last few months of his life Thoreau prepared this and other papers for what he knew was to be posthumous publication. (M.M.)*

At a lyceum, not long since, I felt that the lecturer had chosen a theme too foreign to himself, and so failed to interest me as much as he might have done. He described things not in or near to his heart, but toward his extremities and superficies. There was, in this sense, no truly central or centralizing thought in the lecture. I would have had him deal with his privatest experience, as the poet does. The greatest compliment that was ever paid me was when one asked me what I *thought*, and attended to my answer. I am surprised, as well as delighted, when this happens, it is such a rare use he would make of me, as if he were acquainted with the tool. Commonly, if men want anything of me, it is only to know how many acres I make of their land—since I am a surveyor—or, at most, what trivial news I have burdened myself with. They never will go to law for my meat; they prefer the shell. A man once came a considerable distance to ask me to lecture on Slavery; but on conversing with him, I found that he and his clique expected seven-eighths of the lecture to be theirs, and only one-eighth mine; so I declined. I take it for granted, when I am invited to lecture anywhere—for I have had a little experience in that business—that there is a desire to hear what I *think* on some subject, though I may be the greatest fool in the country—and not that I should say pleasant things merely, or such as the audience will assent to; and I resolve, accordingly, that I will give them a strong dose of myself. They have sent for me, and engaged to pay for me, and I am determined that they shall have me, though I bore them beyond all precedent.

So now I would say something similar to you, my readers. Since *you* are my readers, and I have not been much of a traveler, I will not talk about people a thousand miles off, but come as near home as I can. As the time is short, I will leave out all the flattery, and retain all the criticism.

Let us consider the way in which we spend our lives.

This world is a place of business. What an infinite bustle! I am awaked almost every night by the panting of the locomotive. It interrupts my dreams. There is no sabbath. It would be glorious to see mankind at leisure for once. It is nothing but work, work, work. I cannot easily buy a blank book to write thoughts in; they are commonly ruled for dollars and cents. An Irishman, seeing me making a minute in the fields, took it for granted that I was calculating my wages. If a man was tossed out for life, or scared out of his wits by the Indians, it is regretted chiefly because he was thus incapacitated for—business! I think that there is nothing, not even crime, more opposed to poetry, to philosophy, ay, to life itself, than this incessant business.

There is a coarse and boisterous money-making fellow in the outskirts of our town who is going to build a bank-wall under the hill along the edge of his meadow. The powers have put this

207

into his head to keep him out of mischief, and he wishes me to
spend three weeks digging there with him. The result will be
that he will perhaps get some more money to hoard, and leave
for his heirs to spend foolishly. If I do this, most will commend
me as an industrious and hardworking man; but if I choose to
devote myself to certain labors which yield more real profit,
though but little money, they may be inclined to look on me as
an idler. Nevertheless, as I do not need the police of meaningless
labor to regulate me, and do not see anything absolutely praiseworthy in this fellow's undertaking, any more than in many an
enterprise of our own or foreign governments, however amusing
it may be to him or them, I prefer to finish my education at a
different school.

If a man walk in the woods for love of them half of each day,
he is in danger of being regarded as a loafer; but if he spends
his whole day as a speculator, shearing off those woods and
making earth bald before her time, he is esteemed an industrious
and enterprising citizen. As if a town had no interest in its
forests but to cut them down!

Most men would feel insulted if it were proposed to employ
them in throwing stones over a wall, and then in throwing them
back, merely that they might earn their wages. But many are
no more worthily employed now. For instance: just after sunrise,
one summer morning, I noticed one of my neighbors walking
beside his team, which was slowly drawing a heavy hewn stone
swung under the axle, surrounded by an atmosphere of industry
—his day's work begun—his brow commenced to sweat—a
reproach to all sluggards and idlers—pausing abreast the shoulders
of his oxen, and half turning round with a flourish of his merciful
whip, while they gained their length on him. And I thought,
Such is the labor which the American Congress exists to protect
—honest, manly toil—honest as the day is long—that makes his
bread taste sweet, and keeps society sweet—which all men
respect and have consecrated; one of the sacred band, doing the
needful but irksome drudgery. Indeed, I felt a slight reproach,
because I observed this from a window, and was not abroad and
stirring about a similar business. The day went by, and at evening
I passed the yard of another neighbor, who keeps many servants,

and spends much money foolishly, while he adds nothing to the common stock, and there I saw the stone of the morning lying beside a whimsical structure intended to adorn this Lord Timothy Dexter's premises, and the dignity forthwith departed from the teamster's labor, in my eyes. In my opinion, the sun was made to light worthier toil than this. I may add that his employer has since run off, in debt to a good part of the town, and, after passing through chancery, has settled somewhere else, there to become once more a patron of the arts.

The ways by which you may get money almost without exception lead downward. To have done anything by which you earned money *merely* is to have been truly idle or worse. If the laborer gets no more than the wages which his employer pays him, he is cheated, he cheats himself. If you would get money as a writer or lecturer, you must be popular, which is to go down perpendicularly. Those services which the community will most readily pay for, it is most disagreeable to render. You are paid for being something less than a man. The state does not commonly reward a genius any more wisely. Even the poet laureate would rather not have to celebrate the accidents of royalty. He must be bribed with a pipe of wine; and perhaps another poet is called away from his muse to gauge that very pipe. As for my own business, even that kind of surveying which I could do with most satisfaction my employers do not want. They would prefer that I should do my work coarsely and not too well, ay, not well enough. When I observe that there are different ways of surveying, my employer commonly asks which will give him the most land, not which is most correct. I once invented a rule for measuring cordwood, and tried to introduce it in Boston; but the measurer there told me that the sellers did not wish to have their wood measured correctly—that he was already too accurate for them, and therefore they commonly got their wood measured in Charlestown before crossing the bridge.

The aim of the laborer should be, not to get his living, to get "a good job," but to perform well a certain work; and even in a pecuniary sense, it would be economy for a town to pay its laborers so well that they would not feel that they were working for low ends, as for a livelihood merely, but for scientific, or even

209

moral ends. Do not hire a man who does your work for money, but him who does it for love of it.

It is remarkable that there are few men so well employed, so much to their minds, but that a little money or fame would commonly buy them off from their present pursuit. I see advertisements for *active* young men, as if activity were the whole of a young man's capital. Yet I have been surprised when one has with confidence proposed to me, a grown man, to embark in some enterprise of his, as if I had absolutely nothing to do, my life having been a complete failure hitherto. What a doubtful compliment this to pay me! As if he had met me halfway across the ocean beating up against the wind, but bound nowhere, and proposed to me to go along with him! If I did, what do you think the underwriters would say? No, no! I am not without employment at this stage of the voyage. To tell the truth, I saw an advertisement for able-bodied seamen when I was a boy, sauntering in my native port, and as soon as I came of age I embarked.

The community has no bribe that will tempt a wise man. You may raise money enough to tunnel a mountain, but you cannot raise money enough to hire a man who is minding *his own* business. An efficient and valuable man does what he can, whether the community pay him for it or not. The inefficient offer their inefficiency to the highest bidder, and are forever expecting to be put into office. One would suppose that they were rarely disappointed.

Perhaps I am more than usually jealous with respect to my freedom. I feel that my connection with and obligation to society are still very slight and transient. Those slight labors which afford me a livelihood, and by which it is allowed that I am to some extent serviceable to my contemporaries, are as yet commonly a pleasure to me, and I am not often reminded that they are a necessity. So far I am successful. But I foresee that if my wants should be much increased, the labor required to supply them would become a drudgery. If I should sell both my forenoons and afternoons to society, as most appear to do, I am sure that for me there would be nothing left worth living for. I trust that I shall never thus sell my birthright for a mess of pottage. I wish to suggest that a man may be very industrious, and yet not spend his time well. There is no more fatal blunderer than he who consumes the greater part of his life getting his living. All great enterprises are self-supporting. The poet, for instance, must sustain his body by his poetry, as a steam planing-mill feeds its boilers with the shavings it makes. You must get your living by loving. But as it is said of the merchants that ninety-seven in a hundred fail, so the life of men generally, tried by this standard, is a failure, and bankruptcy may be surely prophesied.

Merely to come into the world the heir of a fortune is not to be born, but to be stillborn, rather. To be supported by the charity of friends, or a government pension—provided you continue to breathe—by whatever fine synonyms you describe these relations, is to go into the almshouse. On Sundays the poor debtor goes to church to take an account of stock, and finds, of course, that his outgoes have been greater than his income. In the Catholic Church, especially, they go into chancery, make a clean confession, give up all, and think to start again. Thus men will lie on their backs, talking about the fall of man, and never make an effort to get up.

As for the comparative demands which men make on life, it is an important difference between two, that the one is satisfied with a level success, that his marks can all be hit by point-blank shots, but the other, however low and unsuccessful his life may be, constantly elevates his aim, though at a very slight angle to the horizon. I should much rather be the last man—though, as the Orientals say, "Greatness doth not approach him who is fore-ever looking down; and all those who are looking high are growing poor."

It is remarkable that there is little or nothing to be remembered written on the subject of getting a living; how to make getting a living not merely honest and honorable, but altogether inviting and glorious; for if *getting* a living is not so, then living is not. One would think, from looking at literature, that this question had never disturbed a solitary individual's musings. Is it that men are too much disgusted with their experience to speak of it? The lesson of value which money teaches, which the Author of the Universe has taken so much pains to teach us, we are inclined to skip altogether. As for the means of living, it is wonderful how indifferent men of all classes are about it, even reformers, so called—whether they inherit, or earn, or steal it. I think that Society has done nothing for us in this respect, or at least has undone what she has done. Cold and hunger seem more friendly to my nature than those methods which men have adopted and advise to ward them off.

The title *wise* is, for the most part, falsely applied. How can one be a wise man, if he does not know any better how to live than other men?—if he is only more cunning and intellectually subtle? Does Wisdom work in a treadmill? or does she teach how to succeed *by her example?* Is there any such thing as wisdom not applied to life? Is she merely the miller who grinds the finest logic? Is it pertinent to ask if Plato got his *living* in a better way or more successfully than his contemporaries—or did he succumb to the difficulties of life like other men? Did he seem to prevail over some of them merely by indifference, or by assuming grand airs? or find it easier to live because his aunt remembered him in her will? The ways in which most men get their living, that is, live, are mere makeshifts, and a shirking of the real business of life—chiefly because they do not know, but partly because they do not mean, any better.

The rush to California, for instance, and the attitude, not merely of merchants, but of philosophers and prophets, so called, in relation to it, reflect the greatest disgrace on mankind. That so many are ready to live by luck, and so get the means of commanding the labor of others less lucky, without contributing any value to society! And that is called enterprise! I know of no more startling development of the immorality of trade, and all the common modes of getting a living. The philosophy and poetry and religion of such a mankind are not worth the dust of a puffball. The hog that gets his living by rooting, stirring up the soil so, would be ashamed of such company. If I could command the wealth of all the worlds by lifting my finger, I would not pay *such* a price for it. Even Mahomet knew that God did not make this world in jest. It makes God to be a moneyed gentleman who scatters a handful of pennies in order to see mankind scramble for them. The world's raffle! A subsistence in the domains of Nature a thing to be raffled for! What a comment, what a satire, on our institutions! The conclusion will be, that mankind will hang itself upon a tree. And have all the precepts in all the Bibles taught men only this? and is the last and most admirable invention of the human race only an improved muck-rake? Is this the ground on which Orientals and Occidentals meet? Did God direct us so to get our living, digging where we never planted— and He would, perchance, reward us with lumps of gold?

God gave the righteous man a certificate entitling him to food and raiment, but the unrighteous man found a facsimile of the same in God's coffers, and appropriated it, and obtained food and raiment like the former. It is one of the most extensive systems of counterfeiting that the world has seen. I did not know that mankind was suffering for want of gold. I have seen a little of it. I know that it is very malleable, but not so malleable as wit. A grain of gold will gild a great surface, but not so much as a grain of wisdom.

The gold digger in the ravines of the mountains is as much a gambler as his fellow in the saloons of San Francisco. What difference does it make whether you shake dirt or shake dice? If you win, society is the loser. The gold digger is the enemy of the honest laborer, whatever checks and compensations there may be. It is not enough to tell me that you worked hard to get your gold. So does the devil work hard. The way of transgressors may be hard in many respects. The humblest observer who goes to the mines sees and says that gold-digging is of the character of a lottery; the gold thus obtained is not the same thing with the wages of honest toil. But, practically, he forgets what he has seen, for he has seen only the fact, not the principle, and goes into the trade there, that is, buys a ticket in what commonly proves another lottery, where the fact is not so obvious.

After reading Howitt's account of the Australian gold-diggings one evening, I had in my mind's eye, all night, the numerous valleys, with their streams, all cut up with foul pits, from ten to one hundred feet deep, and half a dozen feet across, as close as they can be dug, and partly filled with water—the locality to which men furiously rush to probe for their fortunes—uncertain where they shall break ground—not knowing but the gold is under the camp itself—sometimes digging one hundred and sixty feet before they strike the vein, or then missing it by a foot—turned into demons, and regardless of each other's rights, in their thirst for riches—whole valleys, for thirty miles, suddenly honeycombed by the pits of the miners, so that even hundreds are drowned in them—standing in water, and covered with mud and clay, they work night and day, dying of exposure and disease. Having read this, and partly forgotten it, I was thinking, accidentally, of my own unsatisfactory life, doing as others do; and with that vision of the diggings still before me, I asked myself why *I* might not be washing some gold daily, though it were only the finest particles—why *I* might not sink a shaft down to the gold within me, and work that mine. *There* is a Ballarat, a Bendigo for you—what though it were a sulky-gully? At any rate, I might pursue some path, however solitary and narrow and crooked, in which I could walk with love and reverence. Wherever a man separates from the multitude, and goes his own way in this mood, there indeed is a fork in the road, though ordinary travelers may see only a gap in the paling. His solitary path across lots will turn out the *higher way* of the two.

Men rush to California and Australia as if the true gold were to be found in that direction; but that is to go to the very opposite extreme to where it lies. They go prospecting farther and farther away from the true lead, and are most unfortunate when they think themselves most successful. Is not our *native* soil auriferous? Does not a stream from the golden mountains flow through our native valley? and has not this for more than geologic ages been bringing down the shining particles and forming the nuggets for us? Yet, strange to tell, if a digger steal away, prospecting for this true gold, into the unexplored solitudes around us, there is no danger that any will dog his steps, and endeavor to supplant him. He may claim and undermine the whole valley even, both the cultivated and the uncultivated portions, his whole life long in peace, for no one will ever dispute his claim. They will not mind his cradles or his toms. He is not confined to a claim twelve feet square, as a Ballarat, but may mine anywhere, and wash and wash the whole wide world in his tom.

Howitt says of the man who found the great nugget which weighed twenty-eight pounds, at the Bendigo diggings in Aus-

214

tralia: "He soon began to drink; got a horse, and rode all about, generally at full gallop, and, when he met people, called out to inquire if they knew who he was, and then kindly informed them that he was 'the bloody wretch that had found the nugget.' At last he rode full speed against a tree, and nearly knocked his brains out." I think, however, there was no danger of that, for he had already knocked his brains out against the nugget. Howitt adds, "He is a hopelessly ruined man." But he is a type of the class. They are all fast men. Hear some of the names of the places where they dig: "Jackass Flat," "Sheep's-head Gully," "Murderer's Bar," etc. Is there no satire in these names? Let them carry their ill-gotten wealth where they will, I am thinking it will still be "Jackass Flat," if not "Murderer's Bar," where they live.

The last resource of our energy has been the robbing of grave-yards on the Isthmus of Darien, an enterprise which appears to be but in its infancy; for, according to late accounts, an act has passed its second reading in the legislature of New Granada, regulating this kind of mining; and a correspondent of the *Tribune* writes: "In the dry season, when the weather will permit of the country being properly prospected, no doubt other rich *guacas* [that is, graveyards] will be found." To emigrants he says: "Do not come before December; take the Isthmus route in preference to the Boca del Toro one; bring no useless baggage, and do not cumber yourself with a tent; but a good pair of blankets will be necessary; a pick, shovel, and ax of good material will be almost all that is required"; advice which might have been taken from the *Burker's Guide*. And he concludes with this line in Italics and small capitals: "*If you are doing well at home,* STAY THERE," which may fairly be interpreted to mean, "If you are getting a good living by robbing graveyards at home, stay there."

But why go to California for a text? She is the child of New England, bred at her own school and church.

It is remarkable that among all the preachers there are so few moral teachers. The prophets are employed in excusing the ways of men. Most reverend senators, the *illuminati* of the age, tell me, with a gracious, reminiscent smile, betwixt an aspiration and a shudder, not to be too tender about these things—to lump all that, that is, make a lump of gold of it. The highest advice I have heard on these subjects was groveling. The burden of it was, It is not worth your while to undertake to reform the world in this particular. Do not ask how your bread is buttered; it will make you sick if you do—and the like. A man had better starve at once than lose his innocence in the process of getting his bread. If within the sophisticated man there is not an unsophisticated one, then he is but one of the devil's angels. As we grow old, we live more coarsely, we relax a little in our disciplines, and, to some extent, cease to obey our finest instincts. But we should be fastidious to the extreme of sanity, disregarding the gibes of those who are more unfortunate than ourselves.

In our science and philosophy, even, there is commonly no true and absolute account of things. The spirit of sect and bigotry has planted its hoof amid the stars. You have only to discuss the problem, whether the stars are inhabited or not, in order to discover it. Why must we daub the heavens as well as the earth? It was an unfortunate discovery that Dr. Kane was a Mason, and that Sir John Franklin was another. But it was a more cruel suggestion that possibly that was the reason why the former went in search of the latter. There is not a popular magazine in this country that would dare to print a child's thought on important subjects without comment. It must be submitted to the D.D.'s. I would it were the chickadee-dees.

You come from attending the funeral of mankind to attend to a natural phenomenon. A little thought is sexton to all the world.

I hardly know an *intellectual* man, even, who is so broad and truly liberal that you can think aloud in his society. Most with whom you endeavor to talk soon come to a stand against some institution in which they appear to hold stock—that is, some particular, not universal, way of viewing things. They will continually thrust their own low roof, with its narrow skylight, between you and the sky, when it is the unobstructed heavens you would view. Get out of the way with your cobwebs; wash your windows, I say! In some lyceums they tell me that they have voted to exclude the subject of religion. But how do I know what their religion is, and when I am near to or far from it? I have walked into such an arena and done my best to make a clean breast of what religion I have experienced, and the audience never suspected what I was about. The lecture was as harmless as moonshine to them. Whereas, if I had read to them the biography of the greatest scamps in history, they might have thought that I had written the lives of the deacons of their church. Ordinarily, the inquiry is, Where did you come from? or, Where are you going? That was a more pertinent question which I overheard one of my auditors put to another once: "What does he lecture for?" It made me quake in my shoes.

To speak impartially, the best men that I know are not serene, a world in themselves. For the most part, they dwell in forms, and flatter and study effect only more finely than the rest. We select granite for the underpinning of our houses and barns; we build fences of stone; but we do not ourselves rest on an underpinning of granitic truth, the lowest primitive rock. Our sills are rotten. What stuff is the man made of who is not coexistent in our thought with the purest and subtilest truth? I often accuse my finest acquaintances of an immense frivolity; for, while there are manners and compliments we do not meet, we do not teach one another the lessons of honesty and sincerity that the brutes do, or of steadiness and solidity that the rocks do. The fault is commonly mutual, however; for we do not habitually demand any more of each other.

That excitement about Kossuth, consider how characteristic, but superficial, it was!—only another kind of politics or dancing. Men were making speeches to him all over the country, but each expressed only the thought, or the want of thought, of the multitude. No man stood on the truth. They were merely banded together, as usual one leaning on another, and all together on nothing; as the Hindus made the world rest on an elephant, the elephant on a tortoise, and the tortoise on a serpent, and had nothing to put under the serpent. For all fruit of that stir we have the Kossuth hat.

Just so hollow and ineffectual, for the most part, is our ordinary conversation. Surface meets surface. When our life ceases to be inward and private, conversation degenerates into mere gossip. We rarely meet a man who can tell us any news which he has not read in a newspaper, or been told by his neighbor; and for the most part, the only difference between us and our fellow is that he has seen the newspaper, or been out to tea, and we have not. In proportion as our inward life fails, we go more constantly and desperately to the post office. You may depend on it, that the poor fellow who walks away with the greatest number of letters, proud of his extensive correspondence, has not heard from himself this long while.

I do not know but it is too much to read one newspaper a week. I have tried it recently, and for so long it seems to me that I have not dwelt in my native region. The sun, the clouds, the snow, the trees say not so much to me. You cannot serve two masters. It requires more than a day's devotion to know and to possess the wealth of a day.

We may well be ashamed to tell what things we have read or heard in our day. I do not know why my news should be so trivial—considering what one's dreams and expectations are, why the developments should be so paltry. The news we hear, for the most part, is not news to our genius. It is the stalest repetition. You are often tempted to ask why such stress is laid on a particular experience which you have had—that, after twenty-five years, you should meet Hobbins, Registrar of Deeds, again on the sidewalk. Have you not budged an inch, then? Such is the daily news. Its facts appear to float in the atmosphere, insignificant as the sporules of fungi, and impinge on some neglected thallus, or surface of our minds, which affords a basis for them, and hence a parasitic growth. We should wash ourselves clean of such news. Of what consequence, though our planet explode, if there is no character involved in the explosion? In health we have not the least curiosity about such events. We do not live for idle amusement. I would not run round a corner to see the world blow up.

All summer, and far into the autumn, perchance, you unconsciously went by the newspapers and the news, and now you find it was because the morning and the evening were full of news to you. Your walks were full of incidents. You attended, not to the affairs of Europe, but to your own affairs in Massachusetts fields. If you chance to live and move and have your being in that thin stratum in which the events that make the news trans-

218

pire—thinner than the paper on which it is printed—then these
things will fill the world for you; but if you soar above or dive
below that plane, you cannot remember nor be reminded of them.
Really to see the sun rise or go down every day, so to relate
ourselves to a universal fact, would preserve us sane forever.
Nations! What are nations? Tartars, and Huns, and Chinamen!
Like insects, they swarm. The historian strives in vain to make
them memorable. It is for want of a man that there are so many
men. It is individuals that populate the world. Any man thinking
may say with the Spirit of Lodin:

> I look down from my height on nations,
> And they became ashes before me;
> Calm is my dwelling in the clouds;
> Pleasant are the great fields of my rest.

Pray, let us live without being drawn by dogs, Esquimaux-
fashion, tearing over hill and dale, and biting each other's ears.

Not without a slight shudder at the danger, I often perceive
how near I had come to admitting into my mind the details of
some trivial affair—the news of the street; and I am astonished
to observe how willing men are to lumber their minds with such
rubbish—to permit idle rumors and incidents of the most insignificant kind to intrude on ground which should be sacred to
thought. Shall the mind be a public arena, where the affairs of
the street and the gossip of the tea table chiefly are discussed?
Or shall it be a quarter of heaven itself—a hypaethral temple,
consecrated to the service of the gods? I find it so difficult to
dispose of the few facts which to me are significant, that I
hesitate to burden my attention with those which are insignificant, which only a divine mind could illustrate. Such is, for the
most part, the news in newspapers and conversation. It is important to preserve the mind's chastity in this respect. Think of
admitting the details of a single case of the criminal court into
our thoughts, to stalk profanely through their very *sanctum
sanctorum* for an hour, ay, for many hours! to make a very
barroom of the mind's inmost apartment, as if for so long the
dust of the street had occupied us—the very street itself, with
all its travel, its bustle, and filth, had passed through our thoughts'

219

shrine! Would it not be an intellectual and moral suicide? When I have been compelled to sit spectator and auditor in a courtroom for some hours, and have seen my neighbors, who were not compelled, stealing in from time to time, and tiptoeing about with washed hands and faces, it has appeared to my mind's eye that, when they took off their hats, their ears suddenly expanded into vast hoppers for sound, between which even their narrow heads were crowded. Like the vanes of windmills, they caught the broad but shallow stream of sound, which after a few titillating gyrations in their coggy brains, passed out the other side. I wondered if, when they got home, they were as careful to wash their ears as before their hands and faces. It has seemed to me, at such a time, that the auditors and the witnesses, the jury and the counsel, the judge and the criminal at the bar—if I may presume him guilty before he is convicted—were all equally criminal, and a thunderbolt might be expected to descend and consume them all together.

By all kinds of traps and signboards, threatening the extreme penalty of the divine law, exclude such trespassers from the only ground which can be sacred to you. It is so hard to forget what it is worse than useless to remember! If I am to be a thoroughfare, I prefer that it be of the mountain brooks, the Parnassian streams, and not the town sewers. There is inspiration, that gossip which comes to the ear of the attentive mind from the courts of heaven. There is the profane and stale revelation of the barroom and the police court. The same ear is fitted to receive both communications. Only the character of the hearer determines to which it shall be open, and to which closed. I believe that the mind can be permanently profaned by the habit of attending to trivial things, so that all our thoughts shall be tinged with triviality. Our very intellect shall be macadamized, as it were—its foundation broken into fragments for the wheels of travel to roll over; and if you would know what will make the most durable pavement, surpassing rolled stones, spruce blocks, and asphaltum, you have only to look into some of our minds which have been subjected to this treatment so long.

If we have thus desecrated ourselves—as who has not?—the remedy will be by wariness and devotion to reconsecrate our-

selves, and make once more a fane of the mind. We should treat
our minds, that is, ourselves, as innocent and ingenuous children,
whose guardians we are, and be careful what objects and what
subjects we trust on their attention. Read not the Times. Read
the Eternities. Conventionalities are at length as bad as impurities.
Even the facts of science may dust the mind by their dryness,
unless they are in a sense effaced each morning, or rather rendered fertile by the dews of fresh and living truth. Knowledge
does not come to us by details, but in flashes of light from
heaven. Yes, every thought that passes through the mind helps
to wear and tear it, and to deepen the ruts, which, as in the
streets of Pompei, evidence how much it has been used. How
many things there are concerning which we might well deliberate
whether we had better know them—had better let their peddling
carts be driven, even at the slowest trot or walk, over that bridge
of glorious span by which we trust to pass at last from the
farthest brink of time to the nearest shore of eternity! Have we
no culture, no refinement—but skill only to live coarsely and
serve the devil?—to acquire a little worldly wealth, or fame,
or liberty, and make a false show with it, as if we were all husk
and shell, with no tender and living kernel to us? Shall our institutions be like those chestnut burs which contain abortive nuts,
perfect only to prick the fingers?

America is said to be the arena on which the battle of freedom
is to be fought; but surely it cannot be freedom in a merely
political sense that is meant. Even if we grant that the American
has freed himself from a political tyrant, he is still the slave of
an economical and moral tyrant. Now that the republic—the *res-
publica*—has been settled, it is time to call after the *res-privata*
—the private state—to see, as the Roman senate charged its
consuls, *ne quid res-*PRIVATA *detrimenti caperet,* that the *private*
state receive no detriment.

Do we call this the land of the free? What is it to be free
from King George and continue the slaves of King Prejudice?
What is it to be born free and not to live free? What is the
value of any political freedom, but as a means to moral freedom?
Is it a freedom to be slaves, or a freedom to be free, of which
we boast? We are a nation of politicians, concerned about the

outmost defenses only of freedom. It is our children's children who may perchance be really free. We tax ourselves unjustly. There is a part of us which is not represented. It is taxation without representation. We quarter troops, we quarter fools and cattle of all sorts upon ourselves. We quarter our gross bodies on our poor souls, till the former eat up all the latter's substance.

With respect to a true culture and manhood, we are essentially provincial still, not metropolitan—mere Jonathans. We are provincial because we do not find at home our standards; because we do not worship truth, but the reflection of truth; because we are warped and narrowed by an exclusive devotion to trade and commerce and manufactures and agriculture and the like, which are but means, and not the end.

So is the English Parliament provincial. Mere country bumpkins, they betray themselves, when any more important question, for instance—the English question why did I not say? Their natures are subdued to what they work in. Their "good breeding" respects only secondary objects. The finest manners in the world are awkwardness and fatuity when contrasted with a finer intelligence. They appear but as the fashions of past days— mere courtliness, knee buckles and small clothes, out of date. It is the vice, but not the excellence of manners, that they are continually being deserted by the character; they are cast-off clothes or shells, claiming the respect which belonged to the living creature. You are presented with the shells instead of the meat, and it is no excuse generally, that, in the case of some fishes, the shells are of more worth than the meat. The man who thrusts his manners upon me does as if he were to insist on introducing me to his cabinet of curiosities, when I wished to see himself. It was not in this sense that the poet Decker called Christ "the first true gentleman that ever breathed." I repeat that in this sense the most splendid court in Christendom is provincial, having authority to consult about Transalpine interests only, and not the affairs of Rome. A praetor or proconsul would suffice to settle the questions which absorb the attention of the English Parliament and the American Congress.

Government and legislation! these I thought were respectable professions. We have heard of heaven-born Numas, Lycurguses, and Solons, in the history of the world, whose *names* at least may stand for ideal legislators; but think of legislating to *regulate* the breeding of slaves, or the exportation of tobacco! What have divine legislators to do with the exportation or the importation of tobacco? what humane ones with the breeding of slaves? Suppose you were to submit the question to any son of God— and has He no children in the nineteenth century? is it a family which is extinct?—in what condition would you get it again? What shall a State like Virginia say for itself at the last day, in which these have been the principal, the staple productions? What ground is there for patriotism in such a State? I derive my facts from statistical tables which the States themselves have published.

A commerce that whitens every sea in quest of nuts and raisins, and makes slaves of its sailors for this purpose! I saw, the other day, a vessel which had been wrecked, and many lives lost, and her cargo of rags, juniper berries, and bitter almonds were strewn along the shore. It seemed hardly worth the while to tempt the dangers of the sea between Leghorn and New York for the sake of a cargo of juniper berries and bitter almonds. America sending to the Old World for her bitters! Is not the sea-brine, is not shipwreck, bitter enough to make the cup of life go down here? Yet such, to a great extent, is our boasted commerce; and there are those who style themselves statesmen and philosophers who are so blind as to think that progress and civilization depend on precisely this kind of interchange and activity—the activity of flies about a molasses-hogshead. Very well, observes one, if men were oysters. And very well, answer I, if men were mosquitoes.

Lieutenant Herndon, whom our government sent to explore the Amazon, and, it is said, to extend the area of slavery, observed that there was wanting there "an industrious and active population, who know what the comforts of life are, and who have artificial wants to draw out the great resources of the country." But what are the "artificial wants" to be encouraged? Not the love of luxuries, like the tobacco and slaves of, I believe, his native Virginia, nor the ice and granite and other material wealth of our native New England; nor are "the great resources

223

of a country" that fertility or barrenness of soil which produces these. The chief want, in every State that I have been into, was a high and earnest purpose in its inhabitants. This alone draws out "the great resources" of Nature, and at last taxes her beyond her resources; for man naturally dies out of her. When we want culture more than potatoes, and illumination more than sugar plums, then the great resources of a world are taxed and drawn out, and the result, or staple production, is, not slaves, not operatives, but men—those rare fruits called heroes, saints, poets, philosophers, and redeemers.

In short, as a snowdrift is formed where there is a lull in the wind, so, one would say, where there is a lull of truth, an institution springs up. But the truth blows right on over it, nevertheless, and at length blows it down.

What is called politics is comparatively something so superficial and inhuman, that practically I have never fairly recognized that it concerns me at all. The newspapers, I perceive, devote some of their columns specially to politics or government without charge; and this, one would say, is all that saves it; but as I love literature and to some extent the truth also, I never read those columns at any rate. I do not wish to blunt my sense of right so much. I have not got to answer for having read a single President's message. A strange age of the world this, when empires, kingdoms, and republics come a-begging to a private man's door, and utter their complaints at his elbow! I cannot take up a newspaper but I find that some wretched government or other, hard pushed and on its last legs, is interceding with me, the reader, to vote for it—more importunate than an Italian beggar; and if I have a mind to look at its certificate, made, perchance, by some benevolent merchant's clerk, or the skipper that brought it over, for it cannot speak a word of English itself, I shall probably read of the eruption of some Vesuvius, or the overflowing of some Po, true or forged, which brought it into this condition. I do not hesitate, in such a case, to suggest work or the almshouse; or why not keep its castle in silence, as I do commonly? The poor President, what with preserving his popularity and doing his duty, is completely bewildered. The newspapers are the ruling power. Any other government is reduced to a few marines at Fort Independence. If a man neglects to read the *Daily Times,* government will go down on its knees to him, for this is the only treason in these days.

Those things which now most engage the attention of men, as politics and the daily routine, are, it is true, vital functions of human society, but should be unconsciously performed, like the corresponding functions of the physical body. They are *infra-*human, a kind of vegetation. I sometimes awake to a half con-sciousness of them going on about me, as a man may become conscious of some of the processes of digestion in a morbid state, and so have the dyspepsia, as it is called. It is as if a thinker sub-mitted himself to be rasped by the great gizzard of creation. Politics is, as it were, the gizzard of society, full of grit and gravel, and the two political parties are its two opposite halves, —sometimes split into quarters, it may be, which grind on each other. Not only individuals, but states, have thus a confirmed dyspepsia, which expresses itself, you can imagine by what sort of eloquence. Thus our life is not altogether a forgetting, but also, alas! to a great extent, a remembering, of that which we should never have been conscious of, certainly not in our waking hours. Why should we not meet, not always as dyspeptics, to tell our bad dreams, but sometimes as *eu*peptics, to congratulate each other on the ever-glorious morning? I do not make an exorbitant demand, surely.

BIOGRAPHICAL INDEX

ALCOTT, Amos Bronson (1799–1888). Pioneer in educational reform, writer, father of Louisa May Alcott. A close friend to Thoreau and Emerson during his residence in Concord from 1840 on.

BEECHER, Henry Ward (1813–1887). Congregationalist minister and one of best-known lecturers of his day. Brother of Harriet Beecher Stowe, he too was a crusader against slavery.

BLAKE, Harrison Gray Otis (1816–1898). From 1848, one of Thoreau's firmest disciples, who lived in Worcester, Mass. They exchanged many visits and letters. Blake inherited Thoreau's manuscript journals upon the death of Henry's sister Sophia.

BRISBANE, Albert (1809–1890). Social theorist and student of Fourier's ideas. A columnist in Greeley's New York *Tribune,* he was influential in the founding of utopian communities.

BROWN, John (1800–1859). Abolitionist who participated in the Free-State struggle in Kansas, and later led the raid on Harpers Ferry in Virginia on October 16, 1859, with the aim of capturing the Federal arsenal and rousing the slaves to join his Gideon's Army. He was captured, tried, and hanged.

BURNS, Anthony (1830–1862). A fugitive slave from Virginia who was taken prisoner in Boston in 1854. Although the abolitionist attempt to rescue him by force failed, it won many adherents to the cause of emancipation.

CARLYLE, Thomas (1795–1881). Scotch-born writer and lecturer noted for his savage essays against materialism and hypocrisy and his book *History of the French Revolution*. He was a close friend of Emerson's. Thoreau wrote an essay on Carlyle.

CURTIS, George William (1824–1892). Author, editor. He lived in Concord briefly after his experience at Brook Farm (1842–1843), and became a friend of Thoreau's.

DEXTER, Timothy (1743–1806). An eccentric merchant of Newburyport, Mass., who dubbed himself "Lord."

DOUGLASS, Frederick (1817?–1895). Ex-slave who rose to international prominence as one of the foremost editors, writers, and orators in the antislavery movement.

EMERSON, Ralph Waldo (1803–1882). Essayist, poet, lecturer, who moved to Concord in 1835. Strong influence on his friend Thoreau.

EVERETT, Edward (1794–1865). Orator and statesman. He was president of Harvard, an editor, Congressman, Massachusetts governor, and United States Senator. His speeches drew immense audiences.

FOURIER, Francis Marie Charles (1772–1837). French sociologist and reformer whose theory of a system of phalansteries, small cooperative communities which were to be associated under a central government, won many followers in the United States, including Horace Greeley and Arthur Brisbane. Brook Farm was strongly influenced by Fourierism.

GANDHI, Mohandas Karamchand (1869–1948). Hindu nationalist leader. He began his first campaign of civil disobedience in South Africa in defense of Asiatic immigrants, and continued the tactic in India as a politico-religious movement of noncooperation with British rule.

GARRISON, William Lloyd (1805–1879). Editor of *The Liberator*, abolitionist newspaper, and a leader of the antislavery movement.

GOODWIN, John (1803–1860). Concord hunter and fisherman.

GREELEY, Horace (1811–1872). Editor of the New York *Tribune*; author; reformer. For several years a friend and literary agent for Thoreau.

HOAR, Samuel (1788–1856). Lawyer, Congressman, and leading citizen of Concord. The squire's sons Edward and George and his daughter Elizabeth were friends of Thoreau's.

HOSMER, Edmund (1798–1881). Concord farmer; friend of Thoreau's.

KOSSUTH, Lajos (1802–1894). Hungarian patriot; leader of Hungarian uprising in 1848–1849. Visited United States in 1851–1852, after revolution was defeated.

LOWELL, James Russell (1819–1891). Critic, poet, humorist, professor, diplomat, editor of *Atlantic Monthly* (1857–1861).

MERRIAM, Francis J. (1837–1865). A young member of John Brown's band at Harpers Ferry who escaped capture. He was the mysterious "X" Thoreau drove to the railway station on his flight north to Canada. Later Merriam served in the Civil War as captain of a Negro infantry company.

MOTT, Lucretia Coffin (1793–1880). A Quaker minister and a leading social reformer, pioneering in the woman's rights and abolitionist movements.

PALEY, William (1743–1805). English theologian and philosopher whose works were read by Thoreau, and are criticized in "Civil Disobedience."

PARKER, Theodore (1810–1860). Unitarian clergyman and transcendentalist, a leader of antislavery and reform movements. He lived in Boston and lectured widely in the United States.

PEABODY, Elizabeth Palmer (1804–1894). Educator, reformer, lecturer. Publisher of *Aesthetic Papers*, the periodical in which Thoreau's "Civil Disobedience" was first printed.

PHILLIPS, Wendell (1811–1884). Bostonian, leading abolitionist, friend and collaborator of William Lloyd Garrison. One of most popular lecturers of the nineteenth century.

PILLSBURY, Parker (1809–1898). Abolitionist; friend of the Thoreau family.

ROGERS, Nathaniel Peabody (1794–1846). A New Hampshire lawyer who became editor of an abolitionist newspaper that was very popular in the Thoreau household.

SIMS, Thomas. A Georgia slave who fled to freedom in Boston and was forced back to slavery in 1851 under the provisions of the Fugitive Slave Law.

SMITH, Gerrit (1797–1874). Wealthy landowner of upstate New York who used his fortune in behalf of many social reforms. He was one of John Brown's friends and backers.

STAPLES, Samuel (1813–1895). Carpenter, bartender, and town jailer of Concord. He arrested Thoreau in 1846 for nonpayment of taxes.

SUMNER, Charles (1811–1874). Senator from Massachusetts, and one of the leading Congressional exponents of Negro emancipation.

VALLANDIGHAM, Clement L. (1820–1871). Politician, editor. An Ohio Congressman in 1858–1863, he was a supporter of states' rights and the Confederacy; Lincoln banished him behind Confederate lines.

WALKER, William (1824–1860). American filibusterer whose sensational forays into Central America ended with his execution in Honduras.

WEBSTER, Daniel (1782–1852). Lawyer, orator, and U.S. Senator from Massachusetts. He was the "godlike Daniel" to New England until he truckled to the slavery interests.

WHITMAN, Walt (1819–1892). Poet, author of *Leaves of Grass*. Emerson was one of the first to recognize his stature, and Thoreau visited him in Brooklyn, N.Y., in 1856.

WISE, Henry A. (1806–1876). Political leader and Confederate general. As governor of Virginia in 1859 he signed John Brown's death warrant.

INDEX

234